THE MISSED KISS

NICOLA LOWE

N.LOWE PUBLISHING

First paperback edition July 2021

Cover design by Jacqueline Abromeit

ISBN - 9781916907911 (ebook)

ISBN - 9781916907904 (paperback)

Published by N.Lowe Publishing

www.nloweauthor.com

Thank you to my gorgeous family for coping with me being glued to the laptop.

Thank you to Ann & Sarah for all the reading and constant messaging.

Huge thank you to Mandi Allen - The Coffeehouse Writer for non stop support, advice and appreciation.

xx

ONE

"*I* changed my mind, I don't want to go." I complained to Cassie as we sat on the Saturday lunchtime train to Manchester, with its musty smell and sticky floor. I didn't even want to think about the state of these seats and what might lurk in them. Cassie rolled her eyes at me dramatically.

"You're not getting out of this Lily," she smiled at me. "I'm not going to let you waste away in that flat of yours any longer."

"I can't believe I let you talk me into this." The train rattled into a dark tunnel. Cassie had persuaded me to let her find me a date. I had agreed to meet one person for one coffee, and even that didn't seem a great idea right now. In her opinion four years of being single was way too much, but it suited me fine. Aged twenty-seven, my life was exactly what I wanted, working as a legal secretary at Draper & Hughes, with the best commute in the world as I rented the flat above the office. My social circle was small but perfect - me and my two best friends. Cassie and I had been inseparable since the first day of high school. Unlike me though she'd settled down in her early twenties and now lived in an insanely beautiful home with her husband and two daughters. My other best friend was Luke - we'd met at work four years ago, we'd been through some pretty major events and were as close as close could be. He was my honorary big brother, he always kept a protective eye out for me.

My face was still screwed up in a sulk. "So, remind me, who am I meeting? Who am I being thrown into the lions' den with?" My stomach was in knots, I knew she meant well but I don't think she completely understood the anxiety this was stirring up in me.

Cassie's face lit up; she loved this. She thrust her phone out, showing me the photograph once again. "Zack, who is also twenty-seven and lives in Cheshire. He's a lawyer."

"Why is that a good thing?" I asked. "It's not like on *Suits* you know. I keep telling you this."

She didn't reply. To be fair to her, he looked lovely. The picture looked like it was taken at a work function. He was wearing a well-cut suit, it looked designer. His brown eyes had a sparkle to them. He was holding a champagne glass which always worked well for me! I really did like his hair - sort of short at the sides and then a longer length and well styled on top - It suited him. It was a gorgeous shade of dark brown, almost matching a dark, chocolatey mocha that I would treat myself to at weekends. I looked up at Cassie and saw she was grinning at me.

"See, you like him! I told you I'd choose someone nice."

I frowned at her. "How tall is he?"

"Five eleven," she replied with a look like she knew I was about to complain.

"I bet he lied, I bet he's only five nine really, so I'll never be able to wear heels with him." I rolled my eyes. Five nine was my height, and it had caused me paranoia for a long time, as my ex-boyfriend had hated me looking taller than him, but I adored heels.

"Lily, why would he lie when he's about to meet you? You'd obviously notice."

I shrugged, knowing I was acting sulky. "Seems short to me."

"It's virtually six foot, stop looking for issues," she scolded.

When the train stopped at the station, we headed straight to the toilets for a last-minute outfit check. I must've tried on twelve outfits, four hairstyles and ten pairs of shoes before we settled on this look - a flattering dark blue, knee-length skater dress. We were meeting for coffee, just casual, so I'd teamed it with a short, distressed-look denim jacket. The outfit was then finished off with black ankle boots in soft leather.

The height difference between me and Cassie was obvious in the mirror, the top of her head just reached my nose. She was so different to me with her blue eyes and blonde bobbed hair, always straightened immaculately. Whereas I tended to look too serious at times, Cassie always looked like she was about to burst into laughter. She had the friendliest face I could imagine.

"We can walk to the coffee shop now. It's five minutes from here. I'll wait outside until I see you're settled," she said, like a mother hen. "Then I'm going shopping! Text me when you're ready and I'll come straight back and meet you."

"OK, Mum." I teased.

"Your make-up looks great," she commented, as she squinted at my favourite black winged eyeliner which emphasised my dark brown eyes. "Natural but gorgeous. You and that perfect skin. Sickening!"

The walk was quick, maybe too quick for my nerves. The early spring sunshine felt so nice on my face, I'd missed it over the long winter. As we approached, I could see a man I thought might be Zack stood outside. I begrudgingly admitted that he looked taller than on the photograph as he leaned against the wall and scrolled through his phone. He wore well-fitted dark blue jeans and a black round-neck jumper that looked, from here, as though it might be cashmere. His hair looked perfect - that same mocha colour from the photograph. Good hair was a weakness of mine.

Zack definitely had the tall, dark and handsome look going on, with a smattering of dark stubble that looked as though he was relaxed about his appearance, but I expected was styled. I snapped out of ogling him as Cassie gave my hand a squeeze and crossed over the road so she could keep an eye on me for a few minutes.

As I headed towards him, focused on not tripping over or otherwise making an idiot of myself, my throat was dry with nerves. I prayed this was in fact him and I wasn't about to approach a complete stranger, waiting for his wife or friend. My chestnut brown hair was in a loose plait, I flicked it forwards over my shoulder as I approached, the ends tickling my collarbone. It was one of those plaits that looked effortless but had taken ages to get right. The man looked up with confident eyes. "Zack?"

I noticed how warm and genuine his smile was as he nodded. "Lily?"

At least I'd got the right person and not approached a random stranger. Now I just needed to relax, my shoulders were so tense. I focused on dropping them down, taking breaths like I'd practised so many times.

"Glad you made it. I figured this would be easier to find than a little independent place," he explained.

"I can find a Starbucks from miles away." I smiled, hoping we could break the ice.

"You're beautiful, I didn't expect you to look like your photograph for some reason," he gazed at me for a second that felt like it stretched to minutes before I saw a subtle patch of pink appear on his cheeks. "Sorry, let's get coffee."

I continued to smile, unsure how to respond as I followed, taking a seat at a table near the window while Zack joined the queue. *How does he not look nervous?* I tapped my foot against the table leg ten to the dozen, instant giveaway of my anxiety. *Breathe Lily.* Legs tucked under me to stop the tapping, I repeated to myself in my head, *it's just a coffee, it's just a coffee*.

This was the same chain of coffee shop that I frequented at home, but this branch was huge in comparison. The male baristas seemed to all share a hipster look: shaggy beards and plug piercings. There was a corner set up for an open mic night later that evening, which was advertised on large posters. There was also a section selling coffee related products and re-usable cups in all the colours imaginable. It seemed as though people from every walk of life were gathered here: teenage girls giggled in noisy groups, parents tried to control toddlers and middle-aged couples gazed wistfully out of the window. I wondered if anyone felt as anxious as me.

"Here you go," Zack placed the delicious-smelling mug in front of me as he sat down opposite with his own. "Hazelnut latte."

"Thank you. I'm a complete coffee addict. This smells so nice. What did you get?" I asked, gesturing to his own mug, wondering what I could read into his coffee choice.

"Mocha," he replied. "I'm a coffee addict too but have such a sweet tooth. Mocha is a good balance."

I smiled, wondering if it was a coincidence that I'd compared his hair to that colour. I noticed more and more about him as we talked.

"I keep thinking about how much I spend in these places and what else I could do with the time, but then coffee made at home isn't quite the same."

"Exactly," I agreed, taking a long sip, conscious of not spilling it, and avoiding a milky foam moustache.

"So, you work in law too Lily?"

"Yeah, I do, but Cassie may have made it sound more glamorous than it is. It's a small family law firm. I'm one of the secretaries. I love working there."

"It's good to love where you work," he smiled. "Sounds completely different to where I am. It's a big office in the city centre, not too far from here. I'm in corporate law."

"How about when you're not working? What do you like to do?" It felt as though I was settling into the rhythm of this now.

"Obviously come out for coffee," he replied. "Love a sporty Sunday with friends, football or whatever, which always ends up in the pub. Just the normal really. Cinema, nights out around here. My flatmate is a games designer, so I know I spend too many hours gaming with him. A few of us from work are wannabe food critics and try out all the posh places. All in the name of research for client events, obviously."

"Corporate sounds more fun. We don't do wining and dining."

"Well, I'd love to wine and dine you," he replied.

I cringed inside at the clichéd comment, and a look on my face must've given my thoughts away as he apologised. Was he one of those guys that schmoozed his way through dates every weekend?

"Sorry, that sounded like such a cheesy pickup line, didn't it?" he frowned and his eyes crinkled up in a really cute way.

"It kind of did, yeah," I grinned at him. I felt glad I wasn't the only nervous one after all.

"What do *you* get up to outside of work then?"

"I love to bake. Our office is always full of goodies on a Monday. I can make amazing brownies. Hanging out with Cassie, my personal matchmaker," I joked. "And her two little girls. Most Sundays I go for a walk or hike with my other best friend Luke, to work off the brownies. Movies and popcorn are always good with me too. Plus yoga and pilates, we go to quite a few classes."

"Have you got a big family?" he asked.

I shook my head. "Only child. Not a spoiled brat though, I promise. My parents live close, so I see a lot of them. You?"

"Four sisters, I'm the middle child," he looked happy as he spoke of them. "I get well and truly hen-pecked when I go home. Always end up escaping to the pub with my dad."

"Wow, big family! Bet it was fun growing up."

"It was," he paused for a moment. "Can I ask you a question?"

I nodded. "Yes. Of course."

"Cassie explained that you weren't fully on board with her idea, and you'd been single for a while. She convinced you to meet someone - I'm glad it was me. She did vet me through a hundred questions, you know?" A quiet laugh escaped his lips. "Is she always that bossy?"

"Always. Was it a bit weird? It was her idea. She wouldn't let it go. I did tell her people would find it odd, like she was trying to pimp me out." I watched him for a response as I sipped my drink.

"It made sense, really, when she explained. At least she was honest. Most people would just go on those dating sites and lie. I was thinking about closing my account, but I got all intrigued by you," he smiled again as he finished speaking and I couldn't help but think how striking he looked. It was really distracting.

"The only bit Cassie didn't want to explain was why," he said tentatively. "Why do you feel like you want to stay single?"

"My last relationship ended in a horrible way. It made me think I didn't want to go through anything like that again. He cheated on me, a lot. Turned out some friends knew and hadn't said. Now ex-friends for obvious reasons. Long story short it ended with a restraining order." I shrugged and concentrated on my coffee for a second, giving him chance to run a mile if he wanted to, which seemed likely. Why would anyone want to work through my baggage with me?

"That's awful. I'm so sorry he did that," Zack reached out and stroked his thumb over my hand for a second. I held my breath. That didn't freak me out like I thought it would. It was such a brief touch, but as he pulled away, I missed the sensation.

"I get why you feel that way, but not everyone is like that, I promise. Believe me, being raised with four sisters, I'd never dare treat a girl the wrong way. They would kill me. Where is he now? I take it the restraining order worked?"

"In Scotland, with a girlfriend and a baby. Feel bad for her," I sighed. "Whenever he had a night out, or went on a lads' holiday, he took home any girl he could. Doubt he's changed. He hasn't bothered me for a long time, he's nothing to worry about. Anyway, how about you? Single through choice or broken-hearted?" I wanted to move the conversation on, close that little box in my mind where those memories lived.

"No horror stories, no baggage. I just haven't met the right person so far," he took another drink of coffee. "I finished with my ex about three months ago, I could tell she wanted it to be more than it was. Didn't seem fair to keep it going when I knew she wasn't right for me."

The conversation got easier from there and before I knew it an hour had passed. As we laughed together, it didn't feel as though he was a stranger. Cassie loitered outside, watching us, I pointed her out to Zack.

"Well, I'd better let you get back," he said.

"I'm glad I came," I admitted, almost wishing he'd touch my hand again. "It was lovely to meet you."

"I'm not going to put you on the spot," he began. "I'd love to go on a proper date. Today has been so nice. I know you aren't sure if it's the right time but think about it and let me know. I can't tell you how much I want you to say yes, but even if it's a no, I'm glad I met you today."

I promised to message him later as we walked outside together, back into the sunshine. Zack turned to look at me, and a wave of nerves crashed into my mind. What was I meant to say? Was he expecting to kiss? I didn't know what to do as he leant forward and placed a single, soft kiss upon my cheek.

"Speak soon I hope," I stood there like a fool, processing how nice this had been. Enjoying this hadn't been part of my plan.

Cassie looked like she was about to burst with excitement, snapping me out of the trance. "Why didn't you reply to my message?"

As I pulled my phone out of my bag, I saw her message pop up, checking if everything was OK, and did I need rescuing. "Sorry, I didn't hear it. We were talking non-stop, and it was loud in there. You know the noise those coffee machines make."

As we headed back onto the train, Lancashire bound, Cassie made me tell her every single detail. I left out the fact that my cheek still felt warm where he'd kissed me, the skin there felt more alive, if that made sense.

"This all sounds so good. I take it you're going to see him again? He looked good, a solid eight and a half, I would say," she winked.

"Cassie!" I scolded, but in my own head I was thinking maybe even verging on a nine. "Well, coffee was one thing, but a proper date? Then he'll want a second date and then, before you know it, it's a regular arrangement and-"

"That's the point!" Cassie interrupted. "That's why most people date silly! You need a boyfriend, and I found a perfect specimen, so just say thank you and message him already," she sat back in the train seat and scrolled through her phone with a smug smile.

I let myself into my flat an hour later, it felt good to have alone time with my thoughts. I loved this place. It had been a mess initially but I needed somewhere to live, so I rented it at a cheap rate from my bosses as part of an agreement to fix it up. My favourite colour, dusky pink had been used to decorate and then accessorised with teal as a contrast. The place felt warm and snug, the vintage accessories I'd collected over time made it feel more homey, rather than cluttered. I switched on the soft lighting before heading through my bedroom and into the bathroom.

The clothes that had been meticulously chosen for the afternoon were abandoned on the wooden floor as I filled the roll top bath with steaming hot water and bubbles. The weekend hadn't been what I expected. Today had been lovely but I still didn't know what to do. Cassie found all of this so easy, and I wished I did too. Zack seemed so sweet and nice, but that didn't mean it couldn't all turn sour, and did I have the strength to face that again? After what had happened last time, my confidence in my own feelings was at rock bottom, and avoidance of situations was preferable to facing them a lot of the time. I didn't trust my own judgement anymore after having got it so wrong. The past four years had been a non-stop cycle of stress and anxiety with me never quite getting to a place of happiness or satisfaction. I knew it had to stop. It was a hell of a scary first step into the unknown.

Luke would know what advice to give, if he were here. I reached over for my phone and tried to call, but there wasn't even a ringtone. He was in Uganda, doing charity work for six weeks, and had said he would be hard to get hold of. It had been an ambition of his for a while. Luke was assisting as a legal volunteer, providing legal support and representation in communities who would otherwise have none. He'd posted a photograph on Instagram a few days ago and looked in his element. He was always at his happiest helping people. It was Luke who had helped me four years ago. He'd only just started working at Draper & Hughes when I went through the breakup.

He found me there late after work, too scared to go home, and when I confessed what was happening, Luke sprang into action. He helped me move, he sorted out legal proceedings - he was like a saviour, especially on that one night…

We became best friends, closer than most siblings, and were pretty much joined at the hip from then on. I must confess, this is where Cassie got her fascination with hot lawyers from. Luke was gorgeous, nobody could deny it. If I'd met him under different circumstances, I probably would've been lusting after him too, but he would always be my bestie.

Whenever we went anywhere, he got all the admiring glances, not me. He was six two and athletic looking. His hair a gorgeous, caramel blonde colour which he always had styled immaculately for work but when left alone would settle into messy beachy waves above the brightest blue eyes which seemed to sparkle when he was happy or excited. The most beautiful thing about him though, was his heart. He'd go out of his way to help anyone who needed it. We often saw sad cases in family law, and he always went the extra mile. On top of his charity work, he was just a truly good person. He was so good at giving advice, but I was going to have to fathom this out alone.

Cosiest pyjamas on, slumped on the couch, I began to type a message. Maybe I was overthinking this. Zack wasn't putting me under any pressure - maybe I should let it play out, see what happened.

Lily: How has the rest of your Sunday been? x
Zack: Nice thank you. Amazing company for coffee put me in a great mood x
Lily: I enjoyed it. Thank you for putting up with me being a nervous wreck x
Zack: You weren't at all, don't worry x I'm sorry I just stood there gawping at you. You took me by surprise, in a good way xx
Lily: Thank you. I think it was me stood there like a fool at the end so don't worry!
Zack: So, Lily ....
Lily: Yes Zack?
Zack: You're really going to make me work for this aren't you? x
Lily: I'm still trying to make my mind up x
Zack: I did mean what I said. No pressure. We had such a lovely time together today though. So how about dinner on Friday evening? Somewhere near you so you aren't on the train alone at night-time xx
Lily: Like a proper date-date? xx
Zack: Yes, a proper date-date xx

At this moment ten thousand butterflies began doing back flips in my stomach. I remembered how nice his eyes looked as he watched me over the coffee-shop table. I thought of his hand brushing across mine and instantly, goosebumps began to appear up my arms.

A conversation between Luke and I, shortly before his trip ran through my mind. Luke had told me that life was short and maybe it was time to start taking chances, to start being brave.

Lily: I would love to xx
Zack: You made my day xx

TWO

The hours on the clock ticked by at a snail's pace for the whole week, the days seemed to blur into slow motion, Friday never getting closer.

Cassie was a bouncing ball of excitement, she sent me hundreds of photos of dresses and hairstyles she thought I should try. I tried getting hold of Luke a couple more times, to no avail. It looked as though I'd have to wait until he returned to tell him what was going on.

My thoughts swung wildly between wishing it were Friday already, and just wanting to call the whole date off. Zack and I talked and messaged a lot during the week. He had a way of putting me at ease, something about him made me feel assured. It was like we already had a connection. By some miracle, Zack hushed the little voices of doubt in my mind.

We agreed to meet at a restaurant near to me, a couple of minutes from the train station. I'd never been, but Cassie assured me it was the epitome of style and romance, plus had amazing cheesecake – my weakness!

When Friday did arrive, it brought a warm, sunny breeze, full of promise. After the longest day ever at work, I styled my hair into soft, relaxed curls and used so much product it shone like it was polished, then I slipped the dress that Cassie had helped me choose over my shoulders. It was knee-length, a stunning emerald-green colour, with short sleeves made of lace. Cassie had even lent me her black Louis Vuitton heels that Guy had bought her for an anniversary gift. Having a best friend with the same size feet and a flawless shoe collection was perfection. Just to add to the pressure, I now also needed to focus on not tripping and breaking said expensive designer shoes. They looked amazing with the dress I noted, glancing up and down my reflection in the full-length mirror.

Was this too dressy? What did people do for dates? I took a selfie in the mirror and sent it to Cassie, hoping for an opinion. Looking at the time though, she'd be putting Ruby and Emilia to bed. As I headed downstairs, I once again wished that Luke was around for moral support.

My heart hammered in my chest as the taxi pulled up outside the restaurant. I felt a moment of apprehension as my phone pinged with a message, I wondered if maybe Zack had changed his mind and wanted to cancel.

Cassie: Drop Dead Gorgeous! I'd do you! Enjoy! x

That girl always made me laugh, and it would seem it was a perfect time to be smiling, when I looked up to see Zack walking the short distance over to me.

"Someone made you smile," he teased, "and it wasn't me?"

"It was just Cassie, messing with me. It's nice to see you

again." I had underestimated how good this would feel, my insides were in knots and I felt like my temperature had risen by about five degrees.

He moved forward and kissed my cheek, causing me to take a deep breath at his touch. He smelled amazing, like citrus and spice. A scent that would stay with me and play on my senses. He wore a dark blue shirt under a matching jacket, with faultless black jeans. He looked good. My eyes travelled down his body and I snapped myself back to the present in the nick of time. As I looked at Zack, I could see him looking at me the same way.

"I still can't believe you're real," he spoke quietly. "You look out of this world."

"You look pretty good yourself." The air felt thick around us, almost as if time moved slower. Zack held his hand out to me and as I took hold of it, a spark zipped around my body. He led me inside and the atmosphere only added to the sensory overload I was already beginning to feel.

One side of the restaurant was like a living wall of dusky peonies and roses. Soft lights cast warm shadows. Each table we passed as we were led to our own was separated from the others by a white crescent-shaped trellis, giving it a feeling of privacy.

A reluctance crossed my mind as I let go of Zack's hand to sit down. What was it about his touch that felt so moreish to me? "I'm sorry, I've gone all weird and awkward again, haven't I?"

"Not at all," he replied. "I know I said it already, but you look stunning."

I smiled, feeling flirtatious and mischievous, sending him

the full-length selfie which had winged its way to Cassie earlier. "There you go, lasting memory."

He grinned back. "We should get one together before the night is out."

We made small talk, but it felt as though there'd been a shift between us since we met for coffee. This felt more real, more invested. Those butterflies in my stomach moved further down my body and awakened feelings I hadn't had in a long time as the evening went on. It could have been a magical spell, it could have been coincidence, who knows. But the wine tasted better than ever. The food was cooked to perfection and Cassie had been so, so right about their cheesecake. It felt as though we were trying to soak each other in, and the time flew by.

As the waiter took our dessert dishes away, Zack's leg pressed against mine, I'd been so careful all night not to brush against him, but now that he'd made the move, I felt the connection of it throughout my entire body. I didn't want it to stop.

"I have to get the last train," he said, as his leg stayed in contact with mine. "Can I see you get home safe first?"

I nodded my head as he stood up and held his hand out to me. The loss I felt at the pressure of his leg leaving mine was soon made up for as he took my hand again, giving it a gentle squeeze. As we split the bill, I sent a message to Cassie.

Lily: He's walking me back before he gets the train. All is good! x
Cassie: Has he kissed you?! x
Lily: Not yet, give me a chance! x

We stepped out into the early spring night and walked slowly (I had no choice in those heels) back towards the town. The days might've gotten warmer over the past week or so, but the evenings were still chilly. Zack wrapped an arm around me.

"That place was amazing, good choice."

"It was, I knew it was popular, but I hadn't realised how beautiful it was inside." I glanced up at him and saw a smile still on his lips. We were only two or three minutes from the train station and the thought I'd been trying to keep at bay all night was getting stronger. I wanted to kiss him so bad.

I guided him towards a bright streetlight on the approach to the station. "We never got that selfie you mentioned. Want one now before the train gets here?"

"Definitely," he said. "Need a lasting memory of this."

I leaned into Zack, my back against his chest and held the phone in front of us, enjoying the warm feeling of him in the cool evening air. "Say cheese." I couldn't help but draw in a sharp breath as he placed his hand on my waist with a feather light touch. This wasn't how I'd expected to feel.

I snapped the photo and shared it to Zack's phone, noting how neither of us moved away from the other. Turning around, but staying close to him, our eyes were almost level. He moved his hand, but I could still feel the subtle warmth where it had been. "The train should only be a couple of minutes so…" I stopped and took a deep breath. "I wondered - is this the kissing bit?"

Zack tilted his head to the side subtly as he looked at me, his intense eyes almost trapped me in his gaze . His hands slid around my back to pull me closer. I was so out of practice, and about to panic when all of a sudden - his lips were on mine and I forgot about everything. The kiss sent tiny shards of fire to my brain, as signals and feelings that had lain dormant for so long shot off throughout my body. His lips teased mine with light, lingering touches and I had no control over myself as one hand snaked up into his hair, the other moved around his back and pressed him to me.

He deepened the kiss in response. The sensation of his breath mingling with mine blocked out the rest of the world, but all too soon, he pulled away.

"Did you hear that?" his voice was soft as he took a breath.

The night air felt cold against my lips now the kiss had ended. "Hear what?" I asked, confused, and still reeling from the delicious sensations.

An announcement rang out from the train station – 'I repeat, due to damage on the line, the last train of the evening has terminated before this station. There will be no more trains through this station tonight.'

We were still wrapped around each other and I stepped back self-consciously as a handful of people exited the station.

"This isn't part of a plan I engineered to stay with you or anything, I promise." Zack looked worried. "I'll sort a taxi or something."

"I didn't think for a minute you were damaging train lines just to try to get into my knickers," I teased. "Don't worry, we can figure it out. I fancied coffee at the restaurant but there wasn't time. Can you cope with homemade coffee and we can figure out what to do?"

He wrapped his arms back around me, much to my

delight. "Are you sure? I don't want you to feel like you have to ask me back."

"I do just mean coffee," I confirmed. "But yes, I'm sure, I think if you were an axe murderer, there would've been a sign by now. Cassie would've figured it out too."

"Lead the way then," he said with a smile.

We walked the five minutes back to my flat in near silence, still holding hands and sneaking glances at each other.

"Home sweet home," I announced, as we crossed the empty office car park, heading to the side entrance which led upstairs. After unlocking the bottom door, I started up the steep stairs, realising that I should've made him go first since he would now be enjoying a close-up view of my bottom.

There was a second door to unlock at the top of the stairs, I felt safe having two big doors between me and the outside world.

Zack's eyes looked around the large living area in surprise. "Wow, when you said a flat above the office, I didn't imagine this. It's so nice, puts mine to shame, you can now never come round," he joked.

"I'm lucky. They could expand and use this for more office space, but they're happy as they are. Perks of working for a small business," I winked. "Tour first, or coffee first?"

"Tour, then coffee, then a plan," he replied

"It's not a great tour to be fair, lounge here, dining area and kitchen at that end. Through here," I walked through the only other door. "Is my bedroom, which I am now hoping and praying I didn't leave in a mess." Phew, the laundry basket was empty and there was no sign of underwear or socks on the floor! "And the bathroom is through here." I motioned to the open door.

"I can see why you love it. And you now can't ever, ever see my place."

"I assume Zack is short for Zachary?" I asked as we stood in the doorway of my bedroom.

A playful look rolled over his face. "Yes. But if you call me that, I feel ten years old, being told off for annoying a sister or two."

"Hmm, interesting to know," I said. "You know Zachary, I haven't been kissed for four years, I didn't know how that was going to go."

As he replied, he had a look on his face as though he was... enchanted. I couldn't comprehend what was happening. "Now I'm feeling the pressure," he pressed his lips together for a brief moment. "So does that mean you enjoyed it or..."

"I think it's a pity that train announcement interrupted us-"

His eyes sparkled as his arms slipped around my waist. "What announcement?" he reached for me, his hand traced a soft pattern up my back, leaving a trail of goosebumps as it went. Then it was like that last kiss had never ended. I felt breathless as he bit my bottom lip with delicious gentleness, his tongue slowly teased at my own. The sensation made me light-headed. I leaned back against the wall and pulled him with me, my hand settled under his shirt, feeling the warm, bare skin of his back. I was intrigued by how strong and firm his body felt. His hands ran down my sides as he pressed me harder against the wall and I knew that these feelings and sensations were going to overpower any trepidation that remained within me.

I gasped as he stopped, his forehead pressed against my own. "It's killing me to say this, but I know you want to take things slow, and that's just too good…" he blew out a soft breath and opened his eyes. "Plus, you promised me coffee. You can't tease a man with promises of coffee." he grinned and kissed my forehead before heading back out into the living room. My insides were like molten lava as I switched on the coffee machine, trying to calm myself down and breathe at a steady pace.

Zack was looking at a large photograph frame that was the focal point of the living room wall. Luke had bought it me a couple of years ago for Christmas and I adored it. A white, heart-shaped frame sat in the middle, made of willow, which then spiralled off into more frames around the edge, to create a bigger heart. Luke had given it me with a photograph of myself in the middle, and I'd filled all the other spaces with the people I loved.

"They're all my favourite people in the world," I explained. "Makes me happy every time I stop and look at it."

"It's lovely," he said. "Maybe I can make it in there one day."

"Maybe so," I replied coyly. "For the longest time, I felt like a huge failure for having so few people in my life. I felt ashamed to be honest. Over time it became apparent I was lucky. It might be a small circle, but it's the best and we'd do anything to look out for each other. I wouldn't swap that."

"I don't blame you." That soft smile lit his face again. "I recognise Cassie, guessing that's work friends? Parents? But why are you up a mountain with a guy who looks like a male model?" he asked the question innocently enough, but I could see something behind his eyes.

"That's Luke, my other bestie," I responded. "We'd struggled to the top of Snowdon. Well, I struggled, he was fine."

"Oh, OK, when you said a lawyer from work who helped you, I imagined a fifty-year-old guy."

"Luke's like my big brother. It wasn't just the restraining order and the legal stuff he did for me. He sat here so many nights when I was scared, he built my confidence back up bit by tiny bit. I can't think of a single occasion he couldn't help me. I didn't want nights out for so long so he and Cassie would have fun nights in with me instead." I cast my eyes downward and bit my lip. "They were horrible times, but I guess it made me who I am today. I know I couldn't have done it without him."

"Sounds like it was an awful time." Zack took hold of my hand.

I nodded, not entirely comfortable at bringing it all up. "Anyway, the couch is calling me, you didn't wear two-inch heels all night."

I sat down, my nerves and worry kicking in again. *Was I sat in the right place? How close was he going to sit to me? Why had I brought an almost stranger home?* Zack snapped me out of my thoughts as he sat and faced me, close enough to be cosy, but not overpowering.

"So, I looked, and I can book an Uber, but it will take about an hour to get here, is that OK?"

"How much will it cost? It's quite a way." I said.

"Estimate is fifty pounds," he rolled his eyes. "Bloody trains hey?"

"That's insane, you cannot spend fifty quid to get home.

Look, just stay here. I'm happy sleeping on the couch, you can have the bed, and get the train tomorrow for a fiver. Honestly, that amount of money is daft." I said, wondering how my brain let me say that so quick before *then* showing me images of axe murderers and psychopaths.

"You're so sweet, but I don't want to put you on the spot. It's only the second time you've met me, and I know you were wary about it." he responded.

I think the two bottles of wine had befuddled my brain, as I pressed my lips to his again to stop his words. "I trust you Zack. Please just stay."

He kissed me back. Maybe I was ready for this? "One condition." His voice was deep and breathy. "I sleep on the couch, the bed is yours."

"Deal." I smiled and sank back into the comfortable cushions, loving that I'd got my own way. "You know what this means?" Zack shook his head.

"Sleepover. How about pyjama's, wine, music, get to know each other better? I've got clothes you can borrow from when we had a team event at work, as long as you can cope with our logo on the t-shirt." I said.

"This sounds intriguing, but I think it'd be classed as a second date," he teased. "Is that OK with you Lily?"

"Coming round to the idea more and more every minute," I replied, but I still felt as if I needed to explain further. "I'm sorry if I seem, dull or whatever for being so cautious about this. My ex... I met him when I was seventeen. He was my first proper boyfriend; he was the first person I slept with. There hasn't been anyone since, on either level. I doubt myself so much after putting everything I had into someone who seemingly, didn't give a toss."

"You don't have to explain yourself, and you don't have to feel like you're being judged," Zack took hold of my hand again. "When Cassie messaged me about you, I figured there was nothing to lose in the crazy sounding idea of hers. But when I met you... I was blown away, and still am by how sweet you are, how well we get on, how utterly gorgeous you are. I wasn't on that dating site for a laugh, or a series of one-night stands, I wanted to meet someone special. I feel like I did. We can take this as slow as you need, I will never put you under pressure. You're in control of this."

"Thank you Zack. Can you grab a bottle of wine from the fridge once you're changed? I only need five minutes to get ready."

He nodded as I closed the door to my bedroom. What had come over me? The girl who wouldn't look at a dating website a week ago. This was insane, yet I was having so much fun. Pyjamas. I needed to find sexy pyjamas, but not too sexy. I wondered if cute pyjamas might be better? After frantically rifling through my chest of drawers, I settled on a dark pink chequered set, which consisted of shorts and a button through top. One quandary after another – should I take off my bra? I never slept in a bra but there was a man here. That being said, the wire was digging into me horribly, so off it went.

I ran my toothbrush over my teeth, fairly confident there was going to be more kissing, and gave my hair a check before I opened the door into the lounge, stomach full of nerves.

"Is this bottle good? You seemed to have a few in the fridge." Zack teased me as he pointed to the wine on the coffee table, not before I noticed his eyes glance up and down my bare legs.

"It's perfect." I slid into the seat next to him and curled my legs up under me, so our knees were touching.

"Did you find what you needed?" I asked.

"I think this flat contains everything I need." his face lit up in a mischievous smile.

We drank the wine and listened to each other's playlists, talking about everything under the sun. In between talking there was kissing, and although his hand drove me insane as he ran it up and down my leg, or his fingers turned me to jelly as they slid up my pyjama top and stroked my back. He was never anything but a gentleman. This was both a blessing and a curse as I was torn between wants.

We must have fallen asleep, as I woke up on the couch, half of me warm and cosy in Zack's arms, but my legs freezing cold. I squinted at the clock; it was two in the morning. Spring may have arrived, but the nights were still cold. I turned myself around, now facing Zack and kissed his ear softly as I whispered. "Zack, I think we fell asleep."

He murmured sleepy, incoherent words as he pressed his lips to my neck.

"Zack," I whispered a little louder. "It's too cold to sleep here. Come and sleep in the bed."

He didn't speak, he just pulled me up with him as he stood. His lips needy on mine he navigated us towards the bedroom. I don't know if I shivered with the cold or the anticipation, as the back of my legs bumped into the mattress. I tried to pull him down with me, but he resisted, instead pulling at the duvet before lowering me down.

He straddled my lower legs, pulling the warm covers up

over us both. His free hand trailed up my body in firm, slow motions, it was driving me insane. Even more so, when he followed it up with tiny, soft kisses. The kisses tickled around my belly button in a soft, slow circle before bypassing my pyjama top and wandering along my collar bone. Then his hands were in my hair as he tilted my head from side to side. He kissed every inch of my neck, almost savouring it. Frustratingly, he then rolled me onto my side and pressed himself behind me in an embrace.

"I hope you feel warmer now," his breath was hot on my shoulder as he dragged his lips over the area.

I could barely speak; I would've done anything he asked of me in that moment. It was apparent he was as turned on as I was, as he pressed against my back. I tried to move my arm to reach for him, but he held it in place, stopping me.

"It's too soon, I don't want you to rush and end up regretting it. I don't want to be a regret," he whispered straight into my ear, his lips brushed my skin and sent a shudder through me. "Thank you for trusting me to sleep here with you, goodnight beautiful."

I pulled his hand up to my mouth, placing a soft kiss on it. I knew what he said made sense, but it didn't stop me aching for more. "Goodnight Zack." I whispered back. He snuggled even closer into me as I fell into the dreamiest sleep I could remember in a long time.

THREE

*M*y eyes flickered open, my brain shot to life… there was a man in my bed. *A man in my bed!* Zack was still asleep, facing towards me with his arm draped over my side. I lay there and took in the detail of him. His face looked strong and sexy. Such full, dark eyelashes, I was almost jealous. His lips were parted as he slept and I traced my finger over the dark stubble on his chin, concentrating on how spiky it felt, amazed at how it had grown while we slept. It was surreal having a man in my bed, but I was delighted about it. Zack's hair was all messed up and I couldn't help but run my fingers through it, starting at the shorter hair above his ear and up into the longer length on top. What would he be thinking about me if he had woken up first? Would he be examining me in a similar way?

That moment felt delicious, I wished I could take a picture, but that would be verging on creepy. I became aware that Zack was awake and watching me. I sucked on my lip, embarrassed at being caught checking him out like that.

The arm that was draped over me pulled me closer,

holding me tighter. "I'm so glad that train didn't arrive," he smiled and looked into my eyes, for a moment we watched each other, the connection I felt there drove me insane. His eyes were the same shade of brown as mine, dark and chocolatey, the pupil hard to differentiate unless you were close up, like this. This was a nice place to be.

"Did I wake you up? I wasn't being weird, promise," I tried to explain. "You just looked, I don't know... I wanted to see what you felt like." A blush spread up my face as I hoped he understood what I meant.

"As far as being woken up goes, that's never going to be an issue," he ran a finger down the side of my face, as I'd done to him a few moments earlier. It brushed over my lips, before he wrapped it in my hair, a playful smile on his face. "I see what you mean. This is nice. How is your hair that soft?" he ran his fingers through the dark strands, watching them fall between the gaps.

Moments like this had been missing from my life for a long time. My breath came faster as I shuffled closer, running my fingers over that rough stubble again. Our bodies were now pressed against each other as I tentatively touched my lips to his, feeling him relax into me with a deep sigh. *How had I forgotten that kissing was this good?* I ran my hand inside the borrowed t-shirt, savouring the feel of his hot skin under my fingertips. I could've stayed there all day, just getting used to how he felt and looked, the effect he had on me every time he touched me - I longed for him to touch me.

The kiss was getting more demanding, my leg slid up around his thigh, willing him to keep doing this to me. He moaned at the movement, rewarding me with hands that skimmed the curve of my bottom, fingers inching inside my shorts, tempting me to keep going.

"Zack…" I whispered into his mouth. Yet he pulled back from me, that sensation of being momentarily lost hit me again, as the contact with him was broken.

"Sorry," he whispered, as he sat up and edged over to the bathroom. "I need a minute."

I smiled sheepishly as it occurred to me that for someone who asked to take things slow, I was really testing him. That had all felt so good. I buried myself back under the covers as I inhaled a deep breath from his pillow.

It was almost lunchtime by the time we found ourselves wandering back to the train station, showered, composed and full of coffee and croissants. Zack wrapped his arms around me as we stood on the platform, placing a kiss on the top of my head, which was at a perfect height now I was back in my Converse. "So, both first date and second date were incredible. How hard is it going to be for me to persuade you to say yes to date number three?"

"Yes," I said. "It's a definite yes. No hard work required."

"Is it ridiculously soon to ask about tomorrow? Only it's going to be tricky this week with work, and next weekend seems too far away," he watched me cautiously, obviously worried about my answer, given how nervous I'd been. There seemed to be more behind his eyes though.

"Tomorrow sounds perfect," I pressed a quick kiss to his lips as the train arrived. "Call me later, we can make arrangements."

It was like I was floating on air as I strolled home, stopping at Starbucks along the way for more coffee. Cassie needed details, and a big thank you!

"So?" I opened the door a couple of hours later to see Cassie holding a bottle of wine with a giant grin on her face.

"Cassie, don't let this go to your head, but I think you may have been right," she squeezed past me with a smile, spotting the wine glasses already laid out on the table, in preparation for her visit.

"You messaged me about eleven to say you were safe and heading home and left all the detail out! Was there kissing in the end? Are you seeing him again?" she bombarded me with questions as she poured the wine. "Why didn't you reply to me last night?"

"Seemed rude to text when I had a guest here," I smirked, knowing she would be loving this.

She gawped at me. "What? You invited him back? I'm shocked! You didn't even want coffee! Don't get me wrong, it's well overdue, I'm just surprised. Hope you were careful?!"

"It wasn't quite like you're imagining," I began to explain. "The train was cancelled, and an Uber was really expensive. It made sense for him to stay. He left at lunchtime today." I blushed at the memory of him being here.

"Oh my god! You should've told me last night though, not the safest thing to do. Luke would lose the plot if he knew. Zack slept on the couch then, did he?" she asked with a raised eyebrow.

"Well, that was the plan, but it was cold, so he slept in the bed with me." Cassie started bouncing up and down on the couch as she grinned from ear to ear with excitement. "Slept, Cassie. We went to sleep, there was no sex."

"Was there other stuff?" She moved closer to me on the couch, I was trapped.

"Sort of," I turned bright red. "And yes, you may have been right that I needed to meet someone. The whole night was lovely."

She threw her arms around me, then filled our glasses up. "This is amazing. When are you seeing him again? I bet he looked good last night too?"

I passed her my phone, rolling my eyes, but actually loving this conversation. It was open on the selfie we'd taken together before we kissed. I'd been staring at that photo and smiling most of the afternoon.

"Aww! You two look so good together." she pulled a soppy face.

"I still feel scared though, don't get mad at me when I say this, I know you did last time I mentioned it," I took a deep breath. "When Zack kisses me, it's crazy intense, I have a sort of reaction to him touching me. I feel like he's really going to know what he's doing in bed; does that make sense?" Cassie nodded. "So, what if... what if I'm absolutely crap in bed? What if that's why *he* felt the need to sleep with all those other girls? What if I get all engrossed with Zack and then he thinks I'm crap too and leaves?"

"Do not start this again! Him being unable to keep it in his pants had nothing to do with you being lacking in any way. Don't let him affect another moment of your life. Judging by the smile on your face every time you mention Zack, and the fact he spent the night in your bed, I'm guessing there's pretty good chemistry going on?"

"Amazing chemistry," My lips pressed themselves

together, hoping there was still a taste of him left behind. "I get goosebumps just thinking about it."

"Then go with it. Don't overthink it, and make sure to give me all the details when it happens," Cassie winked. "When are you seeing him again?"

"Tomorrow. We were on the phone before you arrived. I'm going to go over late morning. There's an artisan market on a Sunday. Weather forecast is gorgeous so we can wander round and eat and drink and talk and-" Cassie cut me off.

"You're completely smitten. I can tell. I should've charged commission," She hugged me again. "I just want you to have what I have with Guy. Imagine the double dates Lily!"

———

The train felt so different to last week. I didn't seem to mind the grubby seats, the weird musty smell or the feral kids having an argument at the other end of the carriage. The nerves this time were positive and excitable. I was looking forward to today so much I felt flustered. The image of Zack in my bed wouldn't leave my mind.

Zack met me at the train station, swooping me into a hug with luscious kisses, and even though we were in public and I would expect to feel uncomfortable, I didn't care. It felt good to be back with him. We chatted in his car like excited kids going on a school trip. In some ways it seemed like the last twenty-four hours had gone painstakingly slow, but in other ways it felt like he'd just left. Either way we seemed as glad as each other to be reunited.

He turned to me as he parked the car outside a modern block of flats. "Do you want to come in or shall we go straight out?" he asked. "It's really basic compared to your place, so I don't want you to think it's awful."

"I wouldn't think that!" I tapped him on the arm with a playful swipe. "Maybe we should go straight out and then see if I feel ready to brave it."

The market was a five-minute walk from Zack's flat and I realised we were in a much more affluent area than I was used to; this was not a standard market. There were a multitude of fancy coffee stands, artisan bakeries, eye wateringly expensive cupcakes and it seemed like at least half the food was vegan; there was even vegan dog food. This wasn't a market with old ladies carrying shopping bags and stalls of knock off goods, it was full of well-dressed people who looked like they belonged. I loved it!

We wandered around as if we had all the time in the world. Holding hands as we talked, the different smells from the stalls luring us to them together. Whenever we stopped to look at the wares, we would exchange touches and looks. The sunshine was out, and I still had that feeling of floating on air. We ended up with aromatic coffee, an antipasti platter with freshly baked sourdough bread and beautiful hand-baked Portuguese pastries.

We headed to a nearby park and settled under an old tree, eating in the shade of its large branches. Everything tasted amazing and fresh, and I couldn't help but equate it to the new experiences I was devouring.

"These pastries are so good," I said as I wiped flaky pastry crumbs from my top and smiled.

"You said you love to bake?"

"Yeah, but I don't have a knack like this for pastry," I replied, wiping a crumb from Zack's cheek. "I'm awesome at brownies, blondies, cupcakes, birthday cakes, the more traditional stuff."

"Do you just do it for fun?"

"Yes. It could be a business I suppose but I don't have a big enough kitchen and it'd take a lot of time to set up. Maybe one day. For now, I'm happy being chief office baker, and sorting out everyone's birthdays," I replied. "Oh, I should've made you something. Next time?" A red flush swept up my face as I heard my words. "I mean, if you want there to be a next time, I wasn't assuming-"

"Lily," he smiled and ran his finger over my lips again. "Please relax, honestly. You don't have to worry or apologise every time you say something. Unless in the next hour you try to mug me or snog my flatmate, I'm pretty sure I want there to be a next time. Especially if it involves brownies."

"Thank you," I said. "It's just nerves. Can I ask though, what does your flatmate look like? Am I likely to want to snog him?" I bit my lip, hoping he could sense the joke.

Zack leaned in close. "You'd better not, I'd rather you mugged me." Another sensuous kiss landed on my lips and we forgot everything else for a few minutes as that deliciousness enveloped me once again.

Zack looked content as he drank more coffee. "You seem like you live in the now," he said. "It's refreshing, so many people obsess about the future and their master plan where they have to achieve certain milestones by a certain age."

"I guess I realised a while ago now, that it's the simple things that make me happy, so I concentrate on those and everything else just happens when it's meant to happen."

Zack placed his hand on my knee. "You are literally the loveliest person I ever met," he said, staying close. "While you were waiting for the coffee, I got something too. I figured as you had about twelve bottles in your fridge that you were a fan." He pulled two mini prosecco bottles out of the bag with a cheeky smile.

"Nice, what are you having?" I teased as I took a bottle.

We sat together, leaning against the tree, drinking cold prosecco straight from the bottle. The warm spring breeze washed over us as the fizz from the bubbles added to the excitement in my stomach. For once my world felt serene, in a way it hadn't for a while now.

I rested my head on Zack's shoulder and he kissed the top of my head once again. "Can I ask a question? I don't want to sound stupid though." I said quietly.

"Yes, and I wouldn't ever think you were stupid."

"So, I guess you've dated a lot, this is all new to me. Is it always like this? This feels so natural, and I thought it would be all awkward and weird." I admitted.

Zack looked thoughtful as he spoke. "Trying to think of a good way to word it, but no, it's never like this. Never for me before at least. I haven't been trawling dating sites for years by the way, but when I have been on dates, they've not been great. Girls that either lied about their age or are nothing like they made out. Or you get people that are after someone with money, or often just want sex. I never found the prospect of sleeping with a girl who is working their way through the internet that appealing myself. Sometimes there have been second dates, but there never seemed to be the right connection. I've never been in a relationship with a girl from a dating site, when I have been in a relationship it was after we met in person and got to know each other the normal way." he laced his fingers into mine and rested our hands together, on his knee. "So basically no, it doesn't normally feel anything like this. This is something else entirely…"

"I just wondered," I said. My voice was quiet as I squeezed his hand a little tighter, trying to stop my mind from running away with me as I absorbed his words and what they could mean. Was he feeling this as much as I was?

We strolled back to Zack's flat, holding hands and chatting about anything and everything. As he went to unlock the front door, it opened out and a tall, skinny man with a huge black beard and a mass of black curls escaping from a ponytail stepped outside. There seemed to more hair than man.

"You off out?" Zack asked him.

"Going shopping, you need anything?"

"No, all good thanks. This is Lily," Zack smiled and raised our entwined hands up into the air. "Lily, this is Adam, the infamous hairy flat mate." he then mouthed to me, "no snogging," and smiled with a mischievous glance.

"Lovely to meet you," Adam replied, his face breaking into a cheery smile. "I didn't believe him when he told me the tale about the train either. I'll leave you in peace, catch you later." He waved as he headed away.

"Aww, have you been talking about our date?" I teased Zack as I followed him inside.

"As if. What was your name again?" He pressed a quick kiss to my lips. "This is the living room; the kitchen is through the archway there." Turning, he pointed to two doors leading off the living room. "The left door is my bedroom; the right door is Adam's – please never get them mixed up. Could be awkward."

It wasn't awful like he'd made out at all. It was just... obviously inhabited by men! The walls were cream, a large black leather couch dominated the room, sitting on top of a polished wooden floor. The main focal point of the room was a crazy big television surrounded by various games consoles, controllers, chargers and other gadgets. Zack had mentioned that Adam was a games designer. I guess he took research seriously judging by the amount of equipment he owned.

"You made out it was a total dump, but it's nice," I said. "It's not full of stuff like mine is, you have as many games consoles as I have photographs."

"I would blame Adam, but I don't take much convincing to join in," he watched me closely. "Want to come and see my room?"

I nodded, as he led me over and opened the door. The room had a large window on the adjacent wall, the bed underneath it was covered in soft looking, dark grey sheets. A large, double wardrobe took up another wall. His room was so neat. I walked to the wardrobe and ran my finger along the door.

"If I open this up, is a pile of stuff going to fall on me? Or is it always this tidy?" I grinned.

"Maybe not quite this tidy, but I can promise there won't be an avalanche."

Opening the double doors, I was pleasantly surprised at his organisation skills. There were more suits than I could count, with sections devoted to ties and waistcoats. Then there seemed to be a more casual side with jeans and tops. The bottom of the wardrobe had pull out shelves containing shoes, boots and belts. "I'm impressed," I said. "This is a lot of suits, I like them." The soft material felt nice under my fingertips.

"It's work stuff, no dodgy skeletons in there." Walking over to join me, he put his arms around my waist and rested his head on my shoulder. I turned to face him and slid my arms around him in return.

"I like it here, it's nice." I said.

"It's nicer when you're here," he stepped towards the bed. "Come lie down with me?"

Part of me wanted to pick up where we left off yesterday, but I was worried it'd feel awkward. We lay down, facing each other like we had in my bed. Time moved in strange ways at the moment, I couldn't comprehend what was going on. "Does it seem weird to you that we only met for the first time last Saturday?" I asked.

Zack nodded. "It does. I don't want to sound all cliché again and make you roll your eyes at me," he laughed. "I feel like I've known you a lot, lot longer than a week." Zack pressed his lips to mine, and I felt swept up by him all over again. "I have important questions to ask you though, these could be deal breakers." He leaned up on his elbow and tried to look serious. I raised an eyebrow at him as he began. "Marmite?"

"God no!" I replied instantly.

"Phew!" Zack smiled. "Ben and Jerry's or Haagen Dazs?"

"Tough one. With you I think Haagen Dazs, its smoother. The chunky bits in Ben and Jerry's could get messy." I tried to look as innocent as possible.

"I like flirty Lily, I will add Haagen Dazs to the shopping list right away. Big spoon or little spoon in bed?" He feathered a quick kiss across my lips with his question.

"Little spoon, definitely," I replied, wishing he would keep kissing me. "My turn now! Blondes or brunettes?"

"Brunettes every time." Zack said.

"Sweet or savoury?"

"Sweet. I love sweet."

"Hmm. What about if you had to choose between touching me with your mouth or touching me with your hands? If you could only use one?" I ran my fingers through that dark, chocolatey hair.

"Are we not considering any other body parts in this scenario?" Zack asked.

"Not at the moment we're not."

"Mouth then, definitely mouth." Zack slid his hand into the back of my jeans and pulled me even closer. "It's the big question now," I couldn't concentrate as I felt his hand on the skin of my lower back, pressing me to him. "You didn't want to kiss Adam, did you?" he teased.

I laughed and kissed Zack's neck in between my words. "Definitely... only thinking about... kissing... you." As he rolled on top of me, his mouth hard on mine, I sank into the feeling, it drove me crazy. Our limbs entangled around each other, the weight of him on top of me... I was kicking myself for having had the 'let's go slow' talk.

The front door banged open, we heard Adam putting shopping away, the kitchen cupboards slamming as he hummed to himself. We lay back down on our sides and giggled at the interruption.

"That was nice." I smiled, watching for any reaction Zack might give.

Zack stretched his neck from side to side as he smiled at

me. "I better work on my technique if the only word I'm getting is nice."

"What words would you prefer?" I asked as I ran my finger up his side.

"Actually, I'd prefer to make you speechless," he held himself up on his bent elbow, his mouth hovered over my ear whilst his fingers traced patterns along my stomach. My back arched towards him, willing him to either move up or down, but those fingers just circled and circled, my skin tense underneath them. "I would prefer to hear your breath in my ear, to notice how it catches and changes depending how I touch you. I could spend days working out which touches worked best."

I strained to move my mouth to his, wanting to kiss him and carry this all on. "Slowly Lily, remember?" His voice teased me.

I wanted to take this further but as much as I was beginning to admit to myself how besotted I was with Zack, I still felt scared to make that jump, he was right to make me stick to my own rule. There had undoubtedly been a shift since yesterday. Our kisses were deeper, his hands gripped me firmer and wandered further all the time. After another public display of affection on the station platform, the train took me home. My mind was overflowing with what an incredible weekend it had been, and the fact I was missing Zack already.

FOUR

*T*he next two weeks were exhilarating, filled with a sense that a new chapter of my life was taking off. Zack lived about an hour away, not quite long distance but it did require more planning. I found myself in a flurry of late-night video calls interspersed with dates whenever we could. A movie night snuggled together at mine. Cocktails at beautiful bars near his flat. Long lunches, coffee's, walks, and every single minute of it he drew me closer into him. Workdays were full of messages and cute photographs, planning for when we could see each other next. After each date I'd replay the conversations, the physical touches, over and over in my mind, wanting to cement them there for eternity.

My trust issues and anxieties seemed to dissolve when I was with Zack. All the barriers and shields that had built up around me, just made way for him. He was still insistent we stick to the slow rule. We uncovered new elements of each other, causing me to be saturated with desire. Our bedtime video calls would undoubtedly get steamy, and so night after night my own hands and mind ran riot with fantasies about

Zack. Fantasies where he was not a gentleman and slow wasn't in his vocabulary, well, not in that way at least. I was desperate to feel his presence on me and it seemed like my body was always too hot.

Explaining all of this to Cassie over sandwiches on my lunchbreak, I struggled with my blushes.

"Lily," she looked at me, a glimmer in her eye. "I know it's been a while for you, but all of those signs are textbook you know?"

"Textbook what?" I asked, genuinely confused.

"Textbook falling in love you idiot!"

"What the… Cassie, I know you want to buy a hat and marry me off, but it's been three weeks, I am not in love with him." I exclaimed.

"No," she said. "You're in the process of falling in love, and that's the best, most delicious, amazing bit, so you should enjoy every second of it."

I took a half-hearted bite of my tuna sandwich to save responding. Cassie simply smiled, "No appetite? Textbook!"

"Shush!" I threw a crisp at her.

"How many times in say, an hour, do you think about him?" Cassie asked with a glint in her eye.

"Cassie," I sighed. "You're right, OK, you're right. It's too soon though and I'm majorly stressing. I think about him all the time, I can't concentrate on anything. When I'm at home I look through my photographs of us all the bloody time. Every time he touches me, it's as though all the breath is being sucked out of me. I get so many hot flushes I could be menopausal, and my poor heart is going to be worn out with the palpitations. Sometimes when he speaks to me, I stand there like an idiot because I can't think of words, like I'm lost in his presence. I'm getting carried away and I don't trust myself."

Cassie put an arm around me and squeezed me towards her. "Have a little faith in yourself, stop overthinking and just let it be. It sounds pretty damn amazing to me. It's a long time since I went through that, I'm ridiculously happy for you."

"I don't know if it's the same for him though Cass."

"Pretty sure it is!" she grinned as she reached for her phone.

"What do you mean? Have you spoken to him?" I frowned at her.

"He had my number from when I set up the coffee shop meet. I might've messaged him since..." Cassie chewed her lip and focused on her phone.

"What did you say to him? I can't believe you did that!" I prayed she hadn't said anything to humiliate me.

"It was after you had spent the whole weekend with him, pretty good going for a first date that by the way, 'Mrs I Don't Want A Boyfriend'! I just said thank you to him for meeting up, I know it was a bit weird the way I set it up. And that I was made up to see you couldn't stop smiling."

I frowned at her. "And he said?"

"Well, I don't know if he'd want me to tell you." I glared at her and she sighed before getting her phone out of her bag to read me the message. "He said, 'I can't stop smiling either. She's amazing.'"

I smiled and bit my lip, thinking again how it was crazy, that this was all happening. The little voices telling me to not risk it, to not trust myself, were being driven away at speed.

"I sort of then suggested you two should come round for

45

dinner one night." Cassie pretended to watch the clouds, to save having to meet my eyes.

"Why would you do that?"

"Come on Lily, you know I always wanted to do the double dating thing. From a purely selfish point of view, what that arsehole did to you, it ruined all my plans! I wanted us to be each other's bridesmaids, plan each other's baby showers, take our toddlers to play group together. We ended up out of sync though." She screwed her face up a little. "Sometimes feels like you and Luke get all the fun."

"I'm not sure Luke thinks that way, sure he's sick of being consulted on which handbag I should buy." I smiled at my beautiful friend. "I didn't know you felt like that Cassie. You know what, dinner at yours sounds perfect. I'd love you and Guy to meet Zack."

"Leave it all to me! I'll message him now. I like messaging your boyfriend, he sends me kisses." she grinned cheekily.

"I'm not sure he's my boyfriend yet."

"I am." Cassie squeezed me into a tight hug, before I headed back to work.

———

That Saturday evening, I waited at the train station, I'd got there too early with my impatience. I wore yet another painstakingly chosen outfit, this time involving black skinny jeans which I knew made my bum look amazing, along with a plunge-neck black top. I was determined to evoke a reaction from Zack tonight.

It seemed to work, as he stepped off the train, his eyes grazed over me with a slow longing. I reached for his hand as he neared me, I was caught off guard as he pulled me into a tight embrace.

"You look unbelievable." His voice vibrated into my ear as he turned my face to his and kissed me with a slight roughness.

"Nice to see you too," I smiled as I admired his own tight jeans and shirt. "Normal people say hi."

"Normal people aren't thinking what I'm thinking right now." He took hold of my hand with a grin, as we headed out of the station together.

"Lily, no pressure, I just want to check if you wanted me to stay over tonight?"

My stomach did a complete flip over. "I would love you to stay over."

"You still aren't getting your wicked way with me, don't get too excited." He lifted my hand to his mouth and kissed it with a delicious softness.

We ambled to Cassie's house, happy to be together. As we approached the fancier part of town, Zack began to pay attention to the neighbourhood.

"We call her house the mini mansion, it's gorgeous." I explained.

"What does her husband do again?"

"Guy? I don't understand it, something to do with importing produce, sounds boring. He doesn't bother trying to tell me anymore. Luke would know." I explained.

"Be amazing to have a place like this."

"Well, Guy is five years older than us, so maybe you'll have one in five years." I squeezed his hand.

"Only want one if I have my perfect girl in it too."

"What's she like then?" I asked, enjoying our little game.

"To be honest, she has an incredible arse, and that distracts me so much I couldn't tell you the rest." He slid his hand behind me and squeezed my bottom with a firm touch.

I rolled my shoulders in a circle, aiming to ease the tension. "And there I was thinking you were a gentleman Zachary."

His mouth lifted up at one side in a sexy smile. "I think you know that you're my perfect girl Lily."

My heart fluttered in excited ripples as we stopped outside a large, immaculate, beautiful home. "Here we are. Mini mansion."

Cassie opened the door, her grin reached from ear to ear. I hadn't even had chance to knock. Her eyes locked on the bare skin within my top. "Jesus Lily, I'm going to have to warn Guy!"

"Cassie, Zack. Zack, Cassie." I shot her a warning glare.

Before the poor man knew what was happening, she had pulled him into a tight hug. "It's so good to meet you in person. Come in, what do you want to drink?"

Seated around a beautiful glass dining table, on tall chairs that felt more comfortable than my couch, we ate succulent roast duck courtesy of Guy. Cassie had ordered in loads of different wine, wanting to make everyone feel at home.

Zack cleared his throat. "Cassie, I should thank you for introducing us. As random internet propositions go, it's good."

"I plan to open my matchmaking service next year," she took a theatrical bow.

"I think you should quit while you're ahead." Guy smiled at her, full of adoration. They were such a loved-up couple.

"What is it you do Guy? Lily mentioned imports?"

Cassie rolled her eyes and motioned for me to follow her as the two of them began to discuss work.

"Did you spray those jeans on Lily? Surprised you could eat in them!" she teased.

"I don't know what you're talking about! So, you like Zack?"

"He's gorgeous! I love him. In fact, I found him, so I'm going to keep him. I'm due a trade-up."

"Pfft!" I grinned. "He's great though, isn't he?"

She nodded, as she plated up four beautiful desserts. "I had an interesting chat with Guy before."

"Everything OK?" I asked.

"Yep, we're going to try for another baby!" Cassie's whole face lit up with happiness.

"Amazing news! Give me the nod if you want us to get going," I winked. "You were right, by the way. This is lovely, doing couples stuff together."

"I know! I can already imagine us all, summers in the south of France, kids crashed out while we drink fancy wine outside the villa."

"Let's give it a little longer before you book the next ten years in hey?" We carried the dessert plates through, to find Zack and Guy chatting away like old friends. It wasn't just the wine making me feel warm and fuzzy as we said goodbye later on.

Zack and I fell through the front door of my flat. My hands held his face, to keep his kisses on me, as he gripped at my hips, pulling me against his body.

My heart was about to beat up and out of my throat as Zack pressed me against the wall. His hands slid down underneath me, and I whimpered slightly as I felt him lift me up. My legs wrapped around him, as if on a lustful autopilot. His lips moved from my mouth, down and across my neck.

"I haven't been able to stop thinking about you for a minute," he murmured to me between kisses.

My body felt out of my control as it reacted to him, but my mind wanted to know what he was thinking and feeling, I needed to know if this was as intense for him as it was for me. Or was I being naïve and reading more into the situation we found ourselves in? "What things were you thinking?" I asked as I squeezed my legs tighter.

"Things like this…" he replied as his finger stroked my skin from the top of my neck, down the exposed skin of my breastbone, then all the way back up. "How much I wanted to kiss you all week. That I miss you when we aren't together. Those sorts of things," he watched my reaction as he continued to run his hand up and down. "Also, how on earth you got into jeans that tight and sexy. How about you, what are you thinking?"

As I tried to speak, he pressed needy kisses along my collarbone, one of his hands squeezing the top of my thigh to hold me steady, as his other teased at my skin. A scorching flash of heat shot upwards through me as I tried to control my breath. "I think that… I don't know what you're doing to me, it's like you're taking me over, and I don't want you to stop." Zack carried me to the bedroom and placed me onto the bed, his mouth and hands never left me.

"Intrigued as I am by how tight these jeans are, I'm even more interested in how they come off," he kissed the bare skin of my stomach as his hands grabbed the waistband and began to slowly wriggle them off me.

"You're so beautiful, you take my breath away." I saw a

shiver pass over him. "It isn't time yet, but there's no harm in a little warm up?" He pressed his lips to mine as his hand skimmed across my now bare thighs, they scarcely touched me yet left a trail of desire. That trail continued up, as he reached into the black La Perla thong that I had worn, in case this happened.

His fingers applied a moment of delicious pressure, then he stopped, holding them there as he spoke. "Are you happy with this?" I nodded as I tried to catch my breath, praying he wouldn't stop. "Still going slow, don't try to trick me into more madam." I laughed and felt his fingers move against me. "Just hands today, Lily."

I gasped for air as he brought every single nerve ending to full attention, with fingers that teased, caressed and lingered in all the right places. I was shaking as I undid the buttons of his jeans. There had been a few occasions now where I had felt him through his clothes, the hardness of him against me when we woke up in the morning for example. My anxiety bubbled up within me, what if this didn't go well? *Now or never Lily.*

Sucking his bottom lip, I glanced into his eyes as my fingers ran down him. I marvelled at the silkiness of his skin as I sensed the blood pulsing through him. My whole body hummed with desire, I wanted him so badly.

"Hands are nice, see?" Zack's voice awoke me from my thoughts as his fingers pressed harder. My head cradled into the nook of his neck as I felt drunk on the feeling. "I said I'd like you speechless, remember?"

I nodded as I concentrated on him, relishing how he strained against my hand. "Wondering how I make you speechless in return." My words just about came out in the right order as he pressed his thumb onto me.

Zack pulled me tighter against him, I wrapped my leg over his hip, my body wanted more. Yet at the same time this was too much, I basked in the feeling as Zack gave me what I craved. Moaning un-intelligible words into his ear as my whole body melted against him. He grabbed me with an urgency and kissed me, his breath ragged in my mouth as I felt a hot, stickiness in my hand. I'd never known that could turn me on so much.

Neither of us moved from our intimate locations as we stilled. Our lips still kissed at each other's mouths softly as our eyes locked. Heart rates returned to normal, breaths slowed down, but our eyes never moved.

"All good?" Zack asked cautiously.

"Blissful." I replied, as I finally let him go and took a long breath.

"I think this going slow is pretty damn sexy," he smiled contentedly as he wrapped his arms around me tightly, cuddling us up ready for sleep. "Night, perfect girl."

FIVE

*E*arly on Wednesday afternoon, I dashed into work after a distracting lunchtime call with Zack. A delivery man followed me in through the main entrance with the most amazing bunch of dark red roses, the colours in them bright and vivid. Their scent flowed throughout the reception area.

"They alright here love?" He plonked them heavily down on the reception desk before I could answer.

I checked the card to see who they were for, hoping they were mine, but knowing probably not likely. That little white envelope didn't let me down, Miss Lily Forshaw. The burgundy red blooms were stunning, separated by sprays of pure white Gypsophila. I couldn't even count how many roses there were in the tight hessian wrap.

"Oh my god Lily!" mouthed Petra, the receptionist.

"I know!" I blushed.

Petra looked past me to the door in surprise, "Luke!" she almost shouted, as she stood up. "You're back!"

"What?" I didn't understand what Petra was saying. I

turned around, holding the most romantic and expensive bouquet imaginable, and found myself eye to eye with my best friend, all the way back from Africa.

Luke looked at me with that cheeky smile, how I'd missed it! His blonde hair had always darkened over winter, but now he was back from the sunshine it was full of ice blonde highlights that would cost a fortune to try to recreate with dye. His white t-shirt, which I recognised from a gig we'd gone to together, was crumpled and creased which wasn't like him. His eyes flicked to the flowers in my hands and then back to me, with confusion. There was a lot to fill him in on. I put them down on the desk and excitedly crossed the reception to him, smiling as he grabbed me into a tight hug.

"I missed you so much!" I said as I squeezed him tight. "We weren't expecting to see you until next week."

"There were problems with the flights," he replied. "So, I had to come back now or stay an extra week. I knew I had appointments here I needed to be back for. Feels like I've been gone months to be honest."

"You look all tanned, lucky thing!" I grinned, then noticed his bags behind him. "Did you come here before going home? That's dedication."

"I can't find my house keys, must've packed them too well. Could I nip upstairs for your spare set?" he asked.

"Of course, I'll come up with you. You OK for a few minutes Petra?"

"Sure am, don't forget your flowers," she grinned at me.

I blushed and saw Luke frown at the bouquet again as I picked it up and headed outside, chattering animatedly as we walked to the side entrance.

"Help yourself to a drink while I find them if you like." I

shouted over as I began to look through the sideboard drawers.

"I'm fine, don't worry," he replied. "Just exhausted from the flight so want to sleep to be honest. It's going to be so nice to sleep in my own house again. The beds there were not good."

"It'll feel amazing!" I wrapped him into another giant hug. "I missed you so much! If you feel up to it later, I could come over and you can tell me all about the trip?"

"I'll see how long I sleep for," he yawned as he backed out of the hug. "Better dash or I'll l be sleep walking back. Is everything good with you?" I saw his eyes dart around the living room, as if looking for something out of place.

"Yeah, all good. Great. I'll fill you in soon, you look like you can barely keep your eyes open." I smiled and pressed his keys into his hand. "I think Scarlet will be glad you're back, yoga attendance has been through the floor without you there for the ladies to impress."

Luke shot me a beautiful smile and laughed to himself before heading downstairs. I felt warm inside, knowing he was back. My eyes shot to the bouquet. I grabbed my phone and took a photograph before I opened the card.

To Lily,
I'm so glad you said yes to the date date
Love Zack xxx

Lily: You're so sweet, they're beautiful. Thank you xxxxx
P.S. I'm glad I said yes too x

In the end, the jet lag was too much for Luke, who I didn't hear from until lunchtime the next day. Cassie was desperate to catch up with him too, so we arranged to go to his that evening. I was worried about my Zack news in case it made Luke all overprotective, but I was also excited to have a chance to talk about it all over again.

Cassie's 'falling in love' theory was obviously correct, but I wasn't ready to address that yet. Every now and then the speed of the last month would catch up with me and scare me, on balance those trust issues and fears were still there, they lurked just below the surface. I wanted to escape that cycle.

"Ahh it is SO good to have you back!" I beamed as Luke let me in to his house. He looked more like himself now, dressed in expensive jeans and a slate grey shirt which would never be described as crumpled or creased. "Was the internet that bad?" I raised my eyebrow accusingly, but with a smile.

"Well, we were pretty remote most of the time. I wanted to enjoy the downtime from modern life, you know what I mean?" he said, as we walked through to the living room. I loved Luke's house, it felt like a second home. Despite always being immaculate and a definite bachelor pad, it felt welcoming and warm.

"Yeah, I get that. I saw a couple of the pics you put on Insta, it looked like an amazing trip."

"It was, I want to do it again. But … I sort of get the impression you've been having adventures without me?" He looked serious; his blue eyes seemed darker for a moment.

"Yeah, I tried to call you while you were away, but I

realised I'd be unlikely to get through. I had to rely on Cassie's guidance so anything could happen now." I giggled hoping it'd break the tension.

"So, you met someone?" Luke asked as he handed me a large glass of cold white wine. I sank down into the deep cushions of his soft, rolled arm sofa.

"Well, I promised Cassie I'd meet one person she chose from this dating site she was harping on about. More to shut her up than anything because you know I didn't want to meet anybody or get involved..." I was rambling but couldn't seem to stop. "He seemed so sweet when we went for coffee and I had to make a decision about whether to see him again. I remembered what you said before you left, about it being time to be brave so... I said yes."

Luke looked at me, his eyes focused and intense. "That wasn't what I meant with that advice but carry on."

"One date became a lot of dates and I felt braver each time. I can see what people meant now about me wasting my life away because of what happened. I still feel weird about it sometimes, but it's a good step forward hey?" I hoped he was going to reassure me. "You said I needed to trust my feelings, believe in myself again."

"After four years of being scared to trust anyone, you are happy with trusting a random guy off the internet who Cassie found on a dating site?" His eyes searched mine. "You see why I'm concerned about this Lily? You know your happiness means the world to me," he took hold of my hand with a gentle touch. "Please think how far it will set you back if it turns out he's lying, or cheating, or has a wife, or god knows what else goes on in the world of internet dating?"

"I... I hadn't thought about it like that," I admitted. "I

know he isn't married though; I met his flatmate, I've been to his place."

"A lot of people use those sites for sex. What if you think it's more and it isn't? You deserve better than to just be a fling." Luke was watching me as he spoke.

"I don't think Zack's like that. Besides," I blushed. "There hasn't been any sex yet. I think he would've given up if that was all he was after."

A look I couldn't gauge flashed across Luke's face. "Zack." Luke repeated his name through a long breath out. "Does he know about everything that happened? Does he know about that night?"

I shrugged and took a large sip of wine. "The basic gist of it, I haven't gone into detail."

"Do you think that maybe you should? So that he's more aware? If it doesn't work out, I can imagine you ending up back at square one. Please don't think I'm being horrible Lily. I'm trying to look out for you."

"I know, but the same could be said if I'd met a guy at a bar or through work. You don't instantly know if a person is good or not. Nobody's more surprised than me at the fact I am enjoying this. I trust him, I think he's a good person. I have been backwards and forwards in my head, doubting myself like I always do. Really, unless I got together with someone I already knew, there would always be that risk wouldn't there?" I wanted Luke to tell me he understood and that I was right.

Instead, he sighed and took a long drink. "Maybe that would've been a better option. Please be careful, I wish I'd been here for the start of this. I love Cassie, she is a bundle of pure enthusiasm, but I bet she was more interested in what dress you wore and how high your heels were, than what could go wrong?"

I nodded and put my wine glass down on the table, pressing my hand to Luke's knee as I replied. "You're right, I'll slow down a little, have a think. What would I do without you hey?" I pulled him into another tight hug as we heard the doorbell go. Cassie, and an enormous Chinese banquet, had arrived.

"Hey sexy lawyer dude. Good trip?" Cassie grinned as she waltzed in, holding the box of food out to me before she pulled Luke into a hug.

"Great trip, but nice to be back."

"Guy has been a proper mope without you. Can you play tennis or something with him at weekend, cheer him up?"

"I thought you'd be cheering him up enough at the moment Cassie?" I grinned as I spooned rice onto plates.

Luke put his hands over his ears, "I don't want to know. Why am I cursed with girls for friends?"

Cassie thumped him on the arm good naturedly. "The kids missed you loads, you going to come see them at weekend?"

"Wouldn't miss it," he replied. "You coming over Lily?"

Cassie jumped in before I could speak. "Oh, she'll be too busy dry humping Zack, never see her at weekends now."

"Cassie!" I snapped. "That's not true."

"The dry humping or the not seeing you at weekends?"

Luke looked flustered as he took his plate and sat down.

"Zack's busy this weekend, so yes Luke, I would love to come visit the kids." I stuck my tongue out at Cassie and the three of us attacked the food as though we hadn't eaten in weeks.

"Luke, I'm now officially the world's best matchmaker, so shout when you want hooking up." Bragged Cassie, she was going to revel in this for a long time.

He smiled, but it didn't seem like a true smile. "I'll pass, confirmed bachelor. You know me." We laughed it off, but something felt amiss.

It made my soul happy to have the three of us back together again. Luke's tales from Uganda were incredible and I was so in awe of what he did, I could never be brave enough to go so far away, alone, to help people, but that was Luke all over.

Cassie teased me about Zack, but Luke's words resonated with me a little, I tried to move the conversation on. My mind was busy as Luke walked me the few minutes home, wanting to make sure I was safe.

"Are you sure that you're OK?" he asked as we neared my flat.

I looked up at him. "Yeah, I'm good. I was dreading the date you know? I did it to shut Cassie up, but then it felt like it was working." There was an awkward silence.

"No sexy lawyer ladies in Uganda then?" I asked.

He laughed. "No. Honest, like I said to Cassie. Not interested. Got enough going on."

"Well, I'm crazy glad you're back. Doesn't feel right when you're not here."

I raised up onto my tiptoes as I hugged him, he was about the only person who made me feel short. I knew he'd linger until he saw my light come on upstairs. "I'll call you tomorrow, thanks for seeing me back."

"Anytime Lily-flower. Night."

"Night Luke."

SIX

*I*t was Friday at last! I lived for Fridays now. It took more time than normal to get ready for work, to make sure I looked as good as possible. Once a month, the whole team went for a meal and drinks, and tonight was that night. People often brought partners, I'd never been able to join in like that before, so earlier in the week I'd invited Zack.

He would be at mine early, as we went out straight from work to allow more drinking time, hence I wanted to look my best. I settled on a black jumpsuit with strappy black heels and a smart jacket over the top for work which could be removed later. My dilemma now though was that as Luke was back, he'd be coming along too, and I desperately wanted the two men in my life to be friends. I had a dreadful feeling they weren't going click. I worried all morning and, in the end, sent Luke a message at lunchtime.

Lily: Hey Mr Jetlag. Feeling all good now? x

*Luke: Yeah, all back to normal. Was great to see you and
Cassie, feels like too long since the three of us were
together xx*
*Lily: Definitely! But you were the one who left the
continent x*
*Luke: You have a point! Guess I'll see you tonight anyway,
won't I? Aren't we trying that Moroccan place? xx*
Lily: Yep, we are. I'm really worried though x
*Luke: Why?? Just eat Hummus if you don't like anything
else xx*
*Lily: I already invited Zack. I so badly want you both to
like each other but I feel like you don't already? x*
*Luke: Don't be silly. I haven't met him so I can't judge. I
know he's important to you, I'm looking out for you, that's
all xx*
Lily: OK. Thanks Luke. You better sit next to me! x
Luke: Deal. See you later Lily-flower xx

I bounded up the stairs to my flat after work, checked my makeup and just about had time to put perfume on before I heard the buzzer. I smiled as I opened the door to Zack, trying to mask how nervous I was.

"I missed you," he said as he walked in. He smelled amazing again and I loved how looking at him made me feel, the way I wanted to soak in every detail of him each time we met. He'd come straight from work too and looked so good in a grey tailored suit over a black shirt.

"I missed you too," I replied with a smile as he pulled me close. He kissed me, his hands ran around my waist and pulled me tightly to him. Luke's words of caution vanished from my mind now that Zack was here.

"Quick drink before we go? Shots or wine?" I asked as I grabbed the bottles from the side. I needed Dutch courage.

"Shots," he smiled and came closer. "Seems like the train was a good plan. Are you going to try to seduce me again?"

My eyes rolled as I handed him the shot glass with a smile. "Me? Seduce you? I think you have that the wrong way round."

"I think it was me stopped it going further last week, wasn't it? You were about to jump me, I could tell."

My face flushed red again at the memory. "Well, you were doing such lovely things to me."

"One, two, three…" We downed the shots of French vodka. He looked good as he licked the remnants from his lips, then moved to my own lips and kissed them, setting off every synapse.

"If last week was hands… does that make this week mouths? That's my absolute favourite." He ran his thumb across my lips slowly. "And your mouth Lily, is beautiful."

I kissed the tip of his thumb and smiled. "Not sure we have time sorry, need to leave now."

'You don't have time for me to re-trace everywhere my fingers went last week? Except this time with my mouth?" He raised an eyebrow at me. *Who was I kidding? To hell with punctuality.*

My lips navigated towards his, as if drawn by magnets. Zack undressed me, we bypassed the bedroom as he pushed me down onto the large couch. A fiery heat rose through me again.

He sighed as his kisses travelled down my chest, then moved past my bellybutton. I tipped my head back, my teeth bit at my bottom lip as I felt his warm breath on my thighs.

"I didn't tell you did I, that this is my favourite? Nothing turns me on like this, Lily…" The most incredible heat in the world descended on my core. His tongue, lips and mouth explored every single bit of me, it was the most delicious torture. He dipped in and out and set every single nerve ending on fire. I couldn't tell how long it went on for, it could've been a minute or an hour, I was lost in it as my fingers tangled in his hair and my thighs pressed him deeper into me.

"Don't hold back, honestly, I've been desperate to do this to you. I want to know what you taste like so bad." I couldn't respond, his hands held my thighs down, reminding me how strong he was as his mouth grew firmer and more insistent on me. He was so in tune with me, responding to every appreciative sigh or moan that escaped my lips, giving me more of what I liked.

It was so intense, almost like a panic rising within me, as I exploded into orgasm. My teeth bit into the couch cushion next to me, wanting to find an outlet for the sensations which overtook me.

I lay gasping and hot, trying to catch my breath and wondering when the world would stop reeling as he moved back up my body. "You are so amazing," he whispered. "That wasn't too far, was it?" I shook my head, unable to speak and kissed him fiercely. Was it wrong that I loved the taste of myself on his damp lips? "You get better and better." He whispered.

I blew out a long breath, it was like an out-of- body experience had occurred. Zack grinned, as he headed to the bathroom, the sound of running water followed.

"We better go, proper late now," he shouted through. I

was a little confused as I grabbed my clothes and followed him. "Can you speak yet?" he asked with a smug smile.

"Just about." I couldn't stop grinning, despite noticing my flushed reflection and messy hair in the mirror. "Think you forgot your turn?"

"I don't want to stress you out by being even later. I can wait, maybe find an excuse to leave early?"

"It's a date," I smiled.

We walked into the restaurant a good forty minutes late, still with that warm glow. It was a small place and the glorious smells of cinnamon and paprika emanated from the kitchen and made me lick my lips with hunger. Zack had given me an appetite.

My colleagues looked around with eager faces as we entered, it was pretty intimidating. I instantly began to think how it was too early to have invited Zack, and what an idiot I was for putting myself under this pressure.

"Everyone, this is Zack." I gestured to him with my free hand, as he held the other close to him. "Zack, you probably won't remember these but... Simon, Laura, James, Bea, Petra, Stuart, Fi, Lucy and Luke."

There were two seats left, opposite each other, one next to Luke and one next to Bea. I pointed Zack towards Bea as I sat next to Luke. This was such an awkward moment, and I really didn't fancy Hummus anymore. I felt like I had a big flashing sign over my head letting everyone know what had just happened.

Luke elbowed me. "Thought you'd got lost. Come on then, you going to introduce me properly?"

I sensed a certain tension as I looked up at Luke, then

across to Zack. "Luke, this is Zack. Zack this is Luke. Please don't tell each other embarrassing stories about me."

They shook hands before Zack replied, smiling at me. "Not sure I have any yet. Give me time though."

"I'm just choosing which to start with," Luke teased. "There was that time we shared a tent... or that time you nearly wrecked my car?"

"Oh, not the car again. It was one scratch! You are such an idiot sometimes." I shook my head at him in resignation.

"Well, what's embarrassing to one person, could be endearing to another," said Zack as he stretched his arm out over the table and laced his fingers together with mine. "What type of car did she scratch then?" he asked with a smile as he looked towards Luke.

"It was a Lexus, I hadn't had it long. Worst thing was, she was in an empty car park." Luke smiled across at me, all innocent eyes.

"Maybe I'll keep the car keys hidden then. I upgraded a couple of months back."

That was the two of them discussing cars for the next half hour. I'd never even bothered to buy a car; everything was close by. No wonder I wasn't used to parking when Luke let me have a drive! It was a relief to see they were getting on. I drank more wine and fanned myself, it was so hot in here.

Slowly but surely, I relaxed, everyone was welcoming to Zack, making him feel involved. Petra was positively salivating over him, she was in her forties and happily married but it was common knowledge she loved a good, harmless flirt. Simon and James, my bosses, were making me sound like the best employee in the northern hemisphere, with jokes about how Zack had better not steal me away. I'd been drinking much faster than normal to calm my nerves, but it was catching up with me. On top of the vodka shots there'd been gin cocktails when we arrived. The wine on the table just kept getting emptied and replaced with new bottles. The staff had given us shots of a Moroccan delicacy to compliment the meal. The restaurant was so hot and loud, the food spicy, and I was not feeling good. The sparkling lanterns that looked so pretty earlier now made me feel as if the room was spinning.

Luke noticed and took hold of my hand. I saw Zack's eyes snap to the movement instantaneously, even though he was mid conversation with James.

"You OK, Lily? You look pale." Luke asked with concern as I tried to focus on his eyes.

"Perhaps went a bit eager with the booze." I bit my lip.

"You are daft," he said. "You know you have to drink slow, always been a lightweight." He pinched my cheek with his gentle touch.

"I need air, sorry."

At this point Zack stood up, his chair scraped across the floor, the sharp noise making me close my eyes. "I'll come with you," Zack said tersely, as he moved round to me and helped me up, his arm around me as we walked outside.

I leaned against the outside of the building, dizzier still as the fresh air hit me. "I'm so sorry," I mumbled. "Shouldn't have been mixing drinks."

"It's fine, don't worry," the sentiment didn't quite reach his voice though. "Do you think you're going to be sick?"

I shook my head. "I'll get water in a minute, I'll be fine."

"So, what's the tale about the tent?" Zack asked, his voice serious and low.

"Huh?"

"Luke said he had an embarrassing story about you two in a tent?"

"Oh, it was last summer, at a festival. I got so drunk I passed out across both of our sleeping bags and was blocking the zip to get in. He had to sleep outside because he couldn't wake me up. It was like a mud bath out there, he said he was never sharing with me again, *and* that I snored all night which is obviously a lie." I giggled and poked his chest, the cold air making me feel more drunk. "Didn't snore when you stayed over did I?"

Zack seemed to relax and smiled. "Nope, no snoring. Maybe a bit of dribble."

"I do not dribble!"

Zack wrapped his arms around my waist and pulled me into him. "Maybe you should invite me to stay over again so I can double check."

I stood on my tiptoes and whispered to him, "You can stay over whenever you like. I think I owe you the image of my lips around something, don't I?" I thought I was acting flirtatious and sultry as I nipped his earlobe, pulling his face towards mine for a kiss. It just came across as drunk and clumsy when I stumbled to the side and Zack had to put his arm out to steady me.

"Yeah, I think you might be a little too drunk for that," he sighed.

"Nope, I'm good to go!" I grinned.

"Lily, two drunk people together is one thing. A sober guy and a drunk girl is not my scene. I'm not going to take advantage of you being wasted."

"Aww." I put my head back against the wall and closed my

eyes for a moment. As I looked up, Luke's eyes were on us, he looked away swiftly.

"I think we should head off now, you look like you need to lie down." Zack said.

"OK," I agreed. "I'll go pay the bill."

"You stay here in the fresh air, I'll go. I don't mind." Zack headed inside without waiting for an answer. He seemed annoyed at me, but it could've been the drink clouding my mind, I couldn't tell. My head hurt too much to think about it in any depth.

Zack wrapped his arm around me as we headed home, not before I noticed Luke watching us once more. I waved with a sad smile.

———

My eye opened cautiously. *Why was it hard to swallow?* My mouth felt like the desert and my head was full of banging drums. A quick glance under the duvet told me I was still fully clothed. Zack was in the bed too. I needed to get to the bathroom before he woke up.

I sat on the toilet with my head in my hands, why hadn't I been more sensible? Teeth cleaned, face washed, I climbed back into my bed and wrapped Zack in a huge cuddle. He had that delicious, sexy stubble look going on again.

"I'm sorry," I whispered. "I ruined the whole night."

Zack blinked his eyes open. "It's fine, don't worry. Not the night I imagined but, I still get to wake up here," he kissed my forehead. "I didn't know what to do about your clothes, I didn't want you to think I took advantage of you or anything, so I left them on."

"I know you wouldn't, even though I seem to recall I was encouraging you to," I closed my eyes and enjoyed the movement of his warm chest rising up and down. "I feel like death."

"I was going to get the last train," he explained. "But I was worried about you. You don't mind that I stayed over?"

"Of course not." I snuggled closer. "That's so sweet of you, thank you."

"Was there anything wrong? You seemed tense. I thought we worked all your tension out before we left?" I blushed at the memory.

"I've never introduced anyone to them all like that before. I felt pressure that everyone should get on. I was worried about you and Luke, I want my boyfriend and my best friend to like each other," I explained, then buried my head in the pillow with embarrassment. "Crap, sorry."

"What are you doing?" Zack laughed as he pulled the pillow away. "Sorry for what?"

"I didn't mean to say the b word, I'm sorry, I don't want you to think I'm assuming anything, I don't know how serious you want this to be-" my words were cut off as Zack kissed me.

"You don't realise how special you are," Zack said. "I definitely want to be your boyfriend, sort of hoped I already was to be honest. I just didn't want to put any more pressure on."

I kissed him again, the feel of his minty breath on mine telling me that he must've sneaked out of bed to brush his teeth too. "I feel like I should write you a note, like we're at school," I smiled. "Zack, do you want to be my boyfriend?" I couldn't help but giggle.

"You're crazy... answer is yes by the way." He slid his

hand around me and squeezed my bottom for a second. "I want to undress you right now, but I have to get the train at eleven. I need to get to that stag do, remember?" he asked. "Am I OK to get a shower? Let you rest a few more minutes?"

"Sure," I said sleepily as I snuggled back under the duvet. "So, me and you, this is like official then?"

"Yep, you're stuck with me." He kissed me once more before he went into the bathroom. Just in time for me to remember I was in debt to the tune of one blow job!

"I'm the worst girlfriend in the world." I blurted out as he headed back into the bedroom ten minutes later, wrapped in a towel. "I didn't mean to neglect you."

"You didn't, stop worrying." He sat next to me, his skin hot and damp, as he stroked my cheek. "You got drunk; it doesn't matter. It's one night. We have lots of nights to come, don't we?"

I nodded. "I hope so."

"I know so. I enjoyed what happened as much as you did, so relax."

I threw on jeans and an off the shoulder jumper and tied my hair into a messy bun as we sat at the table with coffee.

"Are you... OK about the stag do? From what you told me about your ex, I don't want you to think for a minute I'd ever do anything like that."

"Zack," I took hold of his hand. "You are the sweetest. In all honesty, yes, it's crossed my mind, yes, it's stressed me out. I'll be imagining strippers and all kinds of madness later. Every thought I've had about you and the stag do, led me back to the fact that I trust you. Just the fact that *you* are worrying about *me* worrying, it speaks volumes." Zack kissed my forehead. "I wouldn't project anyone else's failings onto you, ever."

"Lately, I can't concentrate on anything," Zack admitted. "I think about you all the time. So even if there was a stripper, I'd spend the whole time telling her about how brilliant you are." He smiled as he lifted his coffee mug to his lips again. "The more I get to know you, the nicer this is. You're lovely and you're gorgeous, but it's more than that. The way you've been so honest about your past and how it still worries you. How in spite of that you are so open to this, and to me. Not to mention the insane chemistry! I feel like the luckiest person in the world right now." He paused for a moment. "I need to say sorry too, I was jealous last night, about how close you and Luke are, and I know I sounded stroppy."

"You don't have anything to be jealous of. I know me and Luke are crazy close, but it's no different to how close I am to Cassie." I looked up at him contentedly, playing with his fingers in our intertwined hands. "Sometimes I get panicky about this. I feel like I'm jumping in too deep, too soon. I convince myself I'm being ridiculous. But then when I'm with you..." I looked down at the table, feeling silly. "When I'm with you, it all feels so natural and right. I don't doubt myself when we're together."

Zack tilted my chin up and placed a single, teasing kiss to my lips. "Only one solution to that then, you need to be with me as much as possible. I sort of wish I wasn't going on this stag do so I could stay with you. However, the fact there's a stag do, means there's a wedding."

I nodded and took a bite of cold toast.

"It's in two weeks, in a castle in Scotland. And I have a

plus one…" He raised an eyebrow. "Now as much as I fancy taking Adam, I thought it might be better to ask you. So, would you be my wedding date?"

I grinned. "You had me at castle."

As soon as Zack left for the train, I went straight back to bed to sleep the hangover off. This whole situation got better and better.

*a*n evening eating pizza in my pyjamas with some trashy television was well overdue. It felt good to have time to myself. I thought about Cassie and how she was sure I was falling in love and this was meant to be. I thought about Luke and how he said I was rushing this and needed to think. My specific feelings were a mystery to me, but I did know it was exciting to be invited to a wedding. I hadn't met any of Zack's friends other than Adam, so this would be a big step for us both. As I lay on the couch googling dresses and shoes, my phone pinged with a message.

Luke: Hey, hope you're feeling OK after last night?
Lily: Yeah, lying on the couch eating pizza in my pyjama's
is strangely therapeutic! Did much happen after I left?
Luke: Nah, just the usual. Much for you?
Lily: Passed out basically. Zack had to go, he's on a stag do,
so I can slob now!

Luke: Does that mean you're free tomorrow? Still want to come see the kids with me?

Lily: A Sunday, with my best friends and two gorgeous kids? Sounds perfect!

Luke: Great. I need to talk to you after though, if that's OK?

Lily: Absolutely, are you alright? Can talk now if something's wrong?

Luke: No, tomorrow is fine, sleep well. Remember that cold pizza for breakfast is gross! x

Lily: Damn, you know me so well, I saved half exactly for that purpose! You sleep well too xx

I awoke early, intrigued about what Luke wanted to discuss and excited to spend the day with friends. I suspected he'd either met someone himself or was going away again. Things had felt slightly askew between us since he'd been back. I did, disgracefully, eat cold pizza for breakfast despite his warnings. Not used to time to myself lately, I gave the flat a spring clean and jumped in the longest shower I'd had for ages. Sporting casual grey jeggings and a maroon cross neck top, my hair wavy and wild, I set off to meet everyone in the park.

As I approached, I could see Luke with Ruby and Emilia. His arms swapped between their swings, pushing them high as they squealed in delight. I circled round to approach them from the back, sneaking up to jab him in the ribs.

"I saw you a mile away Lily." he grinned and moved to the side, giving us a swing each.

"Where's Cassie?" I asked as I glanced around.

"She looked tired, so I said we could handle them alone. We *can* handle them, can't we?" he threw me a panicked look and I laughed.

"You coped alone in Uganda, what's the worst two little girls can do?"

"Were you alright on Friday night? You didn't look good." he asked, caution in his voice. "Zack whisked you away before I could check."

"I was fine, stop worrying." I smiled at him as I continued to push the swing. "He isn't a bad guy Luke."

"When I see a man taking a drunk girl - a very drunk girl home, it's a worry. I know what you're like in that state."

I frowned at him. "What do you mean? What am I like when I'm drunk?"

He sighed, delighting Ruby by pushing her even higher. "I'm not going to embarrass you!"

"No, go on. You've not mentioned this before. What do I do when I'm drunk?"

Luke looked at me and sighed. "Sometimes Lily, just sometimes, you sort of..." he ran his hand through his hair, looking bashful. I stared at him; I wasn't going to let this go.

"You, well... you ask for stuff. You get all flirty and suggestive. I know that it passes, and you fall asleep and snore. Another guy might not. Zack might not."

"I've never done that! You're lying!" I nudged my hip into his. He simply raised an eyebrow and smiled. "Anyway, nothing happened. Zack stayed over. He was a perfect gentleman, he just wanted to make sure I wasn't sick. He isn't horrible, I promise."

"If we weren't in a kids' playground, I could tell you a

selection of what you've said while drunk, but it would be obscene," he winked at me.

I laughed to myself. "You're making it up, stop it. I'm starving, can we buy them ice cream? Buy me a sandwich at the same time?"

Luke lifted the two girls out of the swings. In a row of four, we held hands as we headed out of the park and towards the café. All happy, enjoying the moment.

"It's almost their nap time." I said to Luke. "Shall I take them back? You still want to talk?"

As Luke nodded, his blonde hair bobbed on his forehead. "How about I grab Starbucks and meet you at yours?"

"Sounds perfect. You got a key?"

"I do. Caramel Macchiato?" he asked.

"Yep. Don't you dare turn up without whipped cream." I grinned.

Half an hour later, I let myself in, and my heart filled up with happy. I mean, who doesn't want to open the door to find a gorgeous blonde with your favourite coffee?! Luke was still adjusting back to the English springtime after his travels. He wore an unseasonably thick, slate-grey jacket, over jeans and a t-shirt. I wrapped my arms around his middle and squeezed him hard.

"Hey, no complaints, but what's that for?" Luke asked.

"For being you." I smiled as I pulled back. "Now, about that whipped cream?"

He grinned and handed me my coffee from the table.

Luke took a deep sip of his coffee. I could sense a hint of sadness around him.

"Luke, I'm worried about you. Has something happened? There's sadness in your eyes since you got back from

Uganda. What's wrong?" I sat close to him, wanting to fix whatever had made this amazing man sad.

"I'm not sure where best to begin," he sighed and put his coffee cup on the table as he ran his fingers through his hair.

"After everything you've done for me, there isn't anything I wouldn't help you with. Just start at the beginning, I'm sure we can fix whatever it is?" My heart was beating fast in anticipation of bad news.

"So, you remember when we met?" he asked.

"Yeah, I do, when you came to work at Draper & Hughes. You were super young!" I grinned, "I guess we both were."

"Yep! You didn't live up here then, and you had a boyfriend, and I admired you from afar, but we weren't friends as such."

"I remember." I sighed. "Wasn't that way for long though, was it?"

"No. I remember you were off work for a week or so, and people whispered about why. I tried not to invade your privacy. Then when you did come back, over a few weeks, it was like you turned into a shadow of yourself. Do you remember the night you told me what was happening?"

I nodded, concentrating on the colours in Luke's eyes to distract me from the memories that shot across my horizon.

"That's when you told me how bad the situation had got. How scared you were. Hiding away alone. I've never in my life felt such an urge to protect someone. Starting the next day, we got everything in motion, didn't we?"

I nodded once again and smiled. Remembering not the awful times, but how Luke saved me from them.

"You were amazing," I said with absolute sincerity. "I can't imagine what would've happened that night if-" Luke pressed a finger to my lips and shook his head.

"Since then, I've tried everything I could to build your confidence back up, to show you it wasn't your fault. To remind you that you are an amazing and beautiful person." He took hold of my hand.

"You were so patient, even when I didn't deserve it," I wiped a tear from my eye. "Sorry, it still gets me a little."

"I know, I'm sorry to dredge it all up. It's for a reason." He wiped a tear from my cheek and smiled.

"So, Lily, during that year..." He stopped and tilted his head back, his eyes focused on the ceiling. "Don't freak out about this. Just listen before you react. I know what you're like, take a moment."

I sat there in silence. *What had happened during that year that he hadn't told me?* We told each other everything.

He looked back down at his feet as he spoke. I absorbed every single word. "I fell, completely, unequivocally, in love with you. Every single bit of you."

Time went into a spin at this point, as I tried to digest his words. I held my coffee cup to my mouth, not drinking, not speaking.

"It wasn't the time to tell you, you were still recovering. I kept convincing myself to wait a little longer. Give you some space. Maybe when that case at work finished. After summer when we'd have more time. Then I was worried I was 'friend zoned'. In the end I decided that when I got back from Uganda would be the time but... everything changed while I was there." He looked into my eyes and I saw his own tinged with tears that waited to escape as his emotions unburdened themselves.

I couldn't register what was happening here.

"Lily, please say something." Luke took hold of my hand, but I pulled it away as I tried to think, a flash of pain ran across his face as I did so.

My emotions span into overdrive. This was the last thing I'd expected. It was like being humiliated again. Flashbacks zipped into my mind, people who I thought were my friends, people who had known my boyfriend was sleeping around and hadn't told me. Why did people keep secrets? Had Luke been using our friendship to get close to me?

"Just clarify a few things for me. Whenever you stayed over here with me you were in love with me?" I asked, as the tension in my voice rose.

He nodded and sighed. "You aren't taking a moment, are you?"

I continued, ignoring his comment, as more memories appeared. "When we went to Glastonbury and I passed out half naked, you were in love with me?"

He swallowed and blew out a long breath. "When I cried for nights on end and you held me close and said it would all be OK, you were in love with me? When I tried on clothes and let you sit there in the changing room? When the two of us made stupid TikToks to love songs? Were you using our friendship to get close to me?"

Anger hit me like a force. I thought of all the times I had let him see me bare, both physically and emotionally. He had taken that without ever once letting me know he had an ulterior motive. He put his head in his hands again and pulled his blonde hair back.

"You had four years to tell me, but you wait until I've met someone. Finally had a little taste of what a normal relationship could be like after everything I went through?" I stood up and walked over to the window, the normal Sunday afternoon life meandered along. It didn't feel like my life would be normal ever again.

"I didn't wait on purpose, I feared what you would say. A hope of having you, was better than dealing with a reality where you were never mine." He walked over to me. I looked up into those beautiful blue eyes that I'd only ever trusted, and for once, I felt unsure.

"I feel like you abused our friendship." I whispered, not wanting it to be true but at that moment, it was.

He took hold of my hands again. "I'm just asking one thing from you. One thing Lily. Let me kiss you. Let me kiss you once and I know you'll feel what I do. We can sort all of this out. If you don't feel it, I'll go. I'll be the bigger man, smile at you and Zack even though it's killing me. But I know if you kiss me back, you'll feel what we could be."

I looked down at the floor, tears ran down my cheeks. If I said yes, I'd betray Zack. If I said no, I'd destroy the dreams of my best friend, the person who saved me. Why had he put me in this position? His hand grasped my chin and lifted it up, our eyes met. "Please, Lily." Luke had tears in his eyes, and I couldn't think of a way to resolve this situation without someone being hurt. *Why did this have to be happening?*

I placed my hand over his and moved it away from my face. My eyes were downcast, unable to meet his as I answered. "No. No, how could you ask me to do this?"

He took a step back, visibly shaken. "Lily… I don't know what else to say, I love you, I'd do anything for you."

"You've completely taken advantage of our friendship.

You've waited to tell me this, until you see me happy with Zack, how do I know it isn't just jealousy?"

"Of course I'm jealous for fucks sake! I don't sleep at night thinking of you and him, but that isn't why I am telling you. I always planned to tell you when I got back. I wasn't counting on him… and this," he gestured towards me. "I never took advantage of you Lily. Jesus, there have been a hundred times I could've kissed you or seen you naked or made a move, but I never did. Do you even remember how many times you got drunk and suggested stuff? You're an absolute flirt when you're drunk. But you never did it sober, so I never took you up on it. You're my whole world. You are totally fucking infuriating, but you're everything to me."

"Is this why you've never had a girlfriend?" I snapped at him, it wasn't fair, but I was unable to stop myself.

"I'm only human, there've been girls. I always made sure nothing would ever last, and you'd never be aware of it. I only ever wanted you. I've never felt this way about anybody Lily."

I turned my back to him. Hoping for inspiration or answers, not knowing what to say or feel. Finally, I spoke, "I feel like I'm losing my best friend right now."

"We could be so much more…" his voice pleaded with me.

"Zack and I literally had the talk about us being official yesterday. I can't cast aside the past few weeks." I sobbed as the hopelessness of this situation engulfed me.

"One kiss Lily, let me show you?" His voice broke up and as it did, my heart followed.

"I think you should leave now."

"You don't mean that, please." His voice was shaky, I had to shut off my emotions to handle this.

"Please leave." I said, my voice quiet and forlorn. I couldn't look at him as he tried to reach for me, as he walked by, as the front door slammed shut.

It was only when I heard the downstairs door slam that I looked out of the window. I saw Luke in the car park with his head in his hands. That's when I fell to the floor and cried every ounce of my heart out. When it was all cried out and I could summon no more tears I sat there, slouched against the radiator. It went dark, my phone beeped and rang, the streetlights outside came on. I felt empty, looking at the photo frame he had bought me as it hung on the wall opposite me. Luke and I, grinning together after a long hike, arms around each other, carefree and smiling. How had that all been lost?

———

I called work and told them I had a stomach bug the next day, unable to face the situation, unable to face Luke. I repeated the same to Cassie when she queried her unanswered calls. Lying on the couch, wearing yesterday's clothes, staring at my phone, I wondered what the hell I was supposed to do.

I didn't want Luke to be out of my life, but how could anything be salvaged after yesterday? I had no idea how my relationship with Zack would pan out, but he didn't deserve to be cast aside. In the end, I typed a message.

Lily: Are you at work today?
Luke: Yes

Lily: Can you come up after?

Luke: Depends if you are contagious...

Lily: I think we both know I'm not really sick. I'm sorry I upset you

Luke: I'm sorry too... I'll finish a bit early, see you about four x

I hadn't eaten since yesterday lunchtime, but my appetite had deserted me. The mirror showed me blotchy skin, red eyes and tangled hair. I jumped in the shower and made myself presentable again, although concealer was not going to fix this. My phone rang as I was debating whether pyjamas were acceptable in this scenario.

"Hello," I answered.

"Hey beautiful!" Zack's cheery voice sang down the line to me. "I survived. I'm on the train heading home and I needed to hear your voice."

"I'm relieved to hear you survived."

"You ok? You sound quiet." Zack asked with concern.

"Think Friday was the start of a bug, I feel rotten, stayed off work today." I closed my eyes as I lied to him.

"Do you want me to come over? Do you need anything?" He sounded so concerned. *You Lily Forshaw, are a horrible person!*

"No, it's almost gone. I just need a big sleep, wouldn't want to make you ill too."

"OK, but shout if you change your mind. I wanted to talk to you about Friday, I guess when you invited me you weren't expecting Luke to be back? I know I mentioned feeling jealous but, things seemed weird. He seemed almost possessive about you?"

"Luke?" I tried to sound nonchalant as my heart fluttered ten to the dozen, "No, he's a bit over-protective, wants to make sure you aren't messing me around I guess."

"I feel like maybe for him its more," Zack sighed. "Listen, I wanted to say, if there's anything there, then please tell me now. I think the two of us together are amazing, and I loved our talk on Saturday morning. I feel like we're on the cusp of something special. If there's an issue, now would be the time to say."

"No issue," I replied, my eyes still squeezed shut. "He's used to being my safety net, I will ask him to tone it down a little. I think me and you are amazing too."

"Thank you," I could hear relief and happiness in his voice. "Listen, I'm beyond exhausted, think I'll pass out as soon as I'm home. Can I let you know there were no strippers? I thought about you the entire time. I have a couple of days off work, be good to see you if you're up for that?"

"Sounds like a plan," I replied. "You enjoy sleeping it off, speak tomorrow." I opened my eyes after ending the call. How could I tell him about yesterday? There was no way.

The closer it got to four o'clock, the more my heart sank. I never thought the prospect of seeing Luke would bring me misery like this. As I heard a gentle knock on the door, I bit my lip with nerves.

"Hi…" Luke looked as bad as I felt, obviously tired, obviously worried.

"Come in," I headed over to the dining table where I'd already made coffee.

We sat there for what felt like an eternity, not speaking. In reality it was about thirty seconds.

"So, you asked me to come up?" Luke asked with a nervous tremor in his voice.

"Yep, and now you're here I don't know what to say. I haven't slept a wink, just gone over and over everything in my head." He nodded in agreement at my words. "I know you weren't taking advantage of me or our friendship, I should never have said that, I'm sorry."

"I shouldn't have waited so long to tell you. I completely screwed this up. Most important person in my life and I screwed it up by being too scared to tell you."

"Luke…" I held his hand over the table as my voice broke and tears fell down my cheeks. "If you'd come to me a year ago, six months ago, even six weeks ago… I would've been shocked, it would've taken a while to digest. But… I would've kissed you, I would've wanted to give it a go." He swallowed loudly. "But now, I'm in a different situation. I've already had to tell Zack white lies about this and I don't want to be that person Luke. Lying, kissing other people, I can't do that, I can't be that." I was crying so hard now I don't even know if he could make out every word. "I don't want to lose you as my friend, but we can't be more Luke, I'm so sorry, I don't want to hurt you, but I can't give you what you want."

He pulled his hand away from mine and stood up, his coffee untouched. "Thank you for being honest. I don't want to lose your friendship either but, I just… I need time."

I watched him walk to the door through blurry eyes, pausing as he reached for the handle. I ran across the room, wrapped my arms around him and sobbed into his shoulder. He kissed the top of my head and backed out of the door, closing it behind him. My forehead pressed against the cold wood; I cried my heart out. Partially at losing my friend. Partially at thinking what could've been.

Grabbing my phone without thinking, I pressed on Cassie's name.

"Hey you, did you get to that appointment to get your pill sorted? Think we know it's about to get real with Zack." She sang down the phone, bonkers as always, completely unaware of the heartbreak occurring.

"I did, I went last week, but that's not why I'm ringing." There was no hiding the tremor in my voice. "Did you know about Luke?"

"What?" I heard her stop whatever she was doing. "What do you mean? What's wrong with Luke?"

"I need you to make sure he's OK. He... I've upset him. I think I've lost him Cassie." My breath shuddered. "I didn't know he loved me, I didn't know Cassie and now he's so hurt."

"He loves you?! What the actual..." Her voice was tense. "Fuck, fuck, fuck. You know that sort of makes sense though now you've said it. Why didn't he say sooner? Oh god and now you have Zack and... Fuuuuuuuck! What happened?"

"It's a bit of a blur, I told him that I was with Zack and I was sorry... I don't know Cassie I was so shocked. He was crying, I was crying, it was horrid. He'll hate me. How did I not see this?"

"Guy will be home in half an hour. Do you want me to come round?" Cassie asked.

"No," I replied. "I'll be OK, can you go see Luke? I'm scared that we can't be friends now after this. He was so upset Cassie."

"I'll go see him. Are you sure you're alright on your own?" she asked.

"I'll be fine, I need to digest this. That's all." I wasn't sure if I was trying to convince Cassie or myself as I ended the call.

———

The next couple of weeks felt so awkward, I tried to keep away from Luke and give him space. Cassie said he was OK, but it didn't seem that way. It felt as though I was paying a price for having found happiness with Zack, the price being losing Luke. There also wasn't much opportunity to see Zack between family commitments of mine, and pre wedding plans he'd already made with friends, which was frustrating. The time alone just left space for more doubt to enter my mind.

Eventually though, the wedding weekend arrived. Zack was heading to the castle on Friday afternoon to spend time with the groom on his last night as a single man. I was catching the earliest train and meeting him there on Saturday morning. I needed this weekend to work, I needed to prove that I'd made the right choice, because really, I wasn't sure of anything anymore.

EIGHT

$\mathcal{A}$s the taxi approached the castle, my mouth dropped open in awe. The grand building was surrounded by magnificent gardens and there was a hubbub of activity as staff whirled around, busy with preparations. I headed into the traditional, luxurious reception and picked up the key to room two hundred and six, which Zack had left for me.

"Hello," I spoke quietly as I opened the door, paranoid that I either had the wrong room or was disturbing him. Zack's happy face popped out from the bathroom.

"Hey, let me help you," said Zack, eyeing the bulky suitcase and bag behind me. "You know this is one night yeah?"

"Some of us need more than a suit thank you." I raised an eyebrow at him and smiled as he carried the bags through to the main part of the room. I followed him, taking in how gorgeous the surroundings were. Then I was pulled into a deep and sultry kiss. His fingers hooked into the waistband of my jeans and held me against him in a firm grip. My fingers tangled into his hair as he bit my bottom lip, in that way I had come to adore over the past few weeks.

"I missed you, feels like ages since I saw you properly," he said.

"I know, it's been too long," I sucked at my lip where the tingles from his bite were still calming down. "This place is incredible." My eyes travelled around the room again. On the far wall was a huge window which let sunlight flood in as it looked out over the gardens and lake. It was opposite the most amazing four poster bed I had ever laid my eyes on, dark wood polished and gleaming, gorgeous cushions and throws arranged like a work of art. The butterflies returned as I thought of being in that bed with Zack tonight. He must've read my mind and squeezed my hand in reassurance.

"If you think that's nice, wait until you see the bath," he winked at me.

"Well, I do need to go and get ready, so maybe I'll check it out," I stretched up onto my tiptoes and kissed him, loving the reaction it caused. "Won't be long."

I closed my eyes for a second as I locked the bathroom door. *So far, so good*. There was incredible tension between us, it was hot and fiery, and I was ready to implode. I took deep breaths and tried to think rationally. It had been six weeks now since our first date, both physically and emotionally things had been going further and further with us each time we met. Now we were in a castle, with a giant bed, at the most romantic wedding I could've imagined. Tonight was going to be the night - I didn't know if I was more scared or excited.

Cassie had helped me find an amazing dress. It was a rich, deep red, the silky material skimmed my knees. Looking in the mirror, I admired the way it wrapped around at the front to create a beautiful, tight waistline which fed into an elegant bow at the back over the base of my spine. Apart from a thin strap across the top of my shoulder blades the back was cut out, my bare skin exposed. The Talbot Runhof had cost a small fortune but was so worth it.

I opened Cassie's shoe box which I'd guarded with my life, she had let me borrow her gorgeous lucky shoes from my first date again. I noticed a velvet bag which shouldn't be there. I picked it up tentatively and spotted a handwritten note.

Lily,
I know Zack is a good guy, but even the good ones are arse-holes sometimes, so use the condoms! The other bits are just for fun! Dirty Deets when you get home please!
Love Cassie xxx

I was mortified. Underneath the letter I found six condoms, fancy lube and a can of body spray by Tom Ford called 'Fucking Fabulous'. As frustrating as Cassie was, it did smell good. I sprayed it over myself before hiding the bag again.

Make up – check. Hair – check. Dress – check. Ready for this? Debatable.

"Are you almost done? I'm going to drink the champagne all by myself otherwise." Zack called from outside the door.

"Don't you dare! One minute, pour me a glass please." I gave myself a final once over before I stepped back out into the main area of the room. My stomach felt fizzy enough without champagne. "Ta-da," I smiled and did a slow twirl.

"Oh my god, Lily." Zack couldn't take his eyes off me, I grinned as I twirled, revelling in the attention. "You look incredible, like beyond belief... I don't think I can let you leave this room." His fingers were ice cold from opening the champagne as he pressed them to the bare skin on my back, making me gasp. I took his glass with a smile, sipping the bubbles as I looked him up and down. He wore a dark grey, three-piece suit which had a subtle check to it. His hair was styled exactly the way I liked it, practically begging me to run my fingers through it.

"You look pretty good yourself," I smiled coyly. "Think I'll have to keep an eye out in case any bridesmaids try to steal you away." Now I had the heels on again our eyes were level. I placed two kisses along his neck, careful not to mark his shirt with my red lips.

"As if I could have eyes for anyone else. I feel like I'm obsessed with you Lily Forshaw, I can't keep my mind off you."

A cold, nervy shiver moved down me as I took a deep breath, the soft fabric of Zack's shirt tickled at my nose. *He didn't mean it like that, he isn't like that.*

Zack hugged me to him, "I'm so sorry, I didn't think. I didn't mean to say it that way."

"I'm fine don't worry. Does it make it better if I admit to being a bit obsessed with you too?" I smiled and stroked the soft skin on the inside of his wrist, loving the feeling of his hand on my waist. I was determined to not lose another moment of my life to the past.

"Let's take a picture." He led me towards the window. We took selfies in our finest clothes, drinking champagne in a castle, as if this was an everyday occurrence. I looked at the last one, I was smiling so happily at the camera, with the gorgeous garden and sunlight behind me. I thought Zack had been focused on the camera too, but his eyes were only on me as his lips grazed my cheek. It was so beautiful.

"Do you mind if I post some of these online today?" Zack asked.

"Go ahead," I nodded in agreement, noticing him tag me. Just for a moment I felt a pain in my stomach as I realised Luke would therefore see it. I had made my decision though, why shouldn't we be able to post cute pictures online? Why not?

The bride and groom, Becca and Lewis, looked over the moon with happiness. The ceremony was beautiful to see, with Zack holding my hand, his thumb stroking over my skin. For the wedding breakfast we were seated on a large, round table, decorated with beautiful, bright summer flowers and tall, elegant candles. You could tell straight away it was going to be the rowdy table as Zack led me over.

"Lily," he gestured to the table. "I've asked them all to behave. This is the bunch who dragged me through Uni and four years of hangovers. Although thinking about it, they caused most of them. It's a wonder any of us got degrees. This is Samira, Maddy, Tom and George, plus their respective girlfriends, boyfriends, spouses – it will all become clear, Ben, Emily, Chris and Jay. Everyone, this is Lily."

I sat down, immediately feeling welcomed and instantly getting names muddled up! "I'm Samira. It's so good to meet you. We thought he was making you up." Her laugh was loud and genuine as she stuck her tongue out at Zack.

A man opposite me with long blonde hair in an impressive man bun that I had envious feelings about, joined in.

"Yep, when he mentioned you for the millionth time, we definitely thought he was making it up. I'm George." He held his hand up in a short wave and smiled.

"OK, you don't have to humiliate me." Zack held his hands up, but he couldn't hide the slight blush to his face, adorable! He turned and looked at me as he replied to George. "Nobody could keep quiet about a girl like this."

"Can't believe you bumped Adam as your plus one though." Laughed a sporty looking, tanned man, who I assumed was Tom. "I wanted to ask him about those new levels."

With the ice broken and the champagne flowing, the whole meal was an absolute hoot. I learned about all of Zack's friends and each of them told me a different embarrassing story about him. From waking up on a bus two towns away after a night out, to failing miserably at joining in rugby with Tom. The five friends at the table, plus the groom, Lewis, had lived together throughout Uni and all studied Law. They were friends for life. Their partners all seemed used to the camaraderie and it was warming to be included. Many more pictures were taken, online friend requests sent, as they made me feel as if I'd always been with them. Zack had gone to the bathroom when Maddy took his chair and sat close to me. She was stunning with long blonde hair and intense, green eyes.

"I just wanted to say, we're so glad you're here. I know we took the mickey out of him, but he hasn't stopped talking about you. Not seen him like this before," she smiled, her eyes tipsy and unfocused. "He deserves to be happy, he's one of the best. Look after him." She gave me a clumsy hug and hiccupped, moving back to her seat as Zack returned.

As we listened to the hilarious and heart-warming speeches, Zack slipped a hand under the table and ran his finger up and down my upper leg causing such a delicious sensation. I fanned myself as I smiled, my mind conjuring images of what the rest of him could do, if one finger was distracting me like this.

The whole day flowed perfectly. We spent time with so many people and I felt like Zack's friends were my friends too. The evening was hilarious, with a live band and so much dancing I was sure my feet would never recover, they were burning from the beautiful shoes, but I was having too much fun to stop.

We'd all been drinking for hours now; a warm and relaxed sensation filled my mind. With perfect timing the band moved onto slow songs. Zack transitioned instantly, his arms slipped around my waist and pulled me close as we danced together. I leaned my head against his and sighed as I felt him kiss my forehead, his breath tickled at my ear.

"I wanted to talk to you," he said, as his hand stroked the bare skin of my back, holding me close to him. Just another reason to love this dress.

"Is everything OK?" I wondered what this might be.

"Everything's perfect, maybe that's why this is worrying me. I can't believe it's only six weeks since we met, I feel like I've known you forever." He brushed his lips against my ear before continuing. "I normally wouldn't worry about saying this but if I scared you away, I couldn't ever forgive myself."

I moved my hand up and stroked his neck. "You aren't scaring me away, the opposite in fact, you're drawing me in. You have been since day one. Trust me, nobody is more surprised than me."

He took a deep breath and his hand slid inside the back of my dress, his fingers gentle on my skin. "I love you, Lily," His words gave me goosebumps as they travelled through me. "I love you so much, it's driving me crazy."

I turned his face towards me. "I love you too, Zack. I love you." I leaned against his chest and closed my eyes as the dance continued. I was exactly where I should be, and I didn't want anything to change.

As the night drew to a close, full of drunken goodbyes, we headed upstairs to that magnificent bedroom. All of a sudden, I felt cold stone sober and nervous as hell. Zack held the key card up to the door but paused a moment as the sensor flashed green.

"I wanted you to know, there's no pressure tonight, I don't mind waiting for you." He kissed my hand, always the gentleman.

I dived on him in a deep and fiery kiss as we tumbled through the door together, the kisses growing more urgent as we moved towards the bed. The curtains were wide open and the whole room was now illuminated by moonlight, giving it a soft glow.

"I don't want to wait one more minute Zack." My fingers stroked rough patterns through that gorgeous hair. Zack was kissing me with such need, I wanted more. His hand slid firmly up my back as the other stroked the back of my thigh, rubbing across the lace of my underwear, it sent shivers through me. This carried on for a couple of minutes and delicious as it was, I couldn't help but wonder what the next move was going to be, when Zack laughed, full of nerves.

"We aren't doing just hands again, are we?" I teased.

"I don't want to look like a complete amateur, but I'm so

sorry, I need help. How the hell does this dress come off?" I rested my forehead against his, our eyes locked together, our mouths millimetres apart.

I reached around and undid the strap across the top of my shoulder, then took hold of his hand and moved it to the base of my spine, where the bow was. "Zachary. Feel underneath the bow, there's a clasp." My lips grazed against his as I spoke, I sensed a subtle shift in his breath. "Now, feel at the side here, there's a zip." He pulled it down, his eyes never left mine for a second. My heart thumped faster and faster, followed by a swish of silk as the dress fell to the floor. I was standing there with him, in nothing but black lace under-wear, which I really hoped he liked. I don't think he paid much attention however as they dropped to the floor with everything else. His lips were on me again in an instant as I undressed him.

He pulled me close, so our chests were squashed together and stroked the side of my face. "I really do love you." I tried to respond but his mouth covered mine once again as his hands slid under me and lifted me up. I wrapped my legs around his hips and kissed him back with every ounce of wanting in me.

"Tonight is so special, I so want to be with you." He bit my bottom lip again. "Inside you." One finger moved inside me and I gasped for breath again. "Completely a part of you."

I don't know how he did this to me with his hand and whispered words of desire but within minutes my head was pressed into his shoulder as he made me lose all control. He moved on top of me, I smiled as he rubbed our noses against each other in the sweetest eskimo kiss. "Definitely sure Lily?" he asked one last time.

I nodded, desperate to feel more of him, as he reached under the pillow and grabbed a condom. "The things they leave for you in hotels these days," he smiled as he put it on and then …

His eyes were so intense, they took in every reaction as he pushed slowly into me. Nothing had ever felt like this before, I was overwhelmed but also desperate for more. My legs clamped around him, not ever wanting to lose this feeling between us – my body smouldered and my mind burned with love for him, the fiery combination explosive.

He began with such tenderness, kisses and strokes making me feel like the most loved person in the world. Every nerve ending inside me lit up. All caution was soon cast aside, it was as though the world outside of this bed had ceased to exist. Completely lost in each other, he moved faster and deeper, mouths locked together, hands pulled at hot, damp skin, my legs tightened around him, urging him on and on.

The pressure built and grew within me to limits I didn't know I had, as my whole body tightened around him. I took desperate breaths of his scent into me, wanting to never forget it. I don't know if the words that came out of my mouth even made sense as I gasped his name, begged him not to stop, told him how he was everything to me. I was barely recovering as he matched me, moaning into my mouth, his hips pushing me down into the bed with fierce force.

Zack's head dropped to the pillow next to mine as our rapid breaths began to slow, our warm skin stuck together. He smiled as he spoke to me. "Are you alright?"

"So good," I grinned. "Please say we can do that again?"

"I plan to keep doing that to you, over and over." He pressed a sweet kiss to my lips.

"Worth waiting for then?" I asked, hoping it had felt as good for him, as it had for me.

"God yes. Glad we waited. Imagine if it had been after that first proper date? Wouldn't have been anything like that. I knew from that first night I would fall in love with you," he admitted, his face bashful. "I couldn't stop myself. I didn't want to stop myself. I wanted you to feel it too."

"I do feel it. It hit me pretty quick, I was just scared of it. But you have this … magic power over me. You make everything feel safe and right." I sighed with happiness. "I love you so much, it feels good to say."

"Give me two minutes." He ran his finger down my cheek, taking in all the detail of my face before he headed to the bathroom. Returning, with water splashed through his hair, he climbed beside me and wrapped me in his arms, kissing me over and over. "I love you so much, Lily. Get some sleep, I can't promise I'll be able to control myself in the morning."

My eyes fluttered closed. I grinned like the cat who got the cream as I fell into a beautiful dream.

NINE

I had to drag myself downstairs to work on Monday morning. There were so much better things to be doing, and we'd done them quite a few times over the rest of the weekend.

Zack wasn't due back at work today so had driven me home and spent the night with me. It felt surreal to be at my desk, knowing he was upstairs. I'd barely looked at my phone all weekend, so fired off messages to Cassie promising all the details soon, and to my mum and dad letting them know I'd had a great time. My mum replied within a minute, hinting that she couldn't wait to meet Zack after seeing all the photographs of us.

I wasn't ready for any meet the parents' scenario, but I was intrigued about the photographs my mum had mentioned. I knew Zack had tagged me in that one beautiful selfie, but it seemed that now I had 'friended' all his friends, I was tagged in a lot! Zack and I holding hands as the bride walked up the aisle, Zack and I looking into each other's eyes at the wedding breakfast, drinking champagne together on a love seat, him spinning me round the dance floor and our faces full of laughter, slow dancing and his mouth whispering to me, looking hungover together the next morning with all his friends before everyone left.

I heard a cough and put my phone down. Luke stood over my desk, his eyes on my phone screen.

"Hi, morning, how are you?" It all came out too fast as I stood up. "Did you need me to get you something? I don't think I have your files here sorry." *Could he tell I'd been shagging all weekend by looking at my face?*

He glanced at me; his eyes cold. My heart sank. I knew why he behaved this way, it was self-protection. It tore me apart that my best friend was falling away from me and there seemed to be nothing I could do.

"I wanted to make sure you're OK, I heard footsteps upstairs just now," he said quietly.

"Ahh yeah," I replied. "Zack is up there." I saw Luke's face drop as he put two and two together. I wanted to cry at the unfairness of the situation. How had I gone from four years of no love interest at all, to this feeling? He looked at me, his eyes regretful as he turned to leave. "Luke-"

He cut me off with a sharp tongue. "Lily, please don't." I sighed as he closed his office door.

The morning at work was the longest, my emotions swung between ecstatic, exhausted and charged. I was drained. I'd asked Zack to meet me downstairs at twelve o'clock so we could grab lunch before he left. If I went upstairs, we were bound to end up back in bed. My thighs were so sore, but the ache in them every time I moved made me smile with the memory, and pledge to get to yoga more often!

We went to a quiet café, as we ordered large coffee's I knew I had to explain to him what had happened with Luke. He'd wonder why I didn't see my best friend anymore.

"That was the best weekend I could've imagined," I smiled at Zack as we held hands across the table, our legs linked underneath. "I wouldn't want our relationship to have secrets though. I'm going to tell you something and I don't want you to worry. I handled it and it doesn't affect you and me. This is what I want." I watched him as concern flicked across his eyes.

"What's wrong?" He squeezed my hand tight.

I gulped before I began. "Luke has been my friend for a long time, and I've never thought of him as anything more than a friend or a big brother figure. I know you had your doubts," I continued. "He came to me, not long ago, to tell me he was in love with me and had been for a long time. He regretted not telling me sooner." I squeezed Zack's hand again, wanting to reassure him all was OK before I got to the end of the story. "I got really, really angry at him, we had a massive fight. He stormed out. I felt like he took advantage of our friendship and put me in a horrible position, knowing I'd met you and it was going so well."

"Lily-"

I shook my head at him. "It's all fine, promise. Let me finish." I reassured him as best I could. "He stormed out and I was so upset, you were on the stag do so I couldn't burden you with it. Then I didn't know when was best to bring it up. I met him the next day and told him it was you I wanted to be with Zack. We've hardly spoken since, it's tricky at work but it's manageable. I don't think our friendship can be the same again and that hurts me, but he knows it's you I want to be with."

Zack looked a little shaken, I moved to the seat next to him. "I only want you," I kissed him. "Please don't be mad."

"I'm not mad at you. It's not your fault. I did feel there was something weird that night we went out. I was crazy jealous about the way he was with you, making it obvious he knew you so well and bringing up all your happy memories," he blew out a long breath. "Are you one hundred per cent sure that this is what you want?"

"One hundred per cent, Zack."

"I can't say it's my perfect scenario that you work with him five days a week, but I trust you, I love you. Promise me you will tell me if anything else happens, or if he starts being weird or bothering you?"

"I promise, I love you Zack." I meant it wholeheartedly.

———

From there we fell into a serious relationship. Spring turned into a beautiful summer of long days and warm nights. Zack and I were together every weekend and I ended up changing my working hours, so I had Wednesdays off, because frankly the week felt too long without each other. One of those nights, Zack had urgent work to finish and was on his laptop in bed, I lay next to him, my head rested against his side as I read my book. We were both so quiet, doing separate things yet completely together. It made my heart bloom that we felt this good.

We spent time with friends, we met each other's families and I found myself with four amazing new friends in his sisters. It was like a honeymoon period; we still couldn't keep our hands off each other. It felt like I'd been having sex all wrong in the past, because it had never been anything like this. My mind was blown. Cassie and Luke continued to be close, and I know it made it difficult for her that our friendships had segregated, but we rarely spoke of it. I don't think any of us could see a solution. Life had just changed.

My mind was about to get even more confused. At the staff meeting one Friday, Luke announced that he had arranged with the partners to take a twelve-month career break to go backpacking around the world. Everyone was so excited for him, telling him about Thailand, Malaysia and a multitude of places to visit. The excitement was a blessing for me, it allowed me to stay in the background. Luke's eyes met mine as Petra told him a horror story about her neighbours' nephew in a youth hostel, I tried to smile but I wanted to cry. I knew he loved to travel, but he also loved his career. Was he only going to get away from me? Or did I think too much of myself?

As I locked up the office that night, I heard Luke finishing his phone call to a client. I knocked on his door, opened it cautiously and saw his expectant face glance up at me.

"Hi."

"Hi." Luke replied.

Silence ticked by.

"Did you need me?" he asked.

"I wanted to say, the travelling sounds amazing, I bet you'll have the time of your life." I bit the inside of my lip hard, wanting to distract myself from the tears that threatened to appear.

He shrugged, his eyes barely met mine. "Seemed like a

good time to go explore what the world has for me. Anyway, I need to go, sorry."

He stood and brushed past me to get out the door. No amount of lip biting was going to stop the onslaught of tears now.

"You don't have to hate me Luke, I can't bear you hating me." I sobbed, taking giant, ugly gulps of air.

Luke sighed and tilted his head back, before placing his hand on my shoulder. "I could never hate you. I just can't do this. I see how happy you are with Zack, and I'm glad it's working for you, but I don't want a ringside seat, it's destroying me. I'd love to think we can be friends again one day, but that won't happen when I do this every day." He gestured at me in his office. "I could never hate you, if you had any idea the depth of love I have for you, you wouldn't even think that."

"I miss you so much Luke. Can we go for a drink one night? Try to be friends again? That can't all be gone surely?"

So many emotions flashed through his eyes as he looked at me, I wanted to reach out and help him through this, but I couldn't. He'd changed from being the ultimate happy-go-lucky guy, to just carrying a sadness with him. "Maybe next week, I'll think about it over the weekend, Lily. Have a good one."

He walked away as I tried to pull myself together. I was selfish, what right did I have to be crying when he was the one so hurt, so rejected? I hated myself in that instant.

Upstairs, I climbed into the hottest shower I could handle, trying to singe the tears, tension and distaste at myself away. I jumped into jeans and a long black sheer top, before I heard an enthusiastic knocking on the door.

I loved opening the door to Zack on a Friday evening, it was like letting a bundle of energy, enthusiasm and love into my home for the weekend. He wrapped his arms around me and planted kisses all over my face, making me laugh. "It's been so long since Wednesday," he complained dramatically, running my damp hair between his fingers. I sighed and rolled my eyes as I noticed the shopping bag full of wine and treats for a weekend of romantic hibernation indoors. For once, we had no plans this weekend, the two of us alone sounded like heaven.

Zack grabbed me and pushed me toward the large corner section of the couch. "I mean it," he whispered to me. "Wednesday was so, so long ago. I have withdrawal." He was on top of me, kissing me in ways that made my head spin. His hands tickled my stomach as he unbuttoned my jeans, tugging them down as I reached for him to do the same. His strong hands pulled me up by my wrists, kisses trailing down my side as he stopped and bit at the fleshy part of my hip just a tiny bit harder than normal, leaving a beautiful tinge of pain. "I missed you so much," he whispered, as he needily pushed my legs apart.

I closed my eyes and let out a deep, long breath, I knew where this was going. Did I mention that I loved Fridays?!

We lay on the couch together afterwards, warm and naked. "Just imagine," Zack pulled a warm throw over us both. "If you hadn't said yes to that coffee. We could've missed all of this." He kissed the top of my head.

Instantly, images flew through my mind of what life would be like if I hadn't said yes to the coffee. In the blink of an eye, I imagined Luke coming back from Uganda and confessing his love to me. I imagined us becoming a couple. I imagined what had just happened on this couch but looking down and seeing Luke's blonde hair between my legs. I imagined his bright, blue eyes looking into my own as he moved up my body to kiss me. I wondered what his skin would smell like, feel like. *I bet he tastes amazing…*

I sprang back to reality as Zack clicked his fingers. "Hello…sleepy head?" He laughed. "You still with me?"

I blushed and shook my head to clear the images. "Sorry! Long week." I smiled as I stood up. "Do you mind if I go sort my hair out? Then we can get food?"

"Sure." He stretched and yawned happily. "You look gorgeous as it is, but I know you think its frizzy."

I headed into the bedroom, my discarded clothes under my arm. How realistic had that image of Luke between my legs been? *Where the hell had that come from?* It was like my mind was betraying me. Luke was leaving, I'd made my decision, I needed to stop this. Zack was incredible, I shouldn't even think of anyone else.

Zack had placed oversized glasses full of deep red wine on the table, alongside cheese, crackers and olives. I joined him, my blow-dried hair still warm on my shoulders. I felt ravenous, and so glad he was here with me.

"You're perfect," I said as I kissed him. "Thank you. I actually have some news for you, there was an announcement at work today. They are letting Luke take a career break." I always felt guilty even saying his name in front of Zack, I had seen how he glanced at Luke's picture in the heart frame every time he came round. "He's going backpacking for a year. Feels weird, but I guess it'll make work a little less tense?" I popped an olive in my mouth, hoping Zack would speak.

He didn't. "So, I know James wants to retire, I guess he'll wait twelve months and then they'll make Luke a partner." I shrugged and tried to look nonchalant.

Zack rolled his head from side to side. "I know you miss him being your friend, but I'll be glad that you aren't with him every day at work. It's not good for you." He sighed and took a long drink.

"I have said you don't need to be jealous. He barely speaks to me now." I didn't need to be told what was good for me.

"I didn't say I was jealous." He looked out of the window and continued to drink.

"Can we not ruin the weekend? He's leaving, you have nothing to worry about." Maybe I shouldn't have even mentioned it. I stood behind Zack and stroked his hair, moving down to rub his tense shoulders. "I love you Zachary, we have hours and hours and hours alone together now. I'm all yours."

He soon relaxed and our evening returned to a happy feel. His jealous streak could be irritating though. As I nodded off to sleep, cuddled up against Zack's warm body, my mind wasn't quite on board with the idea of being 'all yours'.

I was at my desk but distracted, I didn't want to work. I looked down and realised I was wearing an obscenely short skirt and those lucky heels of Cassie's that I liked to borrow. That was weird, they would cripple me at work. The phone rang, I picked it up with long manicured nails. "Hello?"

"You should come through now." Ordered a deep, male voice. I knew that voice but couldn't place it.

Then I was knocking on Luke's office door. He dragged me in and pushed me up against the wall, kissing me harder than I had ever been kissed, ripping the clothes off me. I was in heels and the raunchiest black lingerie I'd ever seen as he carried me to his desk and pushed me down onto it...

I sat bolt upright in bed, confused, the sun was rising. Zack sat up too, looking concerned. "What's wrong?" he asked, rubbing his eyes.

My heart was pulsating as though it would burst out of me. "Weird dream," I replied. "I'm fine, sorry."

Zack wrapped his arms back around me, like a protective shield as I lay down. Why was my brain so stubborn about Luke?

TEN

*C*assie and I had been messaging each other over the weekend about Luke's news. We arranged to meet for dinner on Monday night so we could talk it all out, in one of our favourite pubs, The Oak Tree. It was an old, traditional place, about ten minutes' walk from both of us. Full of cosy snugs, log fires in winter and a traditional menu with local ales and real home cooked chips. It was impossible to come here without eating chips.

Cassie was already at the table with a bottle of wine for us when I headed in. "Not like you to be early." I nodded towards the wine. "Drinking?"

Cassie rolled her eyes and sighed. "Maybe next month hey? Anyway, I'm so excited to be eating in a place that doesn't serve happy meals or have a soft play attached. I missed you. It's weird not seeing you every weekend now," she smiled, the real genuine smile of an old friend.

"Aww, look at you all soppy! I thought you were made up now I'm officially in love and everything is rosy?" I asked, knowing I was forever indebted to this beautiful lady for finding Zack.

"I am! I still expect a special speech at the wedding to thank me," she grinned. "Right, I'm ordering food and then we can talk. The usual I take it?" I nodded in agreement as I took my phone out of my bag.

Cassie headed to the bar, chatting away to George, the landlord. I heard her order lamb for both of us, our favourite in here. I don't know what their special recipe was, but it was addictive. I was sending Zack a picture of our wine and thinking I needed to bring him here one day, when Cassie returned.

"Leave him alone please and concentrate on me," she pulled a face. "So, honestly, how do you feel about Luke going?"

Sighing, I slipped the phone back into my handbag. "I feel like it's all my fault."

"I think you were a contributing factor, but you know how he loves to travel, he has always been passionate about seeing the world. Perhaps, this is what he needs?" Cassie watched me as she spoke.

"I hate the fact we aren't friends anymore; he can barely look at me in work." I took a long drink of the wine. "I asked him if he wanted to go for a drink one night, but he hasn't answered. I miss our silly laughs, miss him coming to yoga with me, miss us sitting in Starbucks just reading and drinking coffee together."

"He needs time, and space, it'll work wonders. Hopefully he'll come back with a Brazilian goddess, and you two can be friends again? Actually, I think he'd be more suited to a

Swedish girl. Imagine the blonde babies," said Cassie, going completely off on a tangent.

"I can't stop feeling guilty," I admitted.

"You were single, Zack was single, you fell in love. You did nothing wrong. I've spent a lot of time with Luke recently, and he just feels foolish, for not saying anything. He's kicking himself that he left it too late. He'll be OK though, Lily, he will. If I'd known I would've told you. You were so focused on being single, and he never seemed to want more than the odd one-night stand. I never pictured you two together," Cassie licked her lips as plates piled high with hot, delicious food were placed in front of us. "If he'd told you, before you met Zack, what would you have done?"

I gulped more wine. "What would I have done? Luke... repeatedly."

"Shit!" Cassie exclaimed. "Serious?"

"The more time goes on since he told me, yeah. He was always like my big brother, possibly because I felt like a scared little kid when I met him. But lately, since Zack I guess, I feel grown up and sexy and over all that crap." I laughed at myself. "Sounds stupid, but I feel different now, and knowing what I know...I think I'll always feel sad about what might've been."

"Have you said that stuff to Luke?"

I shook my head. "No point. The situation is what it is. Did you already know Luke was going away, before Friday?" I asked.

"Yes, sorry. He made me promise I wouldn't say. He wanted to tell you himself." she replied.

"He announced it in a staff meeting, he didn't make time to talk to me alone or anything." I sounded sulky.

"I don't know what you expect, Lily, he's hurting and everywhere he turns it feels like all he sees or hears is you and Zack. He needs space. I expect Zack isn't going to miss him?"

"Zack's jealous streak about Luke is off the charts. I can barely mention Luke's name." I confessed.

"Instead of feeling guilty, or sad, just think about what an amazing time he's going to have, and how much he needs it. The best thing you can do is wave him off with a smile, and then be ready to be his friend again when he gets back. Can you do that?" Cassie asked.

I nodded. "I can, I will. When he came back from Africa, I had this idea in my head that he and Zack would be great friends, and everything would slot into place. I found a man I'm crazy in love with, why did there have to be a price?"

"Now you're just being dramatic." She grinned as she pinched a giant chip from my plate. "It's all going to be fine, trust me. Plus, you have me, what more does a girl need?" I smiled at her as I stuck my fork into one of her chips in retaliation. "I need more details on what's happening with you and Zack please. Brighten up my dull life!"

She may have joked about her life being dull, and how hard being a mum was, but she was an absolute natural. She loved it and everything that came with it. Cassie and Guy were the most in love, solid couple I could imagine. I envied how easy it had been for her. They'd met when Cassie was at college and had been inseparable ever since. The two of them survived a long-distance relationship through university and then settled into domestic bliss, buying a bigger house every time Guy got promoted, which seemed to be a regular occurrence. As much as she joked about needing details of my sex life to keep her going, I was pretty sure she was satisfied in that department. I hoped she got the baby news she wanted soon.

Cassie hugged me as we split the bill and got ready to head home. "We should make Monday nights a regular arrangement," she smiled. "That was so much fun. Do you promise me you are going to stop stressing?"

"I will." I replied. "But I'm going to miss him."

"We all will, but, we all want our friends to be happy, don't we?" she asked, raising an eyebrow at me.

"Yes, we do, Mum."

"I'll call you in thirty seconds. Love you!"

Whenever we walked home separately, we talked as we walked, making sure each other was safe. It was quiet where we lived, and crime was low, but it was always nice to not feel alone when walking home in the dark.

I arrived back to my gorgeous flat and kicked off my boots, my phone pinged with a message. I opened it, expecting Zack, but it was Luke's name on the screen.

Luke: Sorry I haven't got back to you about the drink, don't know what to do for the best. I can't decide if it's a good or bad idea, but this can't get worse I guess?
Lily: It's been so long since I even got a message from you, I missed seeing your name! x
Luke: What are you up to now?
Lily: Literally just got in from the pub, had tea with Cassie. Why? x
Luke: If I wait, I'll change my mind, feel up to coming back out?

My head was flooded with all the happy hormones, to be able to message my friend again was so nice. The idea of going out at this time on a Monday night reminded me of carefree times.

Lily: This time on a Monday night? There's only one place we could go. Are you ready for that level of slumminess? x
Luke: Born for it! I'll be outside yours in fifteen minutes x

Half an hour later we walked into the local student union bar, the oldest people in there by miles. That still didn't stop a gaggle of eighteen-year-old girls literally stopping in their tracks to gaze open-mouthed at Luke, before moving onto flashing me daggers. The bar was loud and colourful, we'd never known it to be closed. Everything was cheap, from the drinks to the vinyl seating, which worryingly seemed to be wipe-clean for a reason.

I grabbed a booth, smiling at Luke as he walked back over with a pint and a large wine. He was dressed casually, jeans and a t-shirt, I hadn't seen him in anything but a work suit in ages now.

"Feels rebellious being out late on a Monday!" I knocked my wine glass against his. "Cheers."

Luke beamed at me. "I missed this. Our random adventures."

"Me too," I smiled. "You want to talk about stuff? Or

follow my example and pretend it didn't happen whilst getting drunk and locking yourself away for four years?"

He blew out a low whistle. "It's a tough one, but seeing as I'm leaving the country soon, we better go with the first option." He took a drink and I watched him swallow the cold liquid down, his Adam's apple bobbed as he did so, the skin of his throat so smooth. Parts of him I hadn't noticed before.

"How have you been then, really? Cassie seems to have me on limited information, she says I just need to leave you alone."

Luke shrugged, and I saw the heaviness he carried with him. "We're OK now, did she not tell you that we had a huge argument?"

I put my drink down too hard and winced as the glass banged against the cheap table. "No, she never said. What happened? I'm sorry, you should've been able to come talk to me."

"You wouldn't have appreciated it. She came to mine to see if I was alright. I was in a vile mood and ended up telling her it was all her fault, and she was so irresponsible. I mean, you were lucky, Zack was nice, but he could've been anyone. She could have put you in a crazy dangerous situation." He shook his head as he gulped down another drink. "I shouldn't have shouted at her. I've apologised, but my thoughts are still the same."

"Luke, if it's any comfort, she questioned Zack to within an inch of his life before she let him anywhere near me. She wasn't being reckless. I guess…" I looked up into his eyes, feeling the strength of his emotions bleed into me. "I guess, nobody in the world will ever understand our bond, will they? They weren't there, they don't know."

I sensed the internal conflict in him as he reached across and placed his large hand over mine, the skin cold from his drink, but so soft and tender. "Is he good, Lily? Is he treating you how you deserve?"

"He really is, there's nothing to worry about there. But Luke, I don't want you to go away thinking it was anything lacking in you. If I'd known..." I felt like I was betraying Zack even thinking this, let alone saying it. But it was a 'what if' situation, it wasn't any threat to him. "If I'd known how you felt, if Cassie hadn't arranged that meeting. I'm sure we'd be together. I had to make a choice though, and I was already too far down one path. Do you understand?"

I noted how neither of us moved our hands. "I do, it's not your fault. Just not our time I guess."

We sat there for a few moments, nobody spoke. I knew he was going through a torrent of feelings; I could see him struggling with what to do right now. Luke's eyes focused and he looked at me.

"What are you meant to be doing at work tomorrow?" he asked.

"The usual. Why? What are you doing?" I was bemused by the question.

"Pretty much slacking off before I leave. I can tell them I need you to help me get all my files closed off. Then we can sit in my office and skive and drink coffee. Which will help the hangovers we can work on now, if we order shots and join in the midnight karaoke session?" He smiled widely, his eyes twinkled with the challenge.

"I'm up for it if you are, but you know I'm going to kick your arse at karaoke!"

"Challenge accepted." With that, Luke headed back to bar. The same group of girls admiring him.

Two hours later, my throat hoarse from the karaoke, we stumbled outside into fresh air. The muscles in my stomach were tight from laughing. The cocktails at the student union appeared to be pre-mixed and I felt on a high from all the added extra's, the combination of sugar and alcohol created a strange sensation in me. I was sure my heart was beating way too fast. My soul felt mellow just for having my best friend close to me again though.

"Want to stay at mine? It's closer." Luke asked. Drunk brain said yes. I couldn't see any harm in this, I'd stayed at Luke's a hundred times before. I'd also had issues with drunk brain though, I duly noted. Nodding enthusiastically, we carried on laughing about nothing as we stumbled the short distance.

It took Luke four or five attempts to open the front door. Eventually we plonked down onto his couch, still grinning like idiots. "Want another drink?" he asked.

"I don't think I can, we have to be up in a few hours don't we?" I tried to squint at my phone but couldn't figure out the time.

"Maybe. Fuck it. Honestly, when are we going to get to do this again?" Luke was at his most reckless now and I loved it. We were always a bad influence on each other when we got like this. He opened a kitchen drawer and pulled out a chunky, hand rolled joint. "I'm taking this outside, you coming?"

"I haven't known you do that for a long time," I waited, patiently, for a response, even though it hadn't been a question.

"I have trouble sleeping since I got back, it helps." I saw him bite on the inside of his gum as he watched me.

"Well, be rude not to share when I'm a house guest." I jumped up, grabbed onto a lamp and almost broke it, more intoxicated than I realised, before I followed him towards the back door.

Luke had a couple of sun loungers in his back garden, the two of us had spent hours on them last summer, talking afternoons away. He pulled them side by side and motioned for me to lie down. I watched him hold the joint between his lips as he lit it, hypnotised by the proximity to the man who had saved me, the man I had missed.

Luke took a deep breath as he lay down next to me, that man had serious lung power. As he exhaled, the aromatic, dense smell floated over me. He turned to look at me and held it out. "Want some?"

I nodded as I took it from him, aware of how his fingers brushed over mine. I closed my eyes as I took a long drag, the heat invaded my lungs like lava flowing into me. As my head tilted back, I opened my eyes back up, noticing the stars above me twinkling in the sky, like beautiful gems. The twisting pattern of my exhaled smoke floated away in front of me, outlined against the dark night.

Everything was still, everything was beautiful. Luke's breath was steady beside me. My right hand had dropped lazily to my side and soft, warm fingers took hold of it. I liked it. I liked this.

Taking another drag, I looked to the side. Luke's face was… so alive and so aesthetically perfect. I shifted onto my side, passing the joint back to him.

He placed it into his mouth. "You are so, so pretty Luke," I whispered, not entirely sure why I was whispering. Even drunk brain was quiet now as the substance made me feel introspective.

He scratched his head, looking torn. "You're beyond pretty. You're everything."

"I missed this Luke."

"I don't think we've ever lain outside in the middle of the night calling each other pretty before, can't miss something that never happened." Luke tried to look serious, but I could see his eyes twinkling with an internal smile.

"Maybe we should've done. Maybe we should've been doing that all along. Give me more of that." I grinned at him, noticing how as he passed it to me, he ran his fingers over mine once more. "Do you think that you and me, would've worked?"

He reached across and stroked my cheek. "I think we would've been the most amazing couple in the world."

"I'm so sorry Luke." I started to cry, the smoke choked my lungs all of a sudden.

"Please don't cry," Luke reached across and pulled me to him in a hug. We lay there, his arm around me, watching the sky until there were no more drags to take. Even then I recognised that neither of us wanted to move. "Come on, let's get you to bed."

"Are you going to come to bed with me?" I meant it, as I looked into his eyes and our breath mingled together. Neither of us spoke for what seemed to be an eternity.

"Lily, don't …" I saw pain flash across his face, and immediately regretted my words. Even if I didn't regret the intention. "Why would you say that?"

"I could blame it on drink and drugs," I shrugged, feeling

hopeless. "In reality though, I don't think we'll ever get another night like this. I think once you leave, you'll never come back. Is one night better than nothing? I don't know anymore. I feel like we should've had more nights."

"We should have, but we didn't. Lily, there's nothing in the world I want to do more right now than take you to my bed. But you'd hate me tomorrow, and then hate yourself too. If we ever did spend the night together in that way, it'd need to be for the right reasons."

"I know. You'll always be my 'what if'." Fat tears ran down my cheeks.

"And you'll always be my only true love. Come on, this is too much." He sat up, pulling me up alongside him but not letting go of my hand.

"We could pretend I'm all yours, just for tonight. I would've loved to have been yours." I felt beyond devastated at the thought of him not being near me, I wanted to keep him here, as selfish as that was.

"But you're not mine, are you?" Luke snapped. "If you were, I'd be driving you into that bed upstairs right now, over and over again. It's all I can think about when you come to work in those super tight skirts. All tiny waist and curvy hips." His eyes locked on mine in a furious blaze, his pupils huge and dilated against the beautiful blue. "Then I come home alone while you head upstairs to meet Zack."

"Sometimes I think about you though, once I head upstairs," I admitted, for the first time. "I had this dream about you…"

"Lily," he sighed. "You're drunk, and I shouldn't have let you smoke this with me because it's making you say things you wouldn't normally say. This is what I was trying to explain in the park that time."

"Maybe then you should've shared this two years ago. Said things you wouldn't normally say. We wouldn't be in this position now. The things you could've said to me…" I swallowed, nervous as I rubbed my fingers against his.

"You need to stop. I'm not sure what this is now Lily, but I only have so much restraint. You aren't ready for me, trust me."

Luke let go of me, stalking inside towards the stairs as I followed behind. We stood side by side at the bathroom sink, the air heavy, like a huge storm was needed to clear it, but the storm was never going to come. The spare toothbrush I'd always kept there was still in the cup. We brushed our teeth together, looking into each other's eyes through the mirror.

"You'll always be the one who saved me," I said, as he wiped his mouth on a soft, grey towel.

"I would save you a million times over."

"Are you absolutely sure you don't want a thank you blow job?" I grinned, cheekily, aiming to break the tension of the night, but wondering how far I'd go if he took me up on it.

"For fucks sake, where was this Lily twelve months ago? I could've had fun with that," he laughed and placed a kiss on top of my head. "Go on, bed. We have work in four hours."

I don't know about Luke, but I knew I'd never tell anyone about that night, not even Cassie and definitely not Zack. The atmosphere was slightly easier at work, I was so glad we had spent that time together. I hoped Luke was too, but I sensed him becoming more and more distant as the weeks went on. I realised it had been a goodbye, the last night of being best friends.

ELEVEN

*I*t felt as though I blinked and we landed in late summer, which also meant it was time for Luke to leave. He'd refused all offers of leaving do's, drinks or presents. I worked myself up into an absolute state that week, knowing he'd be gone by weekend. On his last day, everyone was in and out of his office, wishing him well and urging him to keep in touch. Petra saw me watching his door.

"Lily, sweetheart, I don't know what happened between you two, but you've been staring at his door all week. Go speak to him before he leaves," she urged as she patted my hand. She pointed at two coffees she had made for us. "Take those if you need an excuse, I'll keep anyone else away."

I murmured my thanks with a smile, heading over to his office with the cups, well-practised at tapping on doors whilst holding drinks for lawyers and clients.

"Come in," I heard his voice through the door.

I pushed open the door with my hip and smiled hopefully.

"Got five minutes?" I asked, holding a cup out as I took a deep breath, feeling the aura of him flow into me.

He looked a little unsure but nodded and gestured to the chair opposite him. "Sure."

"Where are you off to first?" I enquired.

"Singapore, China and Japan are first three stops. I'm keeping it pretty flexible, but want to get to Thailand, Laos, Vietnam. Undecided about Australia and that direction think it might feel like a warmer version of here, with better beaches." For the first time in so long he smiled at me and I saw it reach his eyes, he was excited about this.

"Look after yourself. I'll worry about you. Have the time of your life but come back safe," I said.

"You stay safe too, Lily," he inhaled a deep breath. "I can see you're happy with Zack and I know you're close to his friends, but if anything went wrong, they'd be loyal to him. I hate the thought of you not having anyone to turn to if it goes bad." He looked down again, the sadness back.

"You taught me how to be strong Luke. I'll be fine, you taught me so much."

"Well, I think I missed the lesson where I taught you not to get stoned and offer to sleep with people," His face lit up with mischief. "Don't do that again."

"I won't," I smiled. "I meant what I said though, my 'what if', my extremely pretty 'what if'."

"I meant it all too, Lily." There was silence, then he put his book into his bag, his desk now bare. "I'm going to escape now while it's quiet."

I nodded as tears streamed down my face, unable to speak. I stood to leave, and he twisted me round to him and wrapped his arms around me, just like he had so many times when I'd needed him.

"Stay safe, be happy. Promise?" He rested his chin on top of my head, not moving a muscle, as if trying to commit me to memory.

I nodded my head as I was wracked with sobs. "You too, come home safe."

The door closed behind him. I leant back against the wall of his now empty office and cried like my heart was broken into a million pieces.

I jumped as the door burst back open a minute later. Luke crossed the room to me, kicking the door closed behind him.

"I can't leave without doing this," he took hold of my tear-soaked face between his hands and then, before I could even register what was happening, his mouth was on mine. My breath stilled as our lips touched for the first time. The very first time… One of Luke's hands slid into my hair as he began to kiss me. I couldn't feel anything except this moment.

He pulled me closer as his other hand wrapped around me, my breath was taken away. It was the definition of being lost in a moment. As my teeth teased his lips, his tongue met mine in a divine exchange.

I scattered kisses along his jawline, my lips moving across his neck, feeling the tension in him as I made my way back up to his mouth, looking into his beautiful eyes. He kissed me harder, I was so lost. I felt our wonderful friendship and how it could bloom into an amazing relationship given chance. The chemistry between us was unbelievable, how had I never noticed it? My whole body was on fire as Luke pulled back, resting his forehead against mine as his hot, fast breath slowed down.

His eyes looked down, but his body stayed pressed against mine. I was aware of his heartbeat against my own. "I'm sorry. Please though, tell me you felt that?" he whispered, almost imperceptibly, as though it could've been a silent prayer rather than a question.

I pushed his chin up with my thumb, so his eyes had to meet mine. His pupils were dark and stormy against that beautiful blue which haunted my thoughts. "I felt that Luke, I want to feel that again. Don't apologise. Please don't apologise."

If time had slowed earlier, it now sped. All at once his fingers tangled into my hair, keeping my mouth pressed to his as we met in a frenzy that had been building up for so long. I ran my own fingers up and down his back, feeling skin I hadn't touched before, noticing how his muscles felt and moved under me. I was aware of his hand inside my blouse, reaching for new skin in the same way I had. Everything felt so new. It was like the two of us were trying to catch up on all the missed kisses.

He pulled on my lip with his teeth, "Lily, we need to stop," he said breathlessly. I knew he was right but his lips were setting off every single pleasure cell in my body and it felt so good.

I looked at him, all too aware of how fast my chest rose and fell. "I can't even think of words…"

"Me and you, Lily and Luke, we were meant to be together. I just needed you to see." Tears glinted in his eyes as he continued. "I know the way I feel about you, is the way you feel about Zack though. I'll always want you to be mine."

"Please don't leave Luke, stay. Stay with me."

We both had teary faces as we pressed them together. "I love you Lily, but I have to go," He ran a finger over my lips. "I'll always love you."

Then he was gone. I sank down into his chair. Weak from the moment. Trying desperately to comprehend what had just happened. My hands were trembling, my tears wouldn't stop. How could he be gone? How?

After about ten minutes Petra came in, her face full of concern. "Everyone's headed home. Why don't you go upstairs? I'll close up."

"Thank you," I said as I wiped my eyes on the tissue she handed me.

"Do you want me to come up and make sure you're OK? Do you want to talk?" she asked kindly.

I shook my head as fresh tears sprang. "I'll be OK, thank you though."

"Whatever happened, whatever it is... The two of you will come around to where you're meant to be, I'm sure. Life isn't simple and people aren't simple. Just trust in the fact that if something is meant to be, it will be. When it's ready." I fled to the sanctuary of my flat. Hiding myself under the duvet seemed the only option.

A little while later I heard knocks at the door. *Zack!* I sat bolt upright, with all my upset I had forgotten it was Friday evening. I couldn't let him know that I'd forgotten he was on his way over. I also couldn't hide how upset I was, I was going to have to brave this, not mention that kiss until I understood it myself. I didn't always feel like I understood myself at all where Luke was concerned.

I opened the door a crack, checking it was him. A small

part of me thought maybe Luke had come rushing back. Wishing almost?

When Zack saw me, his face dropped and he pushed the door open wide, he enveloped me in a huge hug which only made more and more tears fall. He helped me over to the couch and held me as I sobbed. My tears left wet marks on his soft t-shirt. "Was it that bad? Did he do something? Say something?"

I shook my head. "No… He just told me to be safe and be happy," I shrugged, gulping down the lie. "It's not nice saying goodbye to a friend, knowing you're the one who forced them away."

"You can't blame yourself for this. You didn't do anything wrong; you can't be responsible for what other people feel and do. Don't let him guilt trip you out of living your life, please, Lily." He kissed me on the lips as I took deep breaths.

"I just… I literally don't know if I'd be here today without Luke." I sighed.

"What do you mean?" Zack looked concerned as he stroked my damp cheek and tucked my hair behind my ear.

I blew out a long, anxious breath. "I need you to understand why I'm so devastated Luke is gone. I don't talk about this, ever. I told you about the cheating, the way my ex wouldn't leave me alone. It got worse than that."

Zack took hold of my hand. "You can tell me anything. If you want to. It's your choice."

"When I found what he'd done, I was so ashamed. I didn't want to admit the vastness of it to my parents. I told them the bare basics of it, said I'd told him it was over. They'd booked this amazing three-week long cruise. They wanted to cancel, but I didn't want them to miss out. I lived alone in a flat in a student building then, but it was summer, so it was deserted. Cassie was heavily pregnant and poorly. I'd lost loads of friends and my boyfriend, so I was about as alone as I could be."

Zack handed me a bottle of water from the coffee table and watched me with concern, as I took a drink and wiped the tears from my cheeks.

"Once I'd found out what he'd done, I dumped him. There was screaming and arguing of course, but we didn't live together so other than maybe an awkward encounter if we bumped into each other, I didn't expect to deal with him again. It started with messages, one after another. First apologising, then demanding I talk to him, and then when I still didn't reply calling me every name under the sun. Then it progressed to phone calls, the phone would ring and ring, so I ended up keeping my mobile off - which isolated me more. He rang work too, I was so scared of getting in trouble, so I didn't tell anyone there."

"I'm so sorry, Lily." Zack looked so concerned, which broke my heart more.

"One day on the walk to work, I could sense someone behind me, not super close but I could tell they were there. I looked back but couldn't see anything. I checked again as I arrived at work, and he was standing there, unashamedly staring at me. It happened again after work. I ran most of the way home and locked myself in, I pressed a chair up against the door. I felt so scared and when I summoned up the courage to look out the window, he was over the road, watching me. It carried on, not every day but most days."

"A short while later, everyone else left work as normal, but I couldn't bring myself to leave. I sat in the staff room and cried, I knew that when I went home, he'd follow me again. I didn't feel I had anyone to turn to. Luke had been working there a few weeks, I hardly knew him. I hadn't even realised he was still in his office. He found me. Just having someone ask me what was wrong, sort of broke a dam. I ended up telling him everything. He was... incredible."

"Luke drove me to my mum and dads place and stayed there with me. The next day he started all the restraining order stuff and never charged me a penny for it. We went to the police together and reported it all. After about a week of Luke staying at my parents with me, I felt brave enough to go back to my flat. Hoping the police and the legal action would've scared him off, it had been a lot quieter."

I took another drink, almost spilling the water with my trembling hands.

"Luke was worried about it, but I was sure it was fine. He went out and got me a new phone so that even if I had to turn my old one off, I could still be in contact with him on a different number. I gave him a spare key to my flat, he made me feel safe, nobody else did. Luke came up with this system, where he told me what he was having for tea." I smiled to myself. "Then he'd message me later in the evening to make sure I was OK. If he'd told me at work that he was having cottage pie for example, I'd reply to his text and say, 'How was the cottage pie?'. If I didn't reply, or replied differently, he'd know I needed him. Like a code word that would change each day, so Luke knew I was safe. I got back to the flat and everything seemed fine. The front door locked from the inside, so, I left my key in the lock as normal. I'm sorry Zack, this is the most convoluted story."

"Don't be sorry, don't you ever apologise for this. I want to kill the guy already, take your time."

"I'd glanced in each room when I got back, but it never occurred to me to check further than that. I went into my bedroom to get changed, and when I came back out, he was on the couch. He must've hidden. I didn't even know he had a key. I looked at the front door, but my key was gone so I knew I couldn't open it. He was looking through my phone. He said that if I'd slept with someone, that cancelled out what he'd done, therefore we could get back together. He was calm, it was eerie. To have been in love with a person, then feel scared to be alone with them. To feel like you don't know them at all. Luke messaged me, as he'd promised, and when he saw the message, he got crazy mad. I felt like the only way to calm him down was to agree with him. So, I apologised, which made me feel disgusting. I said that of course I could forgive him, and we could get back together. I just wanted him to stop shouting, Zack."

"I was scared that the neighbouring flats were empty, nobody could hear what was happening. He went to kiss me, and I froze. I thought I could act, but I couldn't do it. Then things got scary. He started screaming at me, his eyes all crazy, I think he must've been on drugs. He pushed me over and I cut my head on the table, but he didn't even seem bothered. He grabbed at my arms and pinned me down and to this day I don't know what he was going to do, but I have horrible, horrible suspicions."

"With all the chaos neither of us had heard the door open. Before I knew what was happening, Luke grabbed him, they started to fight. Luke easily overpowered him, he was a scrawny little shit." I laughed sadly.

"Luke punched him in the face, hard, and told me to go in the bathroom. I could hear Luke's voice as he pinned him down, but he's never told me exactly what was said. After about fifteen minutes, Luke knocked and told me to come out, he was gone." I shivered. *Almost done, Lily.*

"Luke took me to a hotel, he stayed with me, making endless cups of tea. He told me that he was due to move into the flat above the office that weekend, but he wanted me to move there instead. It was safe, it had alarms and security cameras and two front doors with solid locks. Then, even after I did move in, Luke slept on the couch whenever I felt jumpy. So basically, because of me not answering that silly 'what did you have for tea?' message, Luke knew I needed help. Without him turning up at my flat, I don't know what would've happened to me."

"Lily," Zack hugged me tighter than I'd ever known. "You kind of breezed over it when you first told me, I didn't know it was that bad."

"I hate talking about, I never even say his name. I didn't want you to think of me differently. To feel like you couldn't act normal around me. I know not everyone is like him."

"So, did he disappear?"

I nodded, "I don't know what Luke said, but it scared the crap out of him. Next I knew, he moved away, and the rest is history. Think he just played at being a bit psycho, and as soon as someone stood up to him, he scarpered." I paused and drank more water. "Do you see now why Luke and I have the bond that we do? Why he found it so hard to tell me what he felt? I hate that I've lost him."

"I get jealous about how close you two are, or at least were. Thank God Luke was there though hey?"

"Now you know, can we leave it in the past? I just want to focus on the future."

"I'm here for the good bits and the bad bits. Don't ever apologise for what you feel," he loosened the hug. "I don't know what's best to suggest. Shall we get out of here? Want to come back to mine? Total change of scenery, we can go and get smashed in those nice bars you like?"

"You drove all the way here, you'd be exhausted," I pointed out.

"I'd drive anywhere for you, don't even worry about that," he placed a light kiss on my lips. "Drive to mine, get your sexy clothes on, drink as many cocktails as we can, in as many bars as we can. Then pass out in bed after letting you take advantage of me in any way you like. Tomorrow morning I'll bring you breakfast in bed and we can make plans, I have big plans for us."

"That sounds amazing, too many memories here right now. Thank you, Zack, for everything, for being so understanding."

"I love you, it's what I do," he smiled. "Go pack a bag."

I felt drained as I gathered a weekend bag together. I still felt confused about that kiss too. I know it was Luke's goodbye, but… that kiss had changed something in me. Surely we weren't leaving it at that? I pulled my phone from my pocket.

Lily: Do you think we should talk? x
Luke: I think that kiss said it all x
Lily: How can that be it for us?
Luke: I have to go Lily, I need to do this. That kiss though…

me and you aren't done, not by a long way. A lot can
happen in a year, let's just see. Look after yourself xx
Lily: You too, my ever so pretty 'what if' x

Guilt and confusion bubbled away in my mind, yet it seemed as if right now there was nothing I could do. I shouldn't have kissed Luke back, but I hadn't been able to resist. I needed to talk to Cassie, but Zack was waiting for me. I needed distracting from this situation so maybe his idea was the best plan right now. Since when had fancy cocktails not helped!?

TWELVE

I remember most of the night... I think. Zack's town was gentrified - beautiful bars and restaurants lined the main streets. As I lay in his bed the next morning and swiped through drunken photographs on my phone, I realised we'd visited most of them. *How many selfies had we taken? Who were those people? And what did we take when we got home?* Those were getting filed somewhere secret!

The screen showed me it was gone noon. The significance wasn't lost that Luke's plane would've left. I looked over at Zack, on the pillow next to me, he'd been so amazing last night. He was the right decision, for sure. I snuggled up to him, that gorgeous face and warm body, and remembered how lucky I was.

A soft kiss fluttered onto my cheek as Zack slipped out of bed. I didn't have the energy to move yet, but as I heard the bedroom door open a few minutes later, I opened a sleepy eye. Zack laughed to himself as he brought a tray full of coffee and toast over. He placed it down on the bed and grinned at me, before slipping back under the covers. I couldn't fathom why he looked so happy, I felt like I'd been drowned in tequila.

"Adam just told me something that's either insanely hot or mortifying, I can't make my mind up." Zack smirked at me.

"What? Tell me!" I replied, grateful as I grabbed a coffee and took a large, hot gulp.

"Do you remember getting home last night?" Zack asked, still smiling.

"Ish…"

"I think I couldn't unlock the door and we were laughing, which turned into kissing. Ring a bell?"

"It does. We were doing that kissing, walking, undressing thing on the way to your room," I moved closer to him as I remembered how good that felt. "I love doing that."

"Mmmm," Zack kissed me. "You're a total temptress. Well, apparently we were so carried away, we didn't notice Adam was sitting on the couch in the middle of a raid."

"You're using boy speak again. He was in the middle of a what?"

"A raid. It's like a group event on his game. You work together. The whole group were watching Adam on Zoom because he co-designed it, and so consequently saw us drunkenly dry humping in the background of his call for a good minute." Zack watched me for my reaction.

"Oh my god. Mortified!" I buried my head in my hands.

"Don't worry! They didn't see anything too graphic. Adam thinks it's hilarious. He told them to consider a career in law rather than games design after seeing the differences between our Friday nights. Anyway, after the sounds I've heard from his room, he had this cosplay girlfriend for a while..." Zack pulled a face and I grinned.

"I suppose it's a bit sexy, as long as he isn't mad. I like the idea of dry humping you," I teased.

"Keep being nice to me and I might let you," Zack wrapped the duvet around my shoulders. "I need to talk to you first. There are two parts, I need you to listen to both parts before you answer me. I'm worried about the timing with you being so upset yesterday, but here goes nothing."

"I'm intrigued," I smiled as I reached for more toast. "Fire away."

Zack twitched with excitement as he began. "There are two secretary jobs going at work, one of which is a senior role. I know you could do it with your eyes shut. It's not in corporate so you wouldn't be stuck with me all day or anything." he smiled, but his eyes were nervous. "I was thinking you should apply to give you room to grow, you could do so much at a company like mine and everyone would adore you." He took a deep breath and another glug of coffee.

"The second bit is that Adam told me he wants to move out. He wants to be closer to his new office. So, I wanted to start looking for a house to rent. I'd like to look together. I guess what I'm trying to ask, is, will you move in with me? All of this happening at once, it seems likes something's aligned. I miss you so much when we aren't together, imagine how amazing it would be to have our own place."

He did his best puppy dog eyes at me and I grinned and ruffled his hair. "What if I didn't get the job?"

"Then you should still live with me, there'll be other jobs. That'd just be a bonus. Having a place together, waking up with you every day. That would be the dream. I know we've only been together a few months, but it feels right, Lily. Everything about you, us, feels right. It has done since the first day."

"I'd love to move in with you." The answer came out of my lips before my brain engaged. I wanted this. Luke was gone, I loved Zack, why not do this?

He pulled me close to him, crumbs scattering all over the bed as he rubbed his nose side to side against mine in an eskimo kiss. "Really?" he asked.

"One hundred per cent." I confirmed with a kiss.

"One other thing though," he had a cheeky glint in his eye as he pulled back from the kiss. "I know the job isn't for my secretary, but I think we should pretend you are…" I hit him on the arm. "Now, about that dry humping you mentioned."

———

Monday night had one meaning, The Royal Oak with Cassie. It was a relatively new tradition, and I guessed it was going to have to end when I moved. Cassie was already at our favourite table when I walked in, tapping away on her phone. I saw two large glasses of wine on the table and instantly realised that meant she still hadn't had the news she wanted.

I reached down and hugged her before I took my seat. "How are you doing lovely?"

"Not bad, the normal," she shrugged.

I gestured at her wine glass as I took a sip of my own. "Want to talk about it?"

She shook her head. "We haven't even been trying that long, shouldn't complain. It's just that with the girls it happened pretty much as soon as we made the decision to try."

"Have you been to see the doctor?"

"No, I'll give it a couple more months. See how we go. Anyway, enough about my sex life… which is now set against a calendar and involves me sticking my legs in the air afterwards… what's been happening?" She leaned forward, a glint back in her eye.

"I don't know where to start. Let's rip the plaster off. I had the sexiest, craziest kiss in the world ever with Luke before he said goodbye. Zack asked me to move in with him and I said yes."

Cassie blinked at me. "We need more wine. Start with Zack, you're moving?!"

"Well, hopefully. I have an interview for a job at his firm. Adam's moving out, so we're going to look for a house to rent." I smiled at my happy news.

"And that's what Zack wanted after you had the 'sexiest, craziest kiss in the world ever' with Luke?" She did the air quotes as she mimicked me.

"That hasn't come up in conversation, it was a weird day Cassie." She poured more wine into our glasses and watched me, her face expectant. "It was Luke's last day at work, I went into his office to say goodbye. It was sad, felt horrible. About a minute after he left, he sort of… burst back in like superman and just grabbed me and kissed me and…" I put my head in my hands, simply remembering the way it made me feel.

"Jesus… Lily, what are you going to do?"

I shrugged. "Nothing to do. He said he couldn't leave without kissing me. Afterwards though he said he still had to go but would always love me. What am I meant to do with that, Cass?"

"Next time I speak to him, I'll find out what he meant."

"No, don't put yourself in an awkward position. He's gone, he's surrounded by gorgeous young backpacker girls who'll be all over him. I won't be on his mind. He wanted to go, just… let him go." I grabbed my purse and headed to the bar, reading the wine list over and over while I waited, to distract me from the thoughts that ran through my head.

"Tell me about the kiss." Cassie said the instant I got back to the table with a second bottle.

I licked my lips without meaning to as I contemplated how to describe it. "It took me by surprise. It was full of love, like I could actually feel the love in it. It was intense, incredibly fucking sexy. It went on a lot longer than a goodbye kiss should have. It was… troubling for many reasons. I feel awful about it when I think of Zack, but I didn't instigate it, I couldn't help but respond to it, to him."

Cassie looked worried. "You couldn't have figured out you fancied the arse off him before this point?"

"Everyone fancies the arse off him."

"You know what I mean. Have you spoken since?"

"No, he seems to want to be left alone. I have this amazing opportunity with Zack, who I also fancy the arse off by the way," I grinned. "A big part of me doubts that Luke will even come back, so I can't sit around moping. It was a kiss, just a kiss."

"Hmm," she didn't look convinced. "Let's look at houses. You're going to be all posh and Cheshire!" The sparkle returned to her eyes!

THIRTEEN

*T*wo months later, I realised that leaving my old life behind wasn't quite as easy as anticipated. I cried buckets when I handed my resignation in, despite the whole team being so pleased for me. I followed Luke's example and decided against having a leaving do, much to everyone's disappointment, but with promises of invitations to our housewarming party.

Cassie heaved giant, snotty tears as if the world was ending when she left my flat for the last time, despite me reminding her I was only an hour away and had a spare bedroom for her. I promised her that Zack and I would come and stay soon, and I'd still plague her with messages chronicling my every move.

Standing in the flat on that final Saturday morning, I felt detached from myself. All of my possessions had already gone in a removal van, including the big heart frame, even though I was sure it couldn't go up in the new house. Zack was there already, at our home. *Our home!*

I felt out of sorts. One single memory kept flicking back

into my mind. Moving in, when it was this empty as well. Newly single, with a restraining order against a narcissistic ex and only Luke to keep me safe. This was meant to be Luke's flat, but he'd given it up for me, to give me a safe place. I shivered at the thought of what might've been without him, and what perhaps, could have been our future if he'd spoken to me before I met Zack.

"Goodbye…" I whispered to nobody as I closed the door for the last time.

———

On a crisp, autumnal Friday evening, a few short weeks later, Zack and I arrived home from work together. I'd adjusted to this new life quickly, almost as if it had always been this way. I'd settled into work and the extra responsibility was nice, plus the extra pay of course. The house was looking good, with a splendid mix of my furniture, Zack's possessions and new items we had bought together in fits of giddy excitement. We'd splashed out on gorgeous, tall bar stools for the kitchen-diner. Whilst one of us cooked the other would sit and chat and pour the wine. My cosy corner sofa was in the living room and we'd framed beautiful black and white photographs of us for the wall. Zack had been so right, not having to say goodbye anymore was beautiful.

It was the right time for the housewarming. We bought ridiculous amounts of booze and snacks, acting like giddy kids all day, waiting to show off our happiness to our favourite people. It was going to be a squash, but I didn't think anybody would care. We'd even invited the neighbours, in case the noise annoyed them.

Everyone who arrived brought more drink and gifts, my heart felt so full of love and happiness it might explode. Both sets of our parents were there, Cassie and Guy, Zack's sisters, all the bunch from Draper & Hughes and then some of my new work friends, plus Zack's own best friends who were more and more part of my life.

Zack's sisters were hilarious, they were all individual characters, and I adored them. Isabelle was the eldest, then Hannah. Zack was the middle child of course, followed by his baby twin sisters Leah and Maisie. Isabelle and Hannah had two children each, so I was now an Auntie by default, which I loved! Leah and Maisie were still young and not ready to settle down. From the first time I'd met them all, they'd welcomed me as if I'd always been part of the family. You could tell they all doted on Zack, the only boy of the family, and were made up to see him happy. As I poured drinks for us all, I heard Petra and Fi chatting in the small, back garden over a cigarette.

"Did you see the photo's he sent through on Wednesday?" Petra asked Fi.

"I did," she replied. "It looks stunning. I've never seen him so well. Where was it again? Laos? It looked incredible, so did he." They both laughed and I rolled my eyes, from that one comment I knew they were talking about Luke.

Luke wandered through my mind on a daily basis. I didn't think I'd ever stop yearning for that friendship back. Our random Monday night replayed itself often too, it unsettled me. Because when I'd asked if he was taking me to bed, I meant it, I would've done it. I felt like I was slightly insane, I wanted to know what he felt like, tasted like. I shook my head, trying to get the image out of my mind as I continued to listen.

A thought struck me… That kiss hadn't been a goodbye, it was an appetiser.

"I wouldn't blame him if he never came back," said Fi. "Even less to come home for now isn't there?"

"I thought they'd get together," she sighed. "Anyway, probably not the right time and place to bring that up is it?"

I wondered what she meant; did she mean me? Did she know what had happened? My thoughts were interrupted as I heard Zack's booming, drunken laugh alongside my dad's. They were two of a kind, got on like a house on fire. Every now and then, I would imagine a future where Zack had a matching shed to escape to, just like my Dad. I smiled at the thought and grabbed the drinks, handing them out before heading to Zack for a kiss and a hug. It didn't take long for me to miss the feel of him around me, it was almost like an addiction to his touch.

"I hope you two aren't laughing about me?" I asked as Zack put his arm around me. My dad looked away as Zack's hand rubbed over my hip with slow strokes.

"As if," smiled Zack. "I was preparing *your* dad for the football rivalry that *my* dad is going to bring up any minute."

"Well, as much as I love football talk," I placed a kiss on Zack's cheek. "Think I'll go see your sisters instead."

The evening was glorious, and everyone seemed to have a great time. Cassie was crying once more when she left, sobbing about how much she missed me. Guy rolled his eyes at me as he put her in the car and said they would see us next weekend. As it grew late and the last guests started to drift home, I couldn't stop thinking about the conversation I'd heard. Just seeing people from my old life had brought Luke to the front of my mind again, which was crazy when I was celebrating my new life with Zack.

The party had been everything it should have been, joyful and happy and full of promise for the future. The house was perfect, our literal love nest, well maybe not perfect right now covered in empty glasses and crumbs but that could be fixed. An utterly gorgeous man who adored me was sound asleep upstairs after way too many shots. I'd spent the whole evening surrounded by friends, family and colleagues, all of them celebrating our move and our future. How could the absence of one person hit me so hard?

I knew that Zack felt relief that Luke was gone, and the 'complication' wasn't there for the two of us. I never admitted the way my mind wandered back to happy memories, silly TikToks, movie nights, hikes. The way Luke's eyes crinkled up when he was laughing with me, always with me, never at me.

It felt like grief in many ways. I'd go to message Luke on my phone and realise I couldn't, or at least shouldn't. I'd see a gig advertised and want to invite him. All of me missed him. I thought back to that night in his back garden, and what would've happened if he'd taken me up on the offer.

I'd already had too much to drink, but drunk brain was on form. It wanted me to pour another large glass of Pinot Grigio and obsess at Instagram.

Luke's travel photographs were stunning. The lifestyle worked for him. His blonde hair was now longer, and it suited him, brighter against his tanned face. Freckles that were not noticeable before were now sprinkled across his nose.

One particular picture was so good it didn't look real. Luke was next to a magnificent azure ocean with crashing waves, and I swear his eyes matched the blue of the water to perfection. I shook my head again, trying to chase the thoughts away. *What are you doing Lily?* Scrolling back, I saw another of him laughing, as he waited at an exotic train station. I knew he would have the crinkled up, sparkly eyes underneath his sunglasses. My breath caught as I looked at his sunglasses and saw the reflection of the person taking the photograph. She seemed as happy as him, long blonde beach waves in her hair and a wide smile as she held her phone up. I suppose he had time to make up for. He deserved to be happy. Why did I feel sick?

I put the wine down and closed my eyes, looking for the rational part of my brain. Luke was a good person, the best person, he should be enjoying every minute of it. He'd always been there for me, his strong arms giving me the tightest hugs every time I needed them. Not now though, not tonight, not anymore.

I swiped back to the main page of his Instagram account, the highlights showing that beautiful ocean, those exquisite eyes. My finger moved to the word 'Message' almost without thought. I'd liked a few of his photographs over the past weeks and had posted bright and breezy comments, but there hadn't been any response and he hadn't done the same to my own feed. I blamed it on the constant travel, the lack of wi-fi, the time difference and so on, but in my heart, I knew he was trying to get away from me. Sometimes the internet made the world feel too small.

Lily: That kiss was everything...

I pressed send then turned off the phone and went to bed. Leaving the mess and chaos of the party for the morning. I didn't look at Zack as my head hit my pillow. The spinning room wasn't the only sensation making me feel uneasy.

———

I woke up to the sound of the shower running. A heavy guilt settled on top of my hangover. Perhaps the best course of action was to keep the phone off and stay busy. Quickly putting on a comfy yoga set while Zack finished in the bathroom, I began to tackle the empty wine bottles, the crushed Dorito's in the carpet and the mountain of shot and wine glasses waiting to be washed. I sensed Zack enter the kitchen and felt his warm arms wrap around me, as he kissed my neck on each side.

"Good morning beautiful," he murmured. "You're busy for a girl who drank so much wine last night."

"Ha!" I laughed. "Says the person who pretty much passed out after every form of shot possible. Did I even see our mums join in at one point?"

"Yeah," he grinned. "I won't be popular this morning. Was such a good night. You've still got loads of presents to open later too, I don't need presents, I have you, that's all I need." He twisted me around to kiss me and I held my bubbly hands in the air, not wanting to get his clean clothes wet. "I don't care about the bubbles," he smiled as he squeezed me and I let my arms wrap around him. He was so warm from his shower. Everything was fine, everything was perfect. How lucky was I to be in this house, with this man? This would've felt impossible twelve months ago.

"I'll join in the big tidy up, but I can't function until I've been to Costa. Want me to bring you back a Vanilla Latte? Almond Croissant? Or is the hangover so bad we need to go straight to chocolate brownie?" Zack asked.

"You choose," I replied. "I don't feel so great, I might nip back to bed for a bit."

Zack looked at me with concern. "Do you need me to get you anything? Not like you to feel so rough?"

"No, I'm OK," I replied. "Got enthusiastic with the wine last night. I'll have a lie down while you are out and I'll feel better, I'm sure."

He pulled me to him and kissed the top of my head, taking a deep breath of me in. "I'm going to walk, so I'll be about half an hour," he smiled down at me. "I love you, even if you are rubbish at hangovers."

I smiled and kissed him on the lips. "Love you too, bring me something nice."

I climbed the stairs back to bed as my mind raced. Safely tucked up under the covers, I switched my phone on. Notifications began pinging, messages from party guests home safe, hungover selfies on Insta, tags in many drunken photos from the night before. I couldn't see the notification I was looking for though. I opened my message to Luke from last night and was almost too fearful to look. There were four little letters under the message - seen. Luke had read the message and not replied, that told me all I needed to know. Tossing the phone onto the empty pillow next to me, I held my head in my hands, what was I doing? I must be losing my mind because this made no sense at all, I could've screamed with frustration at myself.

Ping

I felt sick, I knew that ping. I didn't want to look at the phone. I couldn't not look at the phone. *Just pick the phone up woman!*

Luke: Is something wrong? Are you OK?
Lily: I'm fine, promise
Luke: Do we need to talk about what you had for tea?
Lily: God no, nothing like that. I wanted to let you know, it was on my mind, the kiss ...
Luke: Why Lily? What's gone wrong in that perfect world that you and Zack seem to inhabit?

It's hard to judge a person's mood from a message, but I felt as though I could feel his anger burn down the phone to me. I guess he had every right to be mad, but then didn't I too? How was it my fault my best friend kept his feelings secret from me for so long?

Luke: I know you had a housewarming party last night, I've seen people's pictures. Was this message a drunk mistake? Can't believe you've moved in with him already, you know he's just trying to lock you down?

Lily: Please don't be like this. I miss you. Everyone but you being here last night brought that back to me. I miss you

Luke: I have to stop myself from missing you every single day, Lily! I have to force myself to not think about you. To not think about you and him. I'm at the airport, I can't do this right now

Lily: I understand. I don't know what to say. I'm sorry, I won't message again. Safe flight, you look so well and so happy xx

Luke: I'm not here to pick you up when you need it Lily. I'm trying to deal with a lot of stuff myself.

The little green light by his beautiful picture disappeared, he was no longer online. I lay back on the pillow and felt... ridiculous... what had I done? Upset Luke, made myself feel like an idiot and gone behind Zack's back. My phone flashed up with a picture message, a close up of a takeaway coffee cup and my favourite chocolate brownie. I sent a love heart back to Zack, and then deleted Luke's messages with mixed feelings.

FOURTEEN

*Z*ack and I living together felt breath-taking, as life continued along a happy path for us. I didn't hear from Luke, those feelings had to be pushed into a little box, in the back of my mind, left alone. I even eased off on the Instagram voyeurism, it was too simple to picture myself in the photographs with Luke, what an amazing journey that would be.

Our first Christmas in our home together was incredible, so much love and happiness and family in one place, plus the newfound joy of receiving designer shoes under the Christmas tree. Time seemed to spin by in a rush, I still didn't feel like I was at the height of my love for Zack, every day I'd love him a touch more. My heart felt so full, yet more love kept blossoming. We found ourselves back in spring-time, and I couldn't help but remember those first dates and nervous times.

One morning at work, the familiar Instagram ping went again. I picked up my phone expecting it to be Cassie, it was a year now since they'd decided to try for a baby and every time we met, I could see the tension growing in her face. She'd agreed to go to the doctors, so I was hoping for good news soon. This message wasn't Cassie however.

Luke: Hey Lily. I'm sorry it's been a while. I didn't mean for it to be that long. Is there a time I could call you? When you'd be able to talk to me?

My heart beat amplified. I knew what he meant, a time when Zack wasn't around. Oh god... He was coming back married to a gorgeous blonde beach goddess, wasn't he? Cassie had been right. They'd have amazing blonde children. Or... maybe he wasn't coming back at all?

Lily: Hi stranger. Sure, I need to go to the other office this afternoon so will be driving over alone. Would 12 ish work? I don't know the time difference? Is this bad news?
Luke: No, not bad news. Not even news, more of a question. 12ish is fine. Speak to you then

This was going to be a long morning. *Coffee... I need coffee.* By quarter to twelve I couldn't wait anymore and headed out to Zack's car, well, I guess it was our car now, explaining I needed to run an errand on my way. I drove to a nearby park and waited, my mind in overdrive.

I jumped as my phone buzzed to life, a contact I hadn't seen in so long flashing up on the screen. Luke Adamson – Incoming Call. I took a long, deep breath before answering.

"Hi Luke," I bit my lip and tried to focus on not saying anything stupid.

"Hey. It's good to hear your voice, been a while."

"It has. That was an unexpected message this morning."

"I know," he said. "I'm sorry about last time we messaged, I didn't mean to sound so angry."

"No, it was my fault, I shouldn't have sent that, it wasn't fair on anybody." Familiar guilt shivered through me.

"Don't worry. How're you doing? New job going well?" he asked.

"Yeah, I'm good thanks, job still feels strange sometimes, but it's going well. You'll have forgotten how to work by the time you come back!" I joked.

"Ha-ha no chance! Listen, I'm back in the UK. I'm in London for a little while before I come back home."

My heart stopped for a full minute. Luke was back. Luke was coming home.

"I wanted to ask you if you'd meet me? I know that Zack won't be happy. I don't want to put you in a difficult situation, but I do want to see you, Lily."

"Erm, wow, Luke that's a lot to take in. When did you get back?" I wasn't sure where this was going.

"Two days ago, jet lag is just easing off."

I could tell he was smiling as he spoke. I wanted to see that smile. I checked myself in the rear-view mirror, thankful for good make up!

"Before I answer, can I ask a favour? Can we switch to video call? Be so good to see you."

"I look like crap, but of course."

Then the screen sprang to life. There he was. So tanned, so blonde, eyes still sparkly, smile so wide. The slightest hint of trepidation.

"Is this your idea of looking like crap? You look so pretty Luke." I laughed at what felt like an in joke for us. He was once so familiar and now such a rare sight. I snapped out of the trance, as I realised, he was taking in everything about me too.

"Says the prettiest girl in the world. You look more grown-up though, does that sound weird?" he asked.

"No, it doesn't, think I feel more grown up now. Stopped hiding from the world."

I felt like this was one of those Sliding Doors moments where your life can split in two different directions. I should leave this alone, but I couldn't. I'd been pining for Luke for so long now.

"I want to meet. We shouldn't have left this like we did," I admitted.

"We can figure out where and when next week. I guess you need to speak to Zack?"

"Yep. That'll be interesting. I'm so glad you're back safe." I smiled at him.

He smiled back and those freckles looked even more adorable. "Speak soon Lily, missed you." Then he was gone, and I was holding the phone in the car, my hand trembling.

———

The thought of speaking to Zack about this filled me with dread. He had a jealous streak at the best of times, but where Luke was concerned, it was on another level. As we cosied up on the couch together on Friday evening, it seemed as good a time as any.

"Zack…" I said, as I stroked my fingers up and down his arm.

"Mmhmm?" He was busy flicking through hundreds of box sets trying to find one to settle on for the night.

"Luke rang me."

All box set browsing stopped as Zack looked at me. "Where is he?"

"London," I answered. "He'll be back home soon. I said I'd go and see him."

"Why would you say that?" He moved away from me subtly.

"Because he's my best friend and I haven't seen him in almost a year," I shrugged. "You wouldn't ask that if I was going to see Cassie, or you were going to see Maddy."

"The difference being they aren't trying to get into your knickers." Deep frown lines appeared on his forehead.

"You don't trust me at all do you? You know how I feel about cheating, I wouldn't cheat on you."

"I trust you. I don't trust him. You're not going, that's it." He continued to look through the tv options as though that was it. His word was final.

"Excuse me? Since when do I not get a say in my own decisions?"

"When it involves him, you're completely blind. For fucks sake, I know what he did was amazing, do we have to hear about it forever? I would've done it, anyone would've done it."

"Wow…" I couldn't believe Zack had said that. "Of all the shitty things you could've said…"

He shrugged, like a petulant child, the conversation was over for him.

"You know you can't stop me? Can I just check we haven't gone back to the fifties here and you are expecting me to be all *Stepford Wives?*"

"Do you ever think about how it makes me feel?" Zack snapped at me.

"Of course I do. Do you ever think that if it was him I wanted to be with, I would be? I wouldn't have uprooted my life to be here with you, would I?" I yelled back. "You can't keep doing this jealous act."

Zack's breaths were fast as he clenched and stretched his fingers. "How about we see him together? With Cassie and Guy, in a group. I don't want you on your own with him."

"I'll speak to Cassie." I looked at the blank television, preferable to looking at him right now.

"I'm going out. Can we take a rain check on this?" He pointed to the beers and popcorn on the table, all ready for a snuggly night in.

"Sure," I sighed. "If that's what you want. Don't rush back on my account."

Ten minutes later, without so much as a kiss on the cheek, Zack drove away. As Friday nights go, not my greatest.

———

"Stranger!" Cassie teased as she answered my call the next day. "Thought you'd run off on me now you're a big career girl."

"No, it's been chaos lately," I responded, making polite chit chat and listening to her tales of the kids whilst wondering how to broach this. "Cassie, I need to ask you something."

"OK… I figured, you've found out, haven't you?" she sounded stressed.

"Found out what?!" I asked, confused.

"That I have Luke staying here." She said.

"Oh, right, no, I mean yes. I knew he was back, but not with you. That's sort of what I wanted to ask about. We need a catch up, it's been too long, and I also want to clear the air with Luke. So, I was wondering about coming over, Friday night maybe? Kill two besties with one stone and all that?" I hoped I sounded casual enough.

"Sounds good to me lovely, but let me check Luke is OK with it yeah?"

"Of course."

"Only problem is he has the granny flat. You'd have to sleep on a couch if you stayed?" she said. "The spare room isn't finished."

"Not a problem, don't worry. I do love the fact though that nobody over the age of thirty actually sleeps in your granny flat."

"They will one day, I was future proofing, and hoping for built in babysitters. Bloody need them now that you've up and moved!" she teased.

"Love you too," I joked. "I need to go, let me know about Friday asap. I need Zack to come round to the idea."

"Zack would never refuse you anything. I'll speak to Luke when he gets back." She blew an exaggerated kiss and hung up.

I felt stupid and jealous that Cassie would see Luke today. *Lily you are so ridiculous!* I took a deep breath as the importance of this to me settled. I knew, of course, that she'd get the go ahead from Luke.

We made arrangements for the next weekend. I noticed Zack sneak glances at my phone on a few occasions, which only put me in a worse mood. Neither of us had apologised, we'd settled back into a mostly normal routine.

I was dreading the night by the time it arrived, this wasn't how I wanted to see Luke.

Cassie was welcoming as ever of course, inviting us in to her lovely, warm home. The mini mansion, nestled in a gorgeous wide street full of other mini mansions and middle-class children who ate quinoa and pesto. Zack and I sleeping on the sofa for the night wasn't going to work, so I'd driven. If one of us was going to drink, I'd prefer it to be Zack. That way I was more in control of my words.

Guy and Luke were opening up bottles of wine in the kitchen as we walked in.

"Hi," I hugged Guy and then looked at Luke. This was surreal, the last time that face was in front of mine, he kissed me. "Sight for sore eyes. Good trip?" I hugged him, wanting to seem like old friends greeting each other and nothing more.

Luke smiled as Zack greeted them both. "Great trip, thank you. I'll bore you with stories later, they're sick of them." He motioned towards Guy and Cassie. "How are you both doing? You moved in together while I was away?"

Zack jumped in like a shot. "Yep, been a busy year." He smiled as he shook Luke's hand, was it sincere? Who knew?

The floor vibrated, how did tiny feet make such an

impact? Ruby and Emilia barrelled into the room and charged at Zack and I for hugs. It was a welcome relief from small talk when they dragged us both away to play Hungry Hippo's.

We shared homemade pizza's; the girls of course had their toppings arranged into smiley faces. The table was covered in empty wine and beer bottles soon enough, I had stuck to the lemonade, determined to stay in control.

"OK you two, bedtime." Cassie clapped her hands.

"I want Lily to put me to bed," said Ruby.

"I want Luke," sang Emilia.

Cassie looked at us. "That OK with you?" I don't think she knew who to check with.

I looked at Zack, "Do you mind?" I spoke quietly, not wanting it to seem like I was asking permission, but knowing that was exactly what was happening.

"How could you possibly say no to that little face?" He smiled at Ruby. "No problem, don't worry. Guy, shall we nip down the road?" We all knew down the road meant the pub.

I wasn't sure Zack was quite as relaxed as he made out, but I also knew he wouldn't want to let on in front of Luke that he had any issue. Luke and I headed upstairs with two gorgeous little girls.

I whispered to Luke as they brushed their teeth. "I'm sorry, this evening turned out nothing like I planned. I hoped we could talk about what happened."

"It's OK, don't worry. No rush." Luke moved out of their view and brushed his hand against mine. "Are you alright?"

I nodded. "Yes, you?"

"It's so good to see you. Zack seems fine about-"

"All done!" Two little voices shouted at us and cut Luke

off as they ran out of the bathroom.

"Story time then!" I ushered them into Ruby's bedroom, to the story corner, piled high with beanbags, throws and cushions. A gorgeous and overflowing bookcase of beautifully illustrated books dominating one wall.

Luke and I sat next to each other on beanbags, with a child each on our knees. As I began to read them a story about a singing mermaid, he slid his free arm behind me and hugged us all together. I drew out every word, turned the pages carefully, enjoying the feel of him and the happiness radiating from the room. It was still over too soon though. Luke carried Emilia back to her room as I tucked Ruby in. She looked sleepy and angelic.

Switching on her monitor, I tiptoed out, closing her door behind me. Unable to see much in the dark hallway as my eyes adjusted. I heard Luke softly close Emilia's door and tiptoe over to me.

He placed a finger over my lips and shushed, before wrapping his arms around me. I knew the monitors would pick up any words, we needed to be quiet, but there was so much I wanted to say.

As he held me close, my muscle memory kicked in. My head seeking its natural spot against his shoulder. His heart beating against me. My own arms wrapping around his back. An ache spread throughout me, how had I gone so long without this?

His mouth pressed against my ear as he whispered, almost silent. "I missed you so much."

I looked up at him and nodded as I smiled, wanting to portray that I felt the same. Those eyes though... how had I never felt lost in them before? This was dangerous and stupid, but I was drawn to him. My breath caught in my throat as he stroked a finger down my cheek, then his lips were heading towards mine, my brain felt fuzzy.

His lips hovered there, millimetres away from mine, setting every nerve ending on fire. He was torn, as was I. Should this happen or not?

The decision was made for us as the slam of the front door signalled that Zack and Guy had arrived back from the pub, their loud laughter echoed up the stairs. We sprang apart, Luke smiled and headed downstairs. I waited in the bathroom for a few minutes, checking myself in the mirror, as if I'd have a big flashing sign above my head that I'd just been about to kiss my best friend, again.

After composing myself, I found everyone on the sofas with fresh drinks, laughing and chatting. It was a genuine, happy scene. Luke was telling a story about Japan. Zack patted the seat next to him and I joined him, his arm wrapped around me. It felt weird but nice, snuggled up with Zack, listening to them all talk, whilst exchanging smiles with Luke.

By eleven, everyone was drunk, except for me, the designated driver, who was sleepy. Cassie was hanging off Zack's neck and once again insisting that she was the most miraculous matchmaker on the planet. Luke grasped the opportunity and hugged me, I felt him take in a deep breath as he held me close, his hands stroked my back. I swallowed with nerves as I looked at him, I knew him too well, his eyes weren't *that* drunk. I imagined him going back to the granny flat on his own. For a moment, I wished we were staying over, then I could sneak out there and do exactly what I wanted. *Stop it, Lily!*

The air outside was warm, within five minutes of leaving, Zack fell asleep in the passenger seat, which gave me thinking time. I had a horrible feeling life was going to get complicated for us all.

FIFTEEN

I skipped downstairs in my gorgeous new skirt as I heard the familiar rhythmic sound of Cassie knocking on the front door. We were overdue a Saturday night out.

"Hello!" She bubbled with excitement as I let her in. "I'm so ready for time away from the kids. Please say we can go to that gorgeous bar with the gigantic gin cocktails? The bars around here are so much better than at home!"

I hugged her and we walked through to the kitchen, where she proceeded to manhandle Zack once again. He smiled at her with true affection.

"It's good to see you!" she said to Zack. The two of them had such soft spots for each other. "You OK? You look a little peaky?" She held a hand up to his forehead, always in mum mode.

"I'm fine," he answered. "Just been working crazy hours. Looking forward to an early night while you two are out."

"It won't be a late one. Cassie's getting the last train." I explained.

"I know, I'm so sad I can't stay over," Cassie explained. "Kids have got two different parties in two different places in the morning, so we need to take one each. Bloody parents who organise kids' parties early on a Sunday morning." She scowled but I knew she loved being a mum and everything that came with it. I also knew that it was going to be a big topic of conversation tonight.

Zack came to the door to see us out, hugging us both and whispering to me. "Are you going to come home all ginned up and horny?"

"Would you like me to?" I asked with a smile.

"I'll be disappointed if not." he grinned and kissed me goodbye.

We went to a bar that I knew Cassie adored, the one she had mentioned. It had a gorgeous roof terrace and the lovely views meant it was always packed. I spotted a small table near the edge of the roof, nestled amongst groups of glamorous ladies and couples. Cassie brought two oversized, over-priced cocktails over and began telling me lots of mundane news. I nodded and smiled, knowing she was avoiding other subjects.

"Cassie, you haven't said anything about the baby issue in a while. Are you still trying? I see the large gin so guess no news yet?"

She looked down at the table, picking at a napkin. "I went to the doctors. They did blood tests and it wasn't great."

I reached out for her hand. "Did they find something? Are you OK?"

She took a massive gulp of the gin. "It seems my oestrogen levels are way, way down. We're going to go private rather than wait, but I googled, and it freaked me out."

"Cassie, Dr Google doesn't know everything. You need to see what the experts say."

"Dr Google doesn't know everything, you're right. But he does know that oestrogen levels that low at my age indicate early menopause caused by 'primary ovarian insufficiency'."

"Seriously? You're only in your late twenties. When's your appointment?"

"Two weeks. See what they say. I googled it-" she stopped speaking and laughed with nerves, as I raised an eyebrow again at her obsessive googling.

"I'd need to move fast I think, see if there were eggs left that they could freeze and go down an IVF route," she sighed with a deep sadness.

"Cassie, I'm sorry you're going through this. I know I'm only an hour away, but it feels farther when stuff like this is going on. Nothing is definite until you get that opinion from the private clinic though, it might not be as bad as you think."

We were both silent for a minute.

"Is Luke still staying in the granny flat?" I asked, trying to sound casual.

Cassie nodded. "Are you two friends or not now, I can't figure it out."

"Yeah, but we don't speak much because Zack gets in a right strop." I rolled my eyes.

"I can kind of see why."

"I'm allowed to have friends Cassie!" I replied.

"Friends who you have crazy, sexy, intense kisses with?" She drummed her fingernails on the table.

"Zack doesn't know about that."

"I'm sure he can pick up on the tension between you two. I know you were upstairs together longer than you needed to be last week." Her eyes zeroed in on me.

"What are you accusing me of? We hugged, we missed each other, that's all!" I raised my voice, feeling a mixture of indignant and guilty all at once.

"I want you to understand that you and Zack are perfect together. If you aren't careful, you could lose that. He won't put up with you messing around with Luke, why should he?"

"I'm not messing around with Luke. I want to be able to meet my friend, and Zack pretty much said I wasn't allowed which pissed me off." I took a long drink, shaking the lemon slice off my mouth in annoyance.

"I don't like being in the middle of this. You and Luke both tell me subtly different versions of events, I know something is off." Her tone was accusatory.

"Look, I don't know what's going on. I wanted to meet Luke to talk. Zack went all stroppy husband and wouldn't let me. I'm not cheating on him, you know how I feel about cheating, Cassie, don't accuse me of stuff like that."

Cassie nearly spat her drink out. "Jesus, calm down. I need the loo, I'll bring more gin back."

I handed her my bank card as she went. Why did everything have to be so tense these days.

When she returned, laden down with fish-bowl glasses, her face looked a little softer.

"I understand Zack not wanting you to see him. I also understand that the two of you need to talk. Luke is moving back to his house on Wednesday. If you wanted to come over to see me on Friday night, it wouldn't be anyone's fault if Luke dropped by to pick up something he forgot, would it?

Guy is away, so no point Zack joining us unless he wants to talk about early bloody menopause."

"Thank you. You're the best." I smiled.

"Yeah, yeah, remember this if I need to borrow your womb." She grinned, and the rest of the evening passed in good spirits, my mind mostly keeping itself in check with regard to Luke and Zack.

———

As predicted, once Zack knew that Luke had moved out and Guy was working away, he wasn't remotely interested in coming to Cassie's with me. He arranged a boy's night in instead. I surveyed my beautiful coffee table full of playing cards, poker chips, cigars, whiskey and beer.

"All-nighter?" I asked, with a smile.

"For sure. Not often I get an empty house. Need to practise for my stag do anyway, I reckon Vegas."

Neither of us spoke as the realisation of what he'd just said dawned.

"Erm," he began. "Obviously that's not an immediate plan, I just meant, in general…"

He blushed and I pressed a kiss to his lips. "I love you, especially when you blush. Don't gamble the house away, we're only renting it remember. See you tomorrow gorgeous."

I drove to Cassie's in contemplative silence, it had taken me an age to get ready. I wanted to look good for Luke, but not so good that Zack was suspicious about what I was doing. I opted for hair down and slightly wavy, with the classic black winged eyeliner and red lipstick look. My best black skinny jeans and a gorgeous deep red, silk blouse by The Kooples that Cassie had spent way too much on for me at Christmas.

Cassie handed me a large glass of wine the instant I walked through the door. "Kids are already asleep," she said as we sat down together. "I'm going to get an early night, but can we discuss one unbreakable rule before I do?"

"Sure," I smiled.

"Granny flat is all made up for you to stay over. That's you, Lily. I'm not having you two shagging behind Zack's back in there. This is just to talk. I still can't even decide if my best mates shagging is weird or lovely. So don't do it."

"Of course, and I fully agree." I nodded.

"You look gorgeous by the way. I knew that blouse would be perfect on you." She smiled.

"You not wanna stay up and chat for a while?" I asked.

Cassie shook her head. "I'm worn out, it's been a horrible week. To be honest, I want to get to Tuesday so I can see that doctor and get an idea of what's going on. Early night, on my own, is exactly what I need."

"I understand. Maybe in the morning we can take the girls out together? Zack has a big night planned, no point me heading home too quick."

Cassie agreed and gave me the key to the granny flat before she headed upstairs. I smiled as I looked in the fridge, Cassie had left wine and chocolate for me. Just as I was choosing a bottle, I heard gentle knocking at the door. My stomach dropped through the floor.

My palms were sweaty with nerves as I opened the door and looked up at Luke. His hair still highlighted by the sun, those bloody adorable freckles, his tanned arms under a light blue shirt. Had those arm muscles always been so defined? Our eyes were locked in contact as he stepped inside, into my arms.

God, I'd missed this. Those arms had held me a thousand times through good and bad and never let me down.

"You smell amazing," I said as I inhaled his scent. He smelled like a warm Mediterranean night, delicious and sensual. He squeezed me, and then stepped back, his eyes travelling over me again.

"You look beautiful," he said.

"I thought pretty was our word?" As he sat down, I poured us both wine. "You're not driving are you?" I asked, wondering how full to leave the glass.

He shook his head, "I walked."

We sat close and talked about his trip, my job, what our friends had been up to, how the kids had grown, how TikTok wasn't the same anymore… But Zack was never mentioned. It felt like there was so much being left unsaid.

"This feels so surreal. Sitting here with you after everything that's happened." Luke shuffled in his seat as he spoke.

"It does, and I feel like you're going to tell me something awful?" My throat felt dry and constricted.

"No, at least I hope you don't find it awful," he took a deep breath. "What I wanted to ask was… that conversation we had in your flat… it went so wrong. It was a shock, we were both over emotional and I don't want that to define us in any way. I'm not asking this with any expectation of a different outcome, Lily, but could we start that conversation again? You not being in my life for so long has been sad. I want you in my life, in one form or another, and for that to happen we need to iron out what was said."

"I agree. That day was horrible. Still upsets me whenever I think of it. How about we forget that and just start from the beginning? When you asked to meet me that day, when you brought that gorgeous Caramel Macchiato! Let's start from there, but with wine." I smiled at him, trying not to show how nervous and unsure I was at that moment.

"Lily, there's something I've wanted to say to you for a long time now. Which is ridiculous, but I haven't wanted to scare you or push you away. I kept thinking, give it a couple more months. Then I went to Uganda, which feels a lifetime ago. I missed every wonderful chance I had." He gulped loudly and took another long breath, looking down at the glass of wine in his hand.

"I've been in love with you for so long now. Initially when I began to have feelings for you, you were still in a bad place emotionally, you were petrified. I didn't want you to think me helping you was a way to get close to you. Then you grew stronger and happier, and we had the best, best fun and laughter together. We were as close as friends could be, but I had no idea if you felt the same, so I never said anything. I know that now isn't ideal, but I need to know how that makes you feel, have you ever felt the same about me, at all?"

His stunning blue eyes were staring into me, my hand shook as I sipped my wine.

"You saved me from a desperate and low place, and I wasn't always grateful enough, I'm sorry for that. We became the best friends in the world, I loved all the fun and adventures we had together. When you told me you loved me, it shocked me. I had no idea. How could you have gone so long and not said a word?" I asked. "Wouldn't there even have been one drunk night you tried to kiss me? I assumed you weren't interested in me, so I never gave it another thought. I struggle with how you could keep it secret for so long?"

"Me too," he sighed. "I was an idiot."

"I just didn't know you liked me like that. I wish I'd known." I shrugged, saddened and resigned now to the missed opportunities. "Cassie made me promise we wouldn't shag."

He laughed out loud. "I hadn't realised it was on the agenda. You have a boyfriend."

"I know. A boyfriend, and a very, very pretty 'what if', sat here looking like absolute heaven right now." I couldn't take my eyes off his.

"I didn't bring you anything to smoke, gave you all sorts of ideas last time," we both laughed.

I snuggled up against him and took a gulp of the cool sharp wine. "I can't cheat on him Luke," I sighed again. "I know too well how that hurts."

"I wouldn't ever expect or want you to," he murmured; his mouth pressed against the top of my head. "It killed me to say no that night we lay in my back garden, but I had to. I'm not sure where we're going from here?"

A million images landed in my brain all at once, showing how we could be together, how we perhaps should've been together all this time. I remembered how broken Luke had looked back in my flat when I had said no, and I hated myself again. Then I thought about potentially telling Zack it was over and I felt physically nauseous, he'd be shattered. I worried it would break him in the way that my breakup had those years ago. How could I pay that pain forward? But then how could I be without Luke?

"I don't know what we do…"

171

"I don't want to put you in an awkward position, Lily." I raised my eyebrow and shot him a suggestive smile, causing him to laugh. "Not that kind of position, although I do want to do that, I meant-"

"I know what you meant, don't worry. But I'm intrigued about what position you were thinking about." I walked over to the window and looked out at the lovely garden.

Luke walked behind me and slid his arms around my waist, resting his head on my shoulder. "Last time you didn't think. You went straight into panic mode and threw me out. It was my fault, I sprung it on you at a bad time. I'd pretty much given up when you sent me that message after your housewarming, it made me realise there was still hope."

"I thought about you so much while you were gone, I realised, more than I should've been. I wasn't just missing a friend, it made me feel guilty though. For hurting you. For contemplating hurting Zack. Whatever I do here, someone loses." I turned around into his arms.

"That kiss in my office. I know I shouldn't have done it, but I couldn't leave without feeling that, just once."

My breath was coming too fast. I thought of Zack at home, happy with his friends. I thought of Cassie over in the house, stuck between all this despite having her own turmoil.

My voice was quiet, these words should stay in my head. "It was the best kiss I ever had Luke."

"In that case then..." He tilted his head towards mine, the strength of feeling scared me, I didn't want him to stop. I went weak at the knees as our mouths locked together. His kisses soft and slow as they turned my insides to mush.

"I went away to get over you, but I can't," he whispered to me, his lips scattering kisses around my neck and cheek.

I held him close, wanting to breathe in every ounce of him and never let it go. "Zack won't let me see you, it still doesn't seem like it's our time."

"Why are you with someone who is trying to control you?" I gasped and tilted my head back as his fingers traced spirals along my back, his hand sliding inside my blouse.

"He doesn't, Luke," I bit my lip as he kissed the exposed skin of my upper neck. "He has insane jealousy about you, and I think it's fairly valid. Look at us."

"One more minute and I'll stop, I promise." Then his hands were in my hair, his body was pressing me against the wall and his mouth was clashing against mine in an urgent kiss. How could a person taste this delicious? I wanted to kiss every single inch of him, be trapped underneath him while he absolutely devoured me. The throbbing between my legs was insane, I wanted-

All of a sudden, he paused, I gasped for breath as he backed away, smiling coyly. He knew full well what he was doing to me. I needed to handle this properly, like an adult and not a horny teenager.

"I have to stick with what I said Luke, I don't want to cheat on anybody." It killed me to say it.

"I wouldn't ask you to, sorry if I went too far. Come on, let's just have a drink and chill, god knows when we'll get to again."

Unsurprisingly, the second bottle of wine loosened my tongue. We lay together on the bed, talking as we always had in the past. We both loved our beds. "If I left him, would you be with me?" I blurted out, without thinking. It was completely unrelated to the conversation that was in progress.

Luke's eyes focused on my own. "In a heartbeat."

"I'll think about it. My mind is so muddled. I don't want to hurt him, and I have the house and the job, but this… I can't ignore this."

"Everything can be undone Lily. Houses, jobs, relationships. We could go anywhere in the world together."

God, he looked insanely sexy. Drunk brain was well and truly in charge now. I imagined us locked in sexy trysts on beaches, by lakes, on planes, lush hotel rooms. *Breathe Lily!* Drunk brain had an idea.

"I read a sad magazine article the other day."

Luke frowned at me in confusion. "I'm struggling to keep up with this now." He said, pouring more wine. "Go on…"

"This couple, had decided not to have sex before marriage. And on their wedding night," I tried to look serious. "She found out he had a micropenis."

"What's a micropenis?" Luke was studying me like I was insane.

"In this guy it was a congenital issue, really teeny tiny. But he hadn't told her, so she found out the hard way, or not! She divorced him. Feel bad for him."

Luke shook his head in confusion. "And you brought this up because?"

"I was thinking, imagine if I gave everything up, and then you had a micropenis."

"Firstly, can we stop saying that word, it's weird," Luke laughed. "Secondly, you'd only be with me for my penis, is that you're saying?"

"Not only for that of course, but I might find myself thinking about it quite a lot."

"Lily, stop it," Luke warned, but with a smile. "It's not micro, don't worry."

"You would say that though, wouldn't you? Dare you to prove it." I watched him with a smile. We had dared each other a lot of stuff over the years, I knew he didn't like to back down.

He gulped down more wine as his eyes flicked over me. "That'd mean you have to go through with whatever I dare you too."

"Fine with me," I smiled defiantly.

"Turn around then." Luke pushed me to my side, so I had my back to him, talking to me as he unzipped his jeans.

He kissed the crook of my neck as he spoke. "I dare you to answer my questions. How many people have you had sex with, Lily?" One of his hands rested on my hip, I could hear the other moving around in his jeans. This was so hot – damn drunk brain!

"Two. You should know that."

"Just checking I didn't miss anything. Most adventurous place you did it?" Luke asked, his lips still against my skin.

"I'm so dull. A hotel?" I shivered as his fingers tickled my skin.

"Never say you're dull. I'll teach you everything, Lily." Even the sound of him breathing was driving me insane.

"Before I complete my dare, I don't think I should be the only one touching myself," I tried to twist my head around to look at him, but he pushed it back with a soft touch. "No peeking. It's up to you. I'm ready if you are."

I gulped, this would be the point to stop and admit it had gone too far. But Luke had put in so much effort now. I'd promised no shagging to Cassie, this didn't count. This was something else. *Bloody drunk brain and its persuasive arguments!*

I closed my eyes, torn between embarrassment and pure lust as I slid my hand inside my skinny jeans, wishing they weren't so tight. I stopped at the waistband, Luke moved his hand from my hip and placed it on my wrist, pushing my hand lower. "Don't stop," he whispered.

I sucked in a sharp breath as my fingers slid down between my thighs. "That's better," Luke said, as I felt him shift backwards. He tugged at the silky material of my top, pulling it up, so my back was bare.

His hot skin touched the base of my spine and a shiver ran through my entire body. "Definitely not micro," he said as he pressed himself fully against my back. *I mean... Cassie will never know if you break your promise.*

Neither of us moved for a second, I realised this really was too far. Zack was at home thinking I was having a nice chat with Cassie, not figuring out how big my friends' penis was. And it was big...

"Lily, we've gone too far," Luke spoke into my ear as he pulled away. "You know full well I can't resist a dare. I'm going to head home; I want you to stay there and keep doing that. OK?"

"Please don't go," I tried to turn over, but he held me still.

"Shh. I'll see you soon. I love you." I watched him stand and struggle to zip himself back up.

"I love you too," I replied. Scared by how much, as I climbed out of the bed and hugged him.

"That's the first time you said it like that to me," Luke smiled and kissed the top of my head.

"I do love you. Scares me to death but I can't deny it."

"We're going to reach a point of no return, Lily." He kissed me with such sweetness as he left. I knew it was better he went, but I was struggling! After locking the door, I jumped back into bed, and straight back into my underwear. Why hadn't we done dares like that before? Sexiest moment of my life.

SIXTEEN

I spent a gorgeous morning with Cassie and the girls, flying kites at the park and eating ice creams together. It was only as I headed home that the guilt and the loathing began to set back into me as I thought about what we'd done. How it would make Zack feel. I may not have had sex with Luke, but it was still a betrayal. How would I feel if Zack had spent a night like that with another woman? Pressing himself to her like that. I shivered at the memory.

My feet crunched down the gravel to our front door. It felt like I'd been gone weeks, not less than a day. My whole world felt different. Luke was right, my life with Zack could be undone, but was I certain I wanted it to be?

Zack opened the door before I could get my key out and wrapped me in his arms. "I missed you so much," he squeezed me as he spoke.

"Bless you, it was only one night. Ugh, the house stinks." The stench of testosterone, alcohol and cigars hit me as I stepped inside. "Good time I take it?"

"I'm dying," he pulled a sad face. I couldn't help but laugh.

"Did you gamble all our prized possessions away?" I teased as we cuddled up on the couch together.

"It's all a bit blurry to be honest, think we're safe though," he smiled. "How about you? Get up to much?"

"Cassie's struggling with not falling pregnant, she just needed me to listen I think." I lied, and felt hideous for it.

"She's the same age as us. Does it make you worry about when we want babies?" he asked.

What was going on? Talk of stag do's yesterday, babies today. Was he planning to propose? "No, what's going on with Cassie is pretty rare. We have loads of time." I smiled.

"I'd like a few, that's all," Zack kissed me with a grin. "You know I love my big family."

"I'm not past my prime yet, calm down." I joked.

"Maybe we could talk about plans and… stuff, soon?" he asked, with big, beautiful eyes as he reached for me. His kisses became more and more insistent as his hands wandered into my clothes.

"Let's go upstairs," I whispered into his ear. "I've got something better to do than talk."

———

Back at work on Monday, my direct line rang for what felt like the fiftieth time. "Hello, Caddel & Boone. Lily speaking." I trilled, in my well-rehearsed work voice.

"Hi, I'm ringing from Draper & Hughes, not sure if you've heard of us?" Spoke a deep voice from down the line. I smiled to myself, recognising it immediately as Luke.

"Yes, we're aware of the firm. How can I direct your call

today?" I responded, trying to channel the sexiest voice I could muster.

"I think you know precisely where I want to be directed to," Luke teased me.

"That's not always possible without scheduling a meeting I'm afraid." I lowered my voice and held the phone close to me.

"And if I scheduled a meeting, the two of us, would you come?"

"I could check the diary, small meetings like that can be arranged out of hours." I responded, trying to keep my breathing steady.

"I don't know if you could handle me out of hours."

"You'd be surprised at what we can handle here." I kept my eyes down on the desk, hoping nobody was paying attention.

"I miss you, Lily Forshaw, I hope that soon I'll find out exactly what you can handle." Then he ended the call. I felt giddy, hot and silly. I knew it was ridiculous that I was at my desk, downstairs from Zack, having been hugely turned on by a two-minute phone call. I also knew Luke's words had been right, we were going to reach a point of no return. The two of us felt... inevitable.

———

Zack drove us home after work, chattering away about plans for the weekend. I realised I had to start to try to explain the situation to him. The world felt peaceful, I was the monster about to tear it all down.

Within minutes of getting home, he began banging

180

around in the kitchen. He was so messy whenever he cooked, I found it kind of endearing in a weird way. He put so much enthusiasm into it, he didn't see the chaos afterwards.

I walked through to the kitchen, taking a seat at the breakfast bar. I smiled as a large wine was held out in my direction. "I think I'd make a great house husband," he opened to oven, peering inside as he adjusted the temperature.

"I couldn't afford you." I tried to join in, but I didn't know how to act or broach this conversation. It looked like he was planning to cook something lovely, and I knew I couldn't eat. I took a massive gulp of the wine, trying to drown my apprehension.

"You OK? You look stressed?"

I nodded my head and looked down at the worktop. "I need to talk to you."

He immediately put everything down and came and sat on the bar stool next to me. We'd had such fun choosing these together. Tears welled up in my eyes, over a bloody bar stool. "Hey, what's wrong? What's happened?" He put his arm around me and hugged me to him. "You can talk to me, you know that."

"I've done something, and I don't know how to tell you." I grabbed a tissue and wiped my eyes.

The colour drained from his face; his eyes fearful. "What do you mean? What have you done?"

"You remember, not long after we met. When Luke told me that he loved me. I told him I wanted to be with you." I couldn't meet his eyes as I spoke.

Zack stood up. "Fucking Luke, I'm sick of hearing his

name. Did he upset you? This is going too far, I'll sort it out, I'll-"

"Zack, stop," I pleaded. "He turned up at Cassie's the other night."

His eyes flashed with rage. "Why would you not tell me that?"

"I'm telling you now, I should've said before, but I knew you'd react like this."

"How do you expect me to react?" he shouted. I needed to diffuse his anger, but there was no way. "So, come on then, what did you two besties get up to?"

"It's not simple Zack. When he told me how he felt, and I chose you... I don't regret that, because I love you so much, I love our life here together." I said.

"So, what's the problem?" he demanded.

Nausea was bubbling within me, but this needed to be said. "I think I love him too." Zack stared at me; I couldn't judge what was going through his mind.

"Love him like your best friend, which I'd expect, or you are *in* love with him?"

I spoke quietly, my eyes trained on the floor. "I think I'm in love with him."

"You told me you were in love with me." The quiver in his voice was tearing me apart.

"I am, I am in love with you, I adore you. I feel the same about both of you and it's so hard Zack." I began to cry again.

"Are you expecting sympathy here? I don't even understand what this is. Are you breaking up with me?" He sat down, his head in his hands. I reached for him, but he shrugged me away. Anger emanated from his whole being.

"No Zack, no, I love you, I don't want to split up. I need you to try to understand how I feel."

"I don't understand Lily," he bawled at me. "You love me, but you love him, but you don't want to break up? That makes no sense. And you haven't answered the question about what you got up to?" He turned away from me, obviously dreading the answer.

I took a deep breath. "We kissed, and it was then I realised..." My words were cut off as Zack swept the two plates off the breakfast bar. I watched them spin and smash into pieces on the floor, like they represented my life falling apart right now.

"Did you kiss him, or did he kiss you?" Zack demanded as his fist banged down on the worktop.

"Zack, I-"

"Did you kiss him, or did he kiss you?" Zack repeated himself, his tone angry and insistent.

"He kissed me," I looked down in shame. "I'm so sorry." Zack had tears in his eyes.

"He always manipulates you, why can't you see it? Not anymore though. You're not seeing him again, Lily. I'm going to go see him, he can't just turn up and kiss you and expect you to drop your whole fucking life and run to him. He only wants you because he didn't get his own way."

"That's charming. You think nobody would want me just for being me?" I screamed back, the neighbours must love this.

"That's not what I said, for fucks sake. Don't have a go at me when you're the one kissing other people." He glared at me.

"Also, you can't tell me what I can and can't do. You can't ban me from seeing my friend!"

"Actually, when that friend is trying to fuck my girlfriend, I think I can. Screw this, I need some air." He grabbed his phone as he stormed away from the house, slamming the door so hard the walls shook. The car sounded too noisy as he revved the engine and sped away.

I threw a cup down with the smashed plates and screamed. I was so mad. But also… so messed up. What the hell was I doing?

SEVENTEEN

*I*t's amazing how long the night time hours feel, when you're alone, and your mind refuses to shut down. Zack hadn't come home, and his phone was turned off. I'd given up on even trying to sleep, spending the time examining every inch of our bedroom ceiling. Remembering an impossible number of nights in here with Zack, then remembering every touch Luke had placed on me. Was Zack asleep somewhere? Drunk somewhere? Just thinking of him caused my insides to twist up in pain. Was he out shagging a random girl to teach me a lesson? Was he throwing himself off a bridge? I had no idea.

The ring of my phone woke me, sleep must have taken me in the end as the room was now bright. I cautiously opened my eyes; it was ten thirty. My heart missed a beat as I saw Cassie was the caller.

"You need to get here *now* and tell me what's going on." Cassie sounded angry.

"What do you mean? What's up?" I asked, my head groggy.

"When I got back from nursery, Zack was here, screaming the place down. Wanting me to tell him where Luke lived." she began.

"He should be at work, shit, I should be at work!" I jumped up in a panic.

"Lily, I don't give a crap about work right now. Did you shag Luke? Is that why Zack turned up here in that state?"

"No! I told you I wouldn't. Is he still there?"

"Zack isn't no, he's looking for Luke. Luke's in court today though. I obviously didn't tell Zack that. Can you get here and sort this out?"

"I don't have the car, he stormed off in it last night." I explained.

"Have you forgotten where I'm going today? Why the kids are in nursery?" Cassie's voice was trembling.

"Shit, Cassie, I'm so sorry. This is the last thing you need. God, I'm the worst friend." My heart sank at the thought I had let her down.

"Yeah, to be honest Lily, sometimes you are. Sort it out, I need to go."

Fuck! Where to even begin with this. I tapped at my phone in a panic.

Lily: Hi Margaret. So sorry Zack and I aren't at work today. Family emergency, I will call you asap. Really sorry x

Lily: Cassie, I love you, I'm so sorry. I didn't think, story of my life. Good luck at the Docs, I'll call you later sweetheart x

Lily: Zack, Cassie called me. You shouldn't have gone there, she has enough on her plate. Can you please come home so we can talk instead of running around screaming at people?!

Lily: Hey you... Had a chat with Zack, he's on a bit of a rampage. He was looking for you, but Cassie said you're in court? I know you won't be allowed your phone on, can you call me when you get this please? x

I sank back in the pillows. What a mess. I almost dropped the phone as it pinged, but it was only Margaret, less than impressed. Least of my worries right now. After throwing some clothes on, I made an extra strong coffee, trying to ring Zack every few minutes but not getting through. I found an online florist and ordered a huge bouquet of flowers for Cassie, with express delivery, to try to apologise.

Coffee all gone, I dropped my head down onto the breakfast bar, feeling exhausted and clueless about what to do. My stomach somersaulted as the front door opened. Zack's face was tired and drawn as he walked towards me. Neither of us spoke.

"Are you going to say sorry?" I asked.

"For?" Zack was obviously not in a better mood.

"Storming out, staying out all night, screaming at my best friend?" I held my hands up in disbelief.

"The only bit I'm sorry about is that I didn't find Luke. Are *you* going to say sorry for acting as though I mean nothing to you?" He stepped closer to me.

"That's not fair. I was being honest." I rubbed my fingers

over my temples, trying to soften the thumping pain in my head.

"You're not sorry at all, are you? For kissing him, for wanting him. I was a warm-up act. Remember how nervous you were when we met? How slow we took everything? Now you're full of confidence, aren't you? Especially in the bedroom… Did I just get you ready for him?"

I shook my head. "How can you say that? I love you."

"Really funny way to show it, Lily. I'm due on that corporate weekend, I need to get into work and get stuff sorted. Maybe we should have some time apart, figure out what's going on here." He looked past me, out of the window.

"You want to break up?" I squeaked, my voice retreated inside me.

He shook his head. "A break, a breath, I don't know what to call it. We both need to think about what we want. Maybe you aren't the girl I thought you were when I brought up stag do's and babies."

"I would *never* give up on you like this." I shouted as I pushed past him, running upstairs and frantically throwing clothes into a bag. Not caring how much mess I left as clothes and make up cluttered the bed and floor. Stabbing at my phone with my finger, I ordered a taxi and slammed the front door behind me with as much strength as I could. Zack hadn't left his spot, hadn't tried to stop me.

The taxi driver turned to me, looking nervous at my teary face. "Where to love?"

My mind went blank. Cassie was pissed at me. Going to Luke's would only add fuel to the fire. None of Zack's friends or family would want to take my side. I remembered what

Luke had said in his office before he left, about me not having anyone to turn to.

Randomly, I thought of a swanky hotel in town that we'd been to a Christmas party at. I had our joint credit card in my purse, Zack wanted breathing space? Fine. I'd get mine boutique hotel style!

———

I threw myself down onto the oversized hotel bed and buried my face in the pillow. Margaret had rung while I was checking in. Zack was back at work, I explained it was a personal issue and I wouldn't be back until next week. She wasn't happy but I had so much more going on in my head. Didn't even know if I'd be staying in this town.

I grabbed an overpriced and undersized bottle of wine from the minibar and glugged at it. Lessons in how to completely screw up by Lily Forshaw. My phone was utterly silent, like a traitor.

I didn't want me and Zack to break up. The thought of not exploring the possibilities with Luke seemed impossible though. Maybe I just needed to cut myself off from both of them, spend time alone. But then, four years alone did me no good before. I didn't want to be that lonely person again.

The phone pinged and I launched myself at it, wine splashed over the plum bed covers.

Cassie: The flowers are beautiful. It's not your fault Zack turned up. I'm upset you forgot it was such an important day for me

Lily: I'm so sorry. How was it? Want to talk? x
Cassie: Not right now. It wasn't great. I need to digest. You
and Zack ok?

She had enough on her plate without me adding more.

Lily: We'll be fine. Ring me when you're ready to talk,
anytime. Love you Mrs xx

No reply. I sighed and rolled onto my back, hanging my head off the edge, wondering if the rush of blood might get rid of my headache. I couldn't believe Zack hadn't even messaged me. The phone rang and I bolted upright, Luke!

"Hey, are you OK? I got your message, the case went on for ages. What's Zack done?" Luke's words escaped his mouth quickly.

"I told him we kissed and that I was confused about my feelings. This was after work yesterday. He stormed out and didn't come home. Then turned up at Cassie's this morning, screaming and shouting, wanting to know where you lived. It was Cassie's fertility appointment today so then she was all pissed at me, understandably."

"Are you OK, Lily?"

"I'm now in a hotel, let's put it that way." I sighed.

"Where? I'll come to you." His voice was so strong and sure.

"It'll just make Zack angrier." I sobbed.

"I don't care, he's always bloody angry or jealous. How

will he know anyway? Does he know where you are?" Luke asked.

"No, no he doesn't. He didn't seem remotely bothered where I went." I admitted.

"Right, then send me the address and I'll be with you in an hour or so. No arguments. I'm not leaving you upset and alone."

Jumping out of the shower twenty minutes later I realised my hasty packing was a little random. It was either a thick woollen jumper, a yoga set, a hot pink Ted Baker dress or the lovely, black lounge wear set I had bought a couple of weeks back, so soft to sleep in. Luke was used to seeing me in pyjama's, and this set was super cute. Decision made, hair dried, splash of make up on. What the hell was going to happen now?

Reception had assured me they wouldn't give my room number out to anyone. I'd sent it to Luke in a message, so when I heard the knock on the door, I jumped up, confident it was him.

What a sight. God, he looked so good in a suit, and especially when holding two pizza boxes and a bottle of wine. My stomach rumbled, reminding me I hadn't eaten since yesterday lunch time.

"How do you always know what I need?" I smiled, as he came in and put the boxes down on the desk. Why did hotel rooms always have desks?! Then he wrapped me up in his best hug, I was back in my safe place.

"Because I know you, and you won't have had anything but coffee and perhaps wine?" he asked, with a little kiss on top of my head.

"Very true," I smiled. "I'm starving, thank you."

He told me the basics about his day in court while we munched the tastiest pizza. I was famished! We sat on the bed together with a glass of wine, his arm around me, my head leaning on his chest.

"Out with it then, what happened?" he asked.

"You don't want to know every horrible word. The neighbours got a pretty good show. Zack said I'd used him like a warm-up act while I waited for you. He said I wasn't allowed to see you again, as if I was his bloody property. Then after storming off like an idiot overnight and upsetting Cassie in the process, he came back and announced we needed a 'break'," I sighed. "So here I am."

"Has he not rung you to check where you are or anything?" Luke asked.

"Nope. Seemed more concerned about this trip to Iceland with work. Work are pissed at me too, just to add to the list. Told them I wouldn't be back until next week, I can't even think."

"A break is probably what you need. From work, from him. Figure out what's happening in that mind. I've never been able to."

"You know it better than anyone, don't say that." I took hold of Luke's hand.

"Did you tell him about the… thing we did? Because I can kind of understand him chasing me down if so." Luke laughed.

"God no. I still can't believe that. You're such a bad influence." I grinned, as he let go of my hand and poked me in the side.

"As if it was me who started any of that."

"I've tried to call Zack, but it goes to voicemail." I said.

"Lily, it's weird me giving you relationship advice here, but if he said he wants space, give him space. Let him come to you, don't chase him."

"What do you want Luke?" I asked.

"Apart from the obvious," he kissed the top of my head again. "I want to get out of this suit, it's too hot."

"Are you… going to stay? Here, with me?" I asked, not sure what I wanted the answer to be.

"That depends. Would I be staying to help you feel safe, as a friend? Would I be staying because you want to start a relationship with me? Would I be staying because you're 'on a break', to coin a famous phrase, and wanting to make the most of it," he sighed. "I don't know what you want from me."

"I want you to be more than my friend, but I don't know if I'm ready for it. I want you to stay, but I think to be together hours after Zack asked me to leave might be wrong. Would you stay with me if sex was off the cards?" I turned around to face him.

"Of course I would. I agree, it's too soon. So, I'm staying then?"

I nodded and smiled. "Yes please. If you still want to get out of that suit, I can show you where the fluffy hotel bath robes are."

———

Oh my god this bed was comfortable. I wriggled further down under the covers as my mind woke up. Luke and I had talked for most of the evening, and then in such a caring way, he had cuddled me up in bed with a brief goodnight kiss and let me fall asleep.

I rolled over and stretched my arms out, taken aback by how different Luke looked. He was often guarded, or would go into mischievous mode with me, there wasn't always a middle ground. Now though he looked so… vulnerable. His blue eyes closed, that blonde hair flopped over his forehead. His freckles had all but disappeared now I noticed as my eyes grazed down to his lips. His lips were beautiful, and I mean, who wouldn't want a good morning kiss?

I pressed myself against him and stroked the side of his face as I whispered. "Do you mind if I wake you up?"

He shook his head briefly as one eye squinted open. "What are you doing Lily?"

"This…" My lips pressed over his as I ran my hand up into his hair. Our bodies were boiling hot under the heavy hotel duvet and he felt so good against me. He moved into a deeper kiss, sighing as his tongue flicked against my own. I couldn't help but notice the effect this kiss was having on him, but this time it was pressed against my stomach rather than my back. I pulled him on top of me. Desperate to know more of what he felt like.

My fingers gripped at the firm skin of his back as he pushed down into me, kissing me harder, taking the breath from me. He felt as hard as he had that night at Cassie's and involuntarily, my hips rose up against him, setting explosions off inside me.

He shivered and began kissing my neck. "You can't wake me up like this and expect me to know what you want. You're driving me crazy. You said no sex."

Luke was wearing nothing but tight, sexy shorts. I ran my fingers down his sides. "Could we… do some stuff but not all the stuff?" I asked.

"You can't say the words can you?" he smiled and nuzzled his mouth against my cheek. "I'll do some stuff, and if you want me to stop say. But not all the stuff."

I laughed and kissed him again, these kisses were addictive. He slid his hand up inside my top, tickling his fingers over my sensitive skin. "This good?" he asked.

"Definitely." I let out a happy sigh as I slid a leg around his hip, pulling him closer to me. He swiftly pulled my top off and then his mouth followed the same pattern as his fingers, driving me insane.

"I've wanted to get you like this for so long," he moaned as he continued, my fingers wrapped into his hair. "We have to stop before all the stuff anyway because I don't have condoms. I was only going to court when I left the house yesterday, they aren't often needed." His mouth moved back up to mine, kissing me as he spoke, his eyes sparkling with the pure attraction between us. "We don't need to talk about tiny penises again do we?"

I laughed and kissed him, I was addicted to his kiss. "No, we don't, I'm pretty assured in that department."

"You had your back to me, it could've been an aubergine I was holding against you."

I laughed too loudly. "Only one way to find out…" His entire body tensed against me as I slid my hand inside his shorts and took hold of him. He made me nervous, and giddy, and completely horny. His mouth pressed against my shoulder. "How have you kept this from me for so long?" I asked.

"I have no idea. But I need to know what you've been keeping from me." He kissed me with an urgency as his hand flashed down my stomach. He lifted the lacy waistband and delved immediately in between my legs. This was incredible.

"Please don't stop Luke." I pulled him even closer to me if that was possible, desperate for him. "I know I said not all the stuff a few minutes ago. But I want all the stuff."

His tongue wrestled with my own as he pinned me down onto the bed with his mouth. "We can't."

"We can," I whispered. Remembering the zip pocket in my handbag which undoubtedly still had condoms in it, left over from before Zack and I stopped using them. I rolled to the side and rummaged around in my bag, grinning and holding a screwed-up foil package aloft in triumph.

"Lily, I can't cope with you," he sighed and pulled back from me, I tried to follow him with kisses but he shook his head. "What if Zack calls you in half an hour, apologising and asking you to come home? Are you going to be able to tell him what we did?"

All the incredible feelings shooting around my body fizzled out, like damp fireworks that had let a crowd down. I pouted sadly. "How are you so good Luke? Anyone else would've carried on."

"I don't want you hurt," he stroked my cheek and smiled. "But, I do need a cold shower. Want to order breakfast?"

Both showered and a little subdued, we ate breakfast together on the bed. Silently contemplating what was going to happen, where this was going to go. I couldn't believe Zack was still blanking me. Luke was working on his laptop at the desk (so they did have a use after all!) I decided to try to call Zack one more time, if he still wouldn't pick up then that sent a pretty clear message.

Yesterday the phone had been ringing for ages before

cutting to voicemail. Today it rang once and then went straight to the 'leave a message' bit. I threw the phone across the bad, muttering, "Such a twat."

Luke turned around and raised an eyebrow. "Me?"

I laughed, glad he was here. "Definitely not you."

Grabbing the phone back as Luke made a call to the office, I decided to see if Instagram gave me any clues what Zack was up to. Nothing, he wasn't the most prolific poster though. I checked Adam's too, see if they had posted anything when Zack was there, but nope, Adam only posted about games. Sighing I flicked through my feed with lazy swipes, half listening to Luke's phone call and legal jargon.

It seemed as though there had been an impromptu work night out. I was seeing lots of tipsy looking photos taken in the bar around the corner from work last night, people often went for a quick drink at five thirty, and occasionally it progressed. Looked like it had been a crazy night, I flicked through the pictures nosily until I got to one and froze.

It was selfie Anna had taken; she did love a good selfie. I'd always thought she was a bit of a bitch, she thought she was so superior with her bloody law degree. Zack and her were in the same team, so I had to smile and be polite. There she was grinning into the camera, but only filling a portion of the screen which wasn't like her. She'd done it on purpose, because filling the background was Zack… with his tongue down a girl's throat. She was petite and blonde, wearing an impossibly short skirt. His hand was above her knee. She was touching his hair, his hair that I loved. For some reason that made me angrier than anything else.

All these games - this was why I'd wanted to stay single. Screw him. I pressed on the heart to like the picture. Screw

Anna too, she'd done this on purpose. Let them know I'd seen it. I took a screenshot of the evidence and threw the phone down again, Luke glanced my way as he carried on talking.

"I'm going to get us good coffee, back soon," I whispered as I stroked my fingers over his hand, grabbing my bag on the way.

I walked to Starbucks in a daze. Half tempted to detour to the office and tell Zack he was a twat to his face. But was kissing a random blonde any worse than me kissing Luke? Probably not. If I wanted to be with Luke, this was the opportunity, but I didn't know what I wanted. This wasn't a nice feeling.

Had Zack had taken that girl back to our house? He wouldn't, would he?

He was infuriating, the way he got so angry and jealous. Now he was blanking me like I was nothing. I knew I'd been far from perfect, but at least I was honest about it, didn't get caught in a random selfie.

I let myself back into the hotel room half an hour later with two large caramel coffee creations. "Are you alright?" Luke asked.

"Yep, you?"

"You left your phone on the bed. Cassie rang, so I answered. Then I saw that photo…"

I sighed. "It's no worse than what I've been doing is it? He might as well make the most of being on a break I guess."

"I don't think you mean that. Is he still not answering your calls?"

"Nope," I replied. "And I'm not trying again. He's going away tomorrow, so perhaps I leave him alone like you said."

"Why don't you go and stay with Cassie? Be better than being here. She won't mind, you two need to talk." Luke suggested.

"That makes me sad." I looked down and pulled a sad face.

"What?" Luke looked confused.

"I wanted you to ask me to come and stay with you..."

"Lily, I don't think you know what you want right now, I don't want to complicate your life anymore than it already is." Luke replied, sweet as ever.

"We missed all the 'right' times. Maybe, this is our chance and if we don't take it, we'll regret it forever? Take me home... as yours." I took hold of his hand in mine. He didn't speak, he pulled me closer and pressed a deep kiss to my lips. *No turning back...*

EIGHTEEN

I couldn't keep my eyes off Luke as we checked out of the hotel. The sense of my life shifting filled me with apprehension as I settled into the passenger seat of Luke's sleek, black car. Not the one I had scratched a few years back.

"Let's go," he grinned as we headed towards the motorway, onto the familiar route back. I loved Luke's house, it was a Victorian semi-detached in a nice road, neat and well looked after. When Luke gave up the flat for me, he had ended up staying with his parents for an extra few months. Which gave him chance to save a deposit and buy this place. At first glance, the interior was blatantly a bachelor pad, stylish and expensive, kind of like Luke. Just as he had an aura of friendliness though, the house had its own welcome atmosphere.

Luke unlocked the dark blue front door and took my bag from me. I stepped into the familiar hallway and kicked off my boots, as I'd done a thousand times. This time was different though, the enormity of realising that we were alone, properly completely alone, with nothing to stop us going as far as wanted, sent heady mixes of desire, fear and tension running through me. We were still in the hallway. "You look worried," said Luke.

I sucked in a sharp breath and focused myself. "Just thinking, about what we are maybe about to do... and how big a deal that is. You know... all the stuff." I looked down at the polished wooden floor.

He lifted my chin up so I was looking up into his eyes, which were full of mischief. "Are we doing all the stuff, Lily? Nearly killed me to stop this morning."

My eyes flicked between his repeatedly, I was blinking too much. Luke looked serene and calm. I couldn't think of what to say, or what to do. I opened my mouth, but no words came out. He leaned down to me and tucked my hair behind my ear, whispering to me. "Do you want to?"

I shivered as his lips grazed my ear before journeying down to my neck. My eyes closed under the sensation. The hall was narrow, and he pressed me back against the wall with one hand as his other began to pull at my top. "You aren't normally lost for words. In fact, you've been pretty vocal about this lately. Just say if you want me to stop..." He was whispering into my ear again and I twisted my head around, wanting his kisses back on my mouth.

All I could think was of Luke and me, how long our chemistry had been building up to this moment. How he smelled of the ocean and pure invigorating oxygen, how his skin was so warm to the touch and so, so soft. How this was basically, inevitable.

"Please don't stop." I unbuttoned his shirt as he threw my own top to the floor. We moved to the stairs, trapped in a savage kiss that neither of us could break. Luke turned me around as we reached the top, kissing along my hairline, leaving goosebumps all over me as his hands undid my bra and dropped it to the floor. Then before I could take another breath, he pulled me back to face him.

"Still so quiet, Lily?" He slid his finger all the way down my spine, one hand kept me still while the other tugged my jeans and underwear down, following his own. I felt all of his bare skin, pressed against mine. We were wholly naked, and perfectly lost in each other.

My heart felt as though it would burst out of my chest as he led me to the bed. I'd been in this bed before, I'd slept in it side by side with Luke multiple times, but this was utterly different.

He leaned back against the soft, plush headboard and pulled me up. My legs straddled around him, as my kisses touched his forehead, his chin, his nose. I was entranced. I couldn't contemplate how this had not happened sooner, it felt preordained. His hands scratched roughly down my back, drawing me even closer in. A flurry of anxiety shot through my stomach, I realised how inexperienced I was compared to him.

Luke shook his head from side to side, disrupting my kisses and focusing me on his face. I wanted to tell him I loved him, but I felt like words were just meaningless in the midst of all this, our bodies were saying more than my three little words ever could. I opened my eyes, instantly falling in love all over again as those beautiful, never ending pools of blue drank me in. It had to be now, it had to be, I absolutely ached for him.

He reached into the drawer beside the bed. "No offence

Lily. but that screwed up packet you pulled out of your bag this morning looked a little past it's best."

I lifted myself up as he put the condom on, I'd never felt nerves like this in my life. Then Luke's hands firmly held my hips as he drove himself inside of me. I wrapped my arms around him and pressed my face into the beautiful spot where his neck became his shoulder, I couldn't breathe. I'd never experienced anything this intense.

I was putty in his hands, as he held me and moved me where he wanted. He seemed to sense from my breath and my kisses exactly what I wanted and needed; no sound passed my lips. I was unable to think about anything except the feel of him inside of me. It was over so fast, yet at the same time lasted forever, we'd waited so long. As soon as he felt me tense against him, my fingers gripping at him, he let himself go too. Face to face, skin against skin, eyes locked to each other, fingers laced together, we stayed like that for an age, placing soft, tender kisses on each other's mouths. I couldn't bear to move, I wanted him inside me forever.

The room was so quiet as the late afternoon sun floated in through the white curtains. Luke stroked my hair as I held onto him. I studied his face, he looked much more relaxed.

"I never would've imagined spending the afternoon like this." I said, not wanting to break the spell.

I thought back over what had happened, it was so different to being with Zack. I don't know what I had expected, they were completely different people. Luke was such a gentleman in daily life, I guess a darker side came out in the bedroom and I liked it, he took command of me and I loved feeling powerless with him. I trusted him with my life, he had shown me he was worthy of it after all.

"I spent a lot, and I mean a lot of time imagining what that'd be like," Luke confessed.

"I think you should tell me more." I said, running my hand up and down his chest in long, lazy strokes.

"Let's just say, every eventuality I came up with in my mind, was nowhere near as incredible as that was. But… in an effort to make you happy I can act them all out with you?"

I rolled my eyes and smiled. "I was worried it'd feel strange, being with my best friend like that, but no… there aren't words for how that felt."

He kissed me with absolute tenderness, I was desperate to feel him again, but he stood up. "I'm going to go and cook us some dinner, then we can decide what to do."

I couldn't keep my eyes off him as he got dressed and I think he knew it. I loved seeing parts of his body I hadn't noticed before, subtle tan lines that were barely visible, little ripples of muscle as he stretched. I lay in the bed, feeling totally satiated, and desperate for round two.

Music began to play downstairs and I could hear the familiar sound of Luke prepping in the kitchen. I wanted him to want me, constantly, like I did him. I wanted to be irresistible to him, to spiral out of control together. I put on one of his shirts and left the rest of me naked, my hair loose and messed up from being with him as I padded down the stairs.

Luke had left me a glass of wine on the worktop; I took it gladly and sat on a stool, watching him. He was such a good cook and had always despaired of my habits like left over pizza or toasties for a full week. "What are you making?" I asked, frustrated he hadn't noticed me.

"I'm hoping Stroganoff is still on your favourite list,

because that's what I'm making." he said, concentrating on a pan.

"It is when you make it," I answered. "Magic touch in the kitchen." Infuriatingly he still hadn't looked at me. "Not just in the kitchen..."

He glanced over to smile, then did a double take. *Got you!* Turning the hob down he crossed over to me and kissed me roughly, his knee slid between my legs to part them. "Lily... you have to prepare me if you're going to walk in looking like that. I'm going to burn the food..." He rubbed his knee against me, still making me long for more of him. "Food, then you can continue that thought. I'm making sure you eat properly, no arguments." He kissed the tip of my nose as he returned to the pan.

Everything felt flawless as we ate together. We laughed and talked like we always had. The food was so good, and this all came with the added bonus of shared touches, a brief squeeze of a hand, a kiss on the lips as a plate was handed over, legs tangled together through the meal. It felt so natural and so good, I had no problem ignoring the outside world. It pained me to think of it afterwards, but I didn't think of Zack.

"What shall we do tonight then?" I knew he was teasing me. I still longed to know how much he wanted me, and he wasn't going to admit it, I could tell.

"Watch the news, cup of tea in bed, straight to sleep?" I tried to keep as straight a face as I could. Neither of us wanted to cave and be the one to admit what we both knew was a certainty tonight.

"It's certainly an option..." He watched me, the intensity of the air between us felt dangerous and flammable. "You asked me once, how I held back from kissing you when we used to turn the lights off and dance. Maybe we should do that again?"

"Would you show the same restraint though?" I asked.

"Would you want me to?" He shrugged and smiled. "You aren't dressed for dancing, but let's see what happens."

He led me to the living room, swiping at his phone for a minute as music began to play from speakers ensconced around the room. I smiled as I recognised the song from a long-forgotten playlist that we used to share. The lights automatically turned down and began to pulse in time with the music. I rolled my eyes. "You are such a boy, is that a new gadget?"

He nodded and pulled me against him. I felt breathless with anticipation. "I learned a lot about you this afternoon. You don't hold back. I knew exactly what you wanted. You don't sound fake like most girls do, trying to speak or act a certain way." My knees turned to jelly at his words, my pupils dilated with both the darkness of the room and the desire for him. "You are utterly honest, wonderful and sexy as hell. I want to touch and know and love every, single, beautiful inch of your body … what do you say?" I couldn't speak, nobody had ever had that power over me. "What happened earlier, that was like an amuse bouche. You have no idea what else I have in store for you. I needed you right away, but now we can take our time."

I blinked at him, nodding, knowing I was his. Totally his.

———

I winced at the bright sunshine inching through the curtains as my eyes opened the next morning. I felt Luke's warm body as I reached behind me and exhaled with relief – It had been real. I twisted around to cuddle him, wincing as I did, He'd worn me out. I was exhausted and sore, but every ache made me shiver and smile with the memory of how amazing it had been, and exactly what had caused that ache.

Luke shifted in the bed as I cuddled him, waking from sleep. I stayed quiet and still, wanting to see how this would be, not knowing how this would be. The newness of it so exhilarating.

"Good morning." His voice was gravelly and so sexy.

"Morning," this felt surreal, but so good I couldn't stand the torment of it, every nerve in my body was on overdrive. I'd been awake less than a minute and I was desperate for him all over again. "Are you OK?" I asked.

"Mmhmm, just tired," he answered. "The best kind of tired though."

I kissed across his shoulder and down the top of his arm. "I don't think I can walk." I smiled as I lay against him.

"Then stay here with me," he squeezed me tighter to him. "I love you."

"I love you too." I nuzzled into his shoulder and breathed in the scent of him once more, my eyes closing in happiness, the feeling of fulfilment flowing through my mind.

The next I knew, I was alone. Glancing at my phone I saw it was gone lunchtime. I sat up quickly and winced as my thighs ached. *What had he done to me?* I hoped he was going to do it again! I picked up a note that was on the bedside table next to me, admiring Luke's gorgeous handwriting that I knew so well from work.

I couldn't bring myself to wake you, you looked so beautiful.

Had to be at work, but ring me when you're up, we can meet in Starbucks?

I love you – feel a bit like I am dreaming right now Lily-flower xx

I hobbled to the shower grinning like a love-sick teenager, letting the steaming hot water ease my muscles. Stretching my jaw from side to side to ease the ache there too as my fingers untangled the matted hair at the back of my head.

I still only had the pitiful clothing selection with me, so grabbed one of Luke's softest t-shirts, putting it on with my jeans. Even this made me happy, like a little badge that I was his. Picking up the phone to call Luke, the lack of messages or calls from either Cassie or Zack was not a surprise.

"Here," said Luke. Sliding one of his expensive vitamin tablets over the Starbucks table an hour later, as he swallowed his own. "I'll get you looking after yourself, one way or another."

"I need to go buy clothes," I announced as I finished my caramel macchiato, it had to be that drink. "Don't want to go back home for more."

Luke smiled and stroked my hand across the table. "You look good in mine to be fair."

I laughed. "Shall I wait until you finish work? I might even let you pick some of them, want to play dress up?" I teased.

Late that evening we arrived back at Luke's house laden down with bags. Clothes, make up, shoes, pyjama's, lingerie. He had helped me choose everything and I couldn't wait to wear it all for him. Although it betrayed every feminist idea I had ever thought of, I wanted to be his ultimate fantasy and I couldn't grasp my feelings.

Luke pulled me onto his knee as we cuddled up on the couch. "I spoke to Guy this afternoon. He knows what's going on. Want to go over there together on Saturday? Try to get back on track with Cassie? Never known you two fall out like this."

I nodded and leaned into him, feeling his chest rise and fall in a soft rhythm. I was dreading each day passing, I knew there were tough conversations and decisions in the future. Zack would be in Iceland now, was he tucked up in bed with another blonde? I closed my mind to it and focused on the feeling of Luke.

NINETEEN

*I*t felt a peculiar mix of mundane and alien as Cassie opened the front door on Saturday afternoon. She had a strained smile on her face, I saw her glance down, at our entwined hands.

"It's so good to see you both. Lovely weather too. So glad you could make it. Guy is busy in the kitchen, I hope you like the food, of course you'll like the food. Luke, he could probably do with a hand though. You should've been a chef you know." she garbled.

"Cassie!" I interrupted. "Relax, take a breath."

Luke kissed me on the cheek. "I'll go and help Guy." I smiled, touching my cheek where I could still feel him, the novelty of it still enthralled me. Out of the corner of my eye I saw Cassie frown.

We watched each other warily. "How are things?" she asked.

I shrugged. "Amazing but utterly screwed up, all at once. How about you?"

"Heartbroken to be honest." she admitted.

We went into the living room and I wrapped her into a hug on the couch. "Tell me what the doctor said."

"It's what I thought. Primary Ovarian Insufficiency. Give it a fancy name, doesn't make it any better. I'm a menopausal, dried up, old maid basically." Her eyes leaked delicate tears as she spoke, I wiped them away.

"You are not, you're radiant and full of life. When we googled that, it seemed to say they could freeze your remaining eggs and you could use them like IVF. Is that the plan?"

She shook her head. "They gave me these hormones that stimulate the ovaries or something, to release the eggs so they could get them. But...they weren't viable. It's not an option."

I held her close as she cried, not able to imagine the anguish this was causing her. "My mum doesn't even get it," she sobbed as she continued. "She said at least I had the girls so not to worry. Guy hasn't said as much but I think he feels the same."

"Cassie he'll be worried about you."

"I feel insane. They aren't grieving, because we haven't lost anyone. But I'm grieving the babies I never got to have. Is that stupid?"

She was shaking as I held her, her head pressed into me, leaving wet skin on my collarbone. Luke sent me a reassuring look from the kitchen, before going back to a chopping board.

"It's not stupid, don't say that. It's completely understandable. You grieve, you take all the time you need, let people think what they like."

"Sod it, let's get drunk." She jumped up and grabbed a bottle and two glasses.

"That's my limit of talking about it. I'm done." she announced. "Can we talk about why your boyfriend turned up here screaming and now you and Luke are all kissy-kissy?"

"I told Zack about Luke kissing me." I exhaled as I prepared for the emotional onslaught. "He went mad, forbade me from ever seeing Luke again. Which turned into a big fight and he stormed out, spent the night with Adam, I think. He came back the next day, after he'd been here, and said he wanted a break. Didn't even try to stop me when I left."

"Shit! Is that why he was looking for Luke? He knew about the kiss?"

I nodded. "He won't answer my calls, haven't heard anything from him."

"Lily, don't get mad. But is jumping into bed with Luke going to help this situation? In any way?"

"Zack wanted a break Cassie, so he's getting a break." I thrust my phone towards her, with the tongue action photo of Zack and a blonde on screen, zoomed in for good measure.

She bit her lip as she looked at the photo. "When was this taken?"

"The same day I left. He's in Iceland now with work. I dread to think what he's doing."

"Or who he's doing," exclaimed Cassie. "Sorry, that was thoughtless. Listen, I think he's hurt, feeling betrayed. Men act stupid when they're hurt. He'll know you're with Luke."

"He pushed me to Luke." I hadn't realised that until I said it out loud.

"Do you think this is helping though? Are you with Luke for good now? What are you doing about this break with Zack? Everyone is going to get hurt." She didn't mean to lecture me, but it felt like I was in trouble with a teacher.

"I have no idea. No idea. Why didn't you just let me be a crazy cat lady? Then you could've borrowed my ovaries, no problem." I downed the wine as I made the flippant comment, not thinking anything of it. Cassie's eyes zeroed in on me in.

"Let's just clone them into one." Cassie suggested.

"Cloning makes more of them, that's the last thing I need. You mean merge them into one?"

"Yeah! Zuke!!! Or Lack… no! Definitely Zuke."

Luke walked in and grabbed me up off the couch. "Food's ready! What are you two going on about?"

We sat at the outdoors table to eat, enjoying the sun and seeing Ruby and Emilia chase each other around the beautiful garden. There was a tension though, all four of us avoided any contentious subjects, of which there seemed to be plenty at the moment.

I didn't even know where to begin processing how the next week would go, and I felt sick every time I thought of seeing Zack at work on Monday. It had been nice, pottering about Luke's house while he worked, but I couldn't afford to lose my job, I needed to go back.

———

Luke was twitchy all day on Sunday, but in an excited way. I was dreading the weekend being over, but he seemed to have a surprise planned. It got to two in the afternoon, when he grabbed my hands, smiling.

"You trust me, don't you?"

"Yes… why?" I asked, intrigued.

"Go have a long bath, take a glass of wine, a book, don't come down until I shout, promise? And don't look out the window." He grinned, with a sparkle in his eyes.

"Hmm. Is this your way of telling me I need a bath?" I asked,

"Course not, you smell sexy as hell. I'll shout you soon, go on, shoo." He ushered me towards the staircase.

Lying in the hot bubbly water, I could hear banging and clattering outside. *What was he doing?* The bath was good, but I'd rather be in it with Luke than here on my own. Eventually, after what felt like forever, Luke shouted up. "Come down in ten minutes!"

I dried my skin, fingers and toes like prunes and put on a deep blue dress that Luke had chosen when we were shopping. My bare feet were silent on the soft, cream carpet of the stairs as I tiptoed down like a child on Christmas morning.

My breath caught in my throat as I peered around the living room door. Flickering candles adorned every surface, highlighting the dusky wallpaper that Luke and I had agonised over in John Lewis.

The air smelled beautiful, I recognised it as my favourite Pomegranate Noir candle. I'd never told Luke it was my favourite, but it was so like him to have paid enough attention to know. I felt myself tear up as it struck me once again just how much Luke loved me, how much he'd been through. I was imprinted all over the house, thinking back we had chosen almost everything together, painted walls together, why had I never spotted how like a couple we were?

I glanced around, feeling a little guarded. Luke knew I was still jumpy about people catching me unawares and I was confident he wouldn't do that to me, but an element of fear still plagued me. I saw a note on the coffee table, leant up against a champagne bucket.

A streak of desire flashed through me as I unfolded the thick paper, noticing Luke's beautiful handwriting. It was sad that people didn't write letters now, how I'd adore letters of love in his script.

I'm yours, always x

My heart swelled as I read the words, but at the same time it ached that a love so great was being shared.

Underneath the note was a shoe box. Nothing excited me like a shoe box! Especially this shoe box. A white top with black edges and base. Glossy and strong. Five magical letters spelling one of my favourite words… Gucci…

I teased the lid open, rubbing the tissue paper between my fingers with a smile. A smile that grew wider as I unwrapped the amazing heels that I'd been lusting over the other day with Luke. They were stupidly expensive. They were spectacular. They were mine! I ran my finger down the beautiful sole as I felt Luke's breath behind me.

"I just wanted to do something special for you."

I put the box down and jumped straight into Luke's arms. "They're beautiful, this is beautiful. You're beautiful." A giddy laugh escaped my lips as I kissed him. "I love being here."

"I love you being here." Luke smiled as he watched me put the shoes on. "They look perfect, I knew they would. Shall I?" He gestured at the champagne bottle and I nodded. *As if I was going to say no to champagne.*

"Did you go back for them? You shouldn't have spent so much." I was glad he had though!

Luke blushed. "I'm not trying to be flashy or anything. I could see how much you wanted them. If you'd loved the cheap one's I would've got them instead." He grinned, pushing the cork out of the champagne with a familiar pop. Handing me a glass of fizzing bubbles, he spoke. "This part of the surprise looks a little luxurious I admit. But I hope you like my plans for this evening, they aren't quite as fancy."

"I'm intrigued, tell me more."

"If I describe it, it sounds rubbish, so I want you to see it. Wait here, five minutes and I will come get you." He looked excited as he kissed me before disappearing to the kitchen, taking the champagne bucket and his own glass.

I couldn't keep still as I waited. Longest five minutes ever! The bubbles from the champagne were fizzing in my stomach alongside my anticipation. Luke returned with a black scarf and blew the candles out.

"You got my favourite candles too." I smiled at him.

"Can you behave and keep your eyes closed, or shall I put this on?" he asked as he proffered the scarf towards me.

"God, this is mysterious!" I turned around so he could tie

the scarf over my eyes. "I can't behave, so go ahead. You aren't trying to take advantage of me, are you?"

"Don't need a blindfold for that." I felt him take hold of both of my hands and lead me through the kitchen. "Careful on the steps." Warm, fresh air hit my face and I guessed that Luke was leading me down the path into his back garden. A few more steps and I heard the swish of what sounded like canvas, Luke's strong hands were on my shoulders. "I'm taking it off now." He sounded like a child with an amazing surprise, and I was reminded again of how I loved his enthusiasm and zest. He was melting my heart.

I opened my eyes and blinked at the beautiful sight that greeted me. We were in a white, tepee style tent which I knew must take up most of the garden. There were eight wooden poles that slanted upwards to create the peak of the roof and each of them had strings and strings of warm, white rice lights entwined around, giving the inside of the tepee an amazing, luminescent glow. On the far side I saw a den, an assortment of soft blankets, beautiful silk pillows, faux fur throws, and cushions of beautiful colours, creating a beautiful place to sit or lie. Next to Luke and I was a large tray, housing the champagne and all my favourite snacks. Luke knew my favourite everything.

I looked up at his earnest face. "Do you like it?"

"I love it! Can we live like this?" I looked around again, transfixed by how dazzling everything was, Luke included. The soft glow from the lights grew more luscious by the minute.

"When I was travelling, I spent a night like this in the desert. I wished so much you were there to see it. So, I decided to recreate it, as best I could anyway." He ran his hand through his hair looking abashed. "Would you spend the night in here with me?"

"I would spend forever in here with you." He kissed me as we stepped forwards towards the blankets and pillows. Within seconds we were naked and coiled up together, the feel of his body and all the different materials driving me insane.

Time felt endless as we lay together, looking up at the lights, almost like tiny stars in a beautiful sky, not needing to say a word. We spent an age consuming the food, the drink and each other, the air inside the tepee warm and invigorating.

"What are you thinking about?" asked Luke, as he traced his finger lazily around my bellybutton.

I smiled at him. "Just how perfect this is, it's like nothing else exists right now."

"I wish we could stay like this. I wish I knew this was going to turn out right." He closed his eyes and rested his head against me.

"Nobody ever knows what's around the corner for them Luke, that's not only us." I tried to reassure him, but sadly I knew exactly what he meant.

"I think, I should never let you leave." He pressed his lips to mine again. "I'll keep you here as my prisoner." The kisses moved down my neck and across my collarbone. "You'd be the best kept prisoner in the world, I promise. I'd lavish you with food and wine and love and attention." He flipped me over onto a soft, silky pillow, which I buried my face in. My breaths coming fast as his lips glanced light kisses from the nape of my neck down to the base of my spine, before making their back up and whispering in my ear. "Please stay with me, Lily." Then he sucked all the breath out of me once again as I heard him rip open a foil packet. I sighed happily, already in love with what he was about to do.

Afterwards, I lay with my head on his chest, his heart beating quickly in my ear as my own continued to race alongside it. He took a long, deep breath. "Is it like that with him, Lily? Honestly?"

I closed my eyes, knowing this wasn't a good conversation to have. "It's not that simple to answer. It's different, you're different people."

"You're avoiding the question. I wonder, the way we feel about each other, the way we are together, it can't be that special twice over." Luke sounded torn in two as he spoke.

"Luke, I know we can talk about anything, but really, you don't want the intimate details in your head." I said, nervous at where this was going.

"Maybe I need to, to understand how this… isn't enough."

I leaned forwards and rubbed at my tense face. "What are you asking for? Comparisons? Score boards? Why do you want to know? You think I don't wonder how many girls you slept with while you were travelling? I mean, look at you, everywhere we go you could have any girl in the room, and I'm guessing that you did for a while?"

Luke sighed and dropped his head into his hands. "I don't suppose I do want to know really. I drive myself mad with it."

I felt a tear slide down my cheek and splash onto my chest. "I just don't want to hurt anybody."

He sat up and brushed my tears away with his fingers. "I'm petrified of you going to work tomorrow, of him being there."

"I am too Luke, but I have to."

"You don't. I have enough money, just quit. You don't have to go back." Luke's eyes were troubled as he spoke.

"I do have to. I can't sit around here, living off you. I have a job, a house, friends. I'm meant to be making Zack's mum a birthday cake next weekend. I can't abandon my life and move here to be your housewife figure, Luke." I sighed.

"That's not what I meant. I just meant, you don't have to worry about money while you find another job, closer, away from him."

"Almost exactly a year ago, he was saying the same to me, not wanting me to work with you." I said.

"And you moved for him." Luke watched me, his eyes guarded.

"After you left Luke, in case you didn't spot that. You left. Not me." I stood up and slipped my dress over my head.

"I'm sorry, stupid time to bring this up. I didn't mean to upset you. Come back, Lily. I'm worried, that's all. Ignore me."

"I notice you avoided the how many girls question." I gave him a small smile, sitting back down as he wrapped his arms around me. I couldn't be mad at him.

"Yep, and I always will." Luke smiled and kissed my forehead softly.

TWENTY

*T*his was definitely not in my head. People were glancing at me as they walked past my desk. Maybe it was the new dress and the fact I was wearing the stunning Gucci shoes? Thinking back to the Instagram post though, I guessed not.

I sipped at my now cold coffee and tried to focus on my inbox which was overflowing after my time off. A peel of laughter rang out from the staff room and I closed my eyes, I wished everything didn't make me paranoid.

"Hi," I winced involuntarily as I heard Zack's voice speak to me.

I looked up at him, all stubbly and sexy. It was really annoying when I was so mad at him.

"You can speak? Who knew?" I stared at him, defiant.

"Why are you all dressed up?" He looked over the desk at my new dress, my feet were tucked out of view.

"Because I left our house with one tiny bag and had to buy new stuff. Is this the place to have this conversation?" I asked.

"No. I wanted to ask if you'd meet me at lunch. I can book a meeting room."

"Who said romance was dead? Fine. You could've messaged me to ask that." I began typing gibberish into an open email, just to look busy.

"I wanted to make sure you were actually here. Later." He walked off. *Twat!*

I must have looked in a foul mood as nobody bothered me all morning. I messaged Luke to let him know I was OK. Cassie had gone on radio silence again which was weird, I thought we'd resolved our issue.

All too soon it was lunchtime, I headed upstairs, admiring my shoes all the way in the glass bannister.

Zack looked me up and down as I walked in, it put me on edge.

"Nice shoes."

I didn't give him the courtesy of a reply.

"I figured you'd come back to the house while I was away, but nothing had moved when I got back." His voice still had anger in it.

"Why would I go back when you were so glad to see me go?" I snapped.

"I wasn't glad. I was angry."

"You didn't try to stop me, you didn't ask where I was, you wouldn't answer your phone. What the hell was I supposed to think?" I tried to keep my voice down, conscious that we were at work. "What's this breath, this break meant to be?"

He shrugged. "Have you been with him?"

I pulled my phone out of my bag, ready for this. "Yes, I have. Not at first, but when I saw this - I figured I should embrace the break in the same way you were." I slid it across the desk towards him.

He sighed as he looked at it. "I told Anna to take it down. She did it on purpose."

"I know, she's always bitchy to me. Maybe this time it worked in my favour hey?"

"I slept with Anna a couple of years ago, she wanted it to be more, I didn't. She's been a pain ever since. I'm sorry you got caught up in that." He ran his hand through his hair.

"You're sorry I saw it then, not sorry it happened? And Anna? Seriously?"

"Don't start twisting my words again. This is all crap. Crap that's covering up the real issue, which still is and always will be – Luke."

I looked down at the table, knowing he was right but not willing to admit it.

"Why have you come to work dressed all sexy like that? Honestly?" His face softened. I bit my lip as I answered.

"To piss you off. To try to look hotter than that girl." I answered. "Various reasons."

"We never had a proper big fight before, did we? This whole situation is crazy, Lily." He placed his hand over mine, I stayed still as a statue, not sure what to think. "You infuriate me, but I love you. You're still my perfect girl, no matter what I said. I've done stupid things that we need to talk about, and I suspect that you have too. I want you to come home. I want us to work this out."

"As long as I agree to never see Luke again?" I asked, looking up at those gorgeous brown eyes. Despite me being so mad at him, I was still full of love.

Zack nodded at me. "We can draw a line under this. I can

forgive anything that's happened, and I hope you can forgive me too. But if we do this, we do it properly. You'd have to leave him in the past, it's the only way."

I took a long breath as Zack rubbed his thumb over my hand. "Lily, I want us to buy a house and get married, have love and family around us all the time. I want lots of kids, you know that, and I don't want to have them with anyone in the world but you. I want to grow old together and love you every single day. I want us. I just need you to want it too."

I was unable to stop the tears dropping from my eyes.

"You're not saying anything and it's making me nervous. If you want to talk, I'll answer the phone. I need to know soon though, what you want. Is it me or is it him?"

Zack placed a paper light kiss to my lips and left the room. The photo of him and the blonde still open on my phone. My stomach hurt; the words I'd just heard flew around my head.

I didn't care if he'd screwed half of Iceland last weekend, we could put it behind us, we could fix this. But Luke... could I live without Luke? It didn't seem possible.

———

Rush hour trains though – those I could live without. I stood in the cramped carriage on the way back to Luke's, I felt so sorry for myself, and my feet were killing me.

Luke handed me a glass of Sauvignon Blanc as I walked through the door. "I love you coming home to me, especially in sexy shoes."

I kissed him and smiled. "That train is vile though."

We sat down together, and Luke pulled my legs up onto

his knee, rubbing my sore feet. He was an angel. "How was work then?" he asked.

I knew what he wanted to know. "We spoke briefly at lunchtime. I need to call him; he wants to explain more."

"Did he apologise?"

I screwed my face up. "Sort of… it was a bit tense. I need to hear what he has to say, and I need to tell him about this."

Luke concentrated on my feet, not looking at me as he spoke. "This? Are we not an 'us'?"

"We're more than that. Let me talk to him. Until I know the full story, nothing can move on." I stroked his face with my finger, his eyes met mine at last.

"I wouldn't stop you, that's his thing, not mine." I knew Luke had a point. "Why don't you go have a nice bath, then call him. I'll cook dinner. Then see how we can figure all of this out?"

I nodded, pulling him into a long kiss. Petrified in case these kisses were on borrowed time. "Thank you."

Luke laughed as I picked my shoes up to take with me. "What? I love them, they come everywhere with me." I grinned.

———

I ended up out of the bath again within half an hour. Sickness rolled over me when I thought of this phone call, it was time to face up to what I'd done, what Zack had done.

Nice pyjamas and wet hair, I sat in Luke's office, ready to make the call. I rested the phone on a stand as my fingers trembled with nerves.

I gulped as Zack answered the video call. He was in the

kitchen, still dressed in work clothes. Still looking... pretty pissed off.

"Where are you?" he asked, I could see him looking behind me for clues.

"Luke's office." A look of resignation swooped over Zack's handsome features.

The silence was deafening. "You told me to call if I wanted to talk."

He nodded, taking a drink from a glass beer bottle. "Right. I wish I'd never said I wanted a break. I've never been that angry in my entire life and I couldn't think straight. It didn't lift for days. I don't understand how you think it's inappropriate of me to want you to stop seeing him."

"You didn't even try to stop me leaving. You wouldn't answer any of my calls. Then I saw that picture. It seemed a pretty clear message Zack." I don't know if being on the phone made this easier or harder than being in person, but I was about to confirm his worst suspicions. "So, after that, I came to Luke's. I've been... with Luke since."

Zack sat down on one of the bar stools, our bar stools. "I didn't sleep with the girl from the photograph. I did sleep with a girl in Iceland though. For stupid reasons, I was still in that angry rage and I wanted to hurt you. Because I knew you'd be with him."

Our eyes stared into each other. I didn't know what to say anymore. This felt like my fault. I hated what he'd done, but I was the one going on and on at him about Luke beforehand.

"I meant what I said at work." Zack blew out a long breath. "This last week has been screwed up. We can put it behind us though, we can have that life we talked about together."

"With the one condition?" I asked, already knowing the answer.

He nodded. "It's the only way. I'd give up anything or anyone if it was hurting you Lily. I need to see the same loyalty in return. If you can't…" There was no need for him to finish the sentence.

"Zack, I love you. This situation with me and Luke is so complicated. Can you give me a couple of days?"

"Knowing you're in bed with him every night? No." He ran his hand though his hair again.

"What if I go to Cassie's? Have a couple of days away from both of you."

"I don't know what's so hard about this. I've apologised, I've admitted what I did. I've said I'll forgive what you did…"

"I need to be sure. I need to know I forgive you in return. I have pretty crappy feelings about myself right now that I need to come to terms with. I'll have eight thousand questions about what you did." I felt salty tears hit my lips as I realised that I was crying. My heart felt like it had been cracked in two when I thought of him with her. Yet I had carried out the same betrayal. Multiple times over.

"I'll answer anything for you. But I don't want to know a single detail about you and him. I can't have it in my head."

"Tell me about what happened then."

He cleared his throat before he began. "You know what those clients are like. Worked us crazy hard in the day, but at night-time… We were in this amazing hotel and everything was on their expenses account. I'd managed to hide what was going on pretty well, but I got to the point I couldn't."

The beer sloshed against the bottle as he took another drink. "I was sat at the side of the bar, moping, while the others carried on. The girl working there asked me what was wrong. I ended up telling her our whole story. I decided to head to bed, drunk by this point. She asked me for my room number as she was finishing her shift in an hour – and I gave it to her."

My lip felt fat under my teeth as I chewed on it. Knowing I had no right to be mad at him, but it still hurt to hear this. "Was she blonde?" I asked.

"Of all the questions..." He shook his head at me. "Yes, does that make a difference?"

"No. I just wondered, because the bar girl here was blonde too and-"

"Lily," he cut me off. "I have no interest in anyone else, blonde or otherwise. I acted like an idiot, but I think we both know why. You *do* have an interest in Luke. It'll destroy me if this is the end of us, but better that than play second fiddle to him for the rest of our relationship."

"I know," I wiped the tears from my cheeks. "Can I say that I love you?"

"You can always say it, might be time to show it though."

I nodded. "I'll go and stay with Cassie. We fell out too, but it'll be fine."

"Was that my fault?" he asked. "I'm sorry, I shouldn't have gone there."

"Don't worry, as much my fault. A couple of days then?"

Zack smiled, but it didn't reach his eyes. "The way we fell in love Lily ... please don't throw that away. That future we talked about, it's right there. It's in touching distance. You've just got to take that step with me. I love you."

"I love you too, Zack."

I put my head down on Luke's desk as the call ended. I

was devastated by the thought of Zack with another woman, but even worse was the thought of losing him. I loved Luke, to the point I felt like it was taking me over. Yet I had to lose one of them.

I messaged Cassie to ask if I could stay. Receiving a quick response of a thumb's up emoji and the words 'bring wine'.

Now to speak to Luke.

As I walked back downstairs, I saw Luke was on the couch with a book. No sign of any food. He looked up at me with worried eyes.

"I didn't cook in the end, because I had a feeling you'd be leaving."

I sat next to him and wrapped my arms around his gorgeous, warm body. "I'm going to Cassie's. I need to sort this out. I can't do that fairly if I'm here with you."

"Do you want to go back to him?" Luke asked.

"I don't know what I want. He just told me he slept with a barmaid in Iceland. Knocks me sick but then… He's willing to forgive what's happened between me and you."

"Me and you are much more than just sex Lily." Luke stroked my face softly as he spoke.

"I know. I love you so much I feel like its bursting my heart open. But I love him too and we have a whole life together. I don't know what to do, only that losing either one of you will break my heart into pieces."

"I meant what I said, your life there… everything can be undone. We can build a life together here, or anywhere you want in the world. Just imagine us together forever Lily."

"I know Luke. I'm scared of how I feel for you. It's so intense. I want to be with you, I want to start again some-where together. I want to feel this love forever, but I'm petrified of failing, and I'm worried I'm not strong enough to go through a breakup with Zack."

He sucked all of his breath in and held me close. "I understand. Can I walk you?"

I nodded into his chest.

"The beds going to feel like the loneliest place in the world. How quickly I adjusted to having you in it with me."

"I don't know how I choose between you." Just when I thought I was all cried out, the tears started again.

Luke stroked my hair. "Shh, it's OK. You do what's right for you. Concentrate on what you feel is right. Don't be distracted by what other people say or do, or what the world says your life should be like. Make this decision for you."

We walked the short distance to Cassie's at a slow place, quiet and contemplative. Our hands wrapped around each other's, as if in preparation for the world to tear us apart. Luke stopped at the front gates.

"A couple of days then?"

"Yes. I love you so much Luke. It hurts."

He kissed the tears from my cheeks before placing his damp lips onto mine in the softest kiss imaginable.

"I love you. I always will. I'm only minutes away if you need me."

———

Cassie opened the front door holding a massive tub of ice cream.

"Actually, I love you more than any boy." I laughed through tears. "Shall we get married instead?"

She screwed her face up. "You haven't got the right equipment for me sweetheart, otherwise yes!" We sat on the couch, wine in hand. "I knew it'd come to this Lily. How are you going to choose?"

"I have no idea," I admitted. "My boss is pissed at me already, so I asked for the rest of the week as annual leave, it would be too weird bumping into Zack. Am I OK to stay while I figure it out?"

"Of course, as long as you need."

"He shagged some blonde girl in Iceland." I sighed.

"The girl from the picture?" Cassie's face was full of shock.

"Nope, that was a different girl. He didn't sleep with that one."

Cassie wrapped her arm around me. "Are you OK?"

I shrugged. "Not really, feel horribly sick whenever I think about it but... have no right to be do I?"

'That doesn't mean it doesn't hurt Lily. This whole thing is so screwed up."

I nodded and rested my head against her.

I sort of... wanted to ask you a question anyway." She had a weird look on her face, I couldn't place it.

"Fire away." I smiled back.

"You know I've always been jealous of your perfect skin." I laughed and nodded. "Well, turns out I'm more jealous of your perfect ovaries."

"What the... we don't even know they're perfect for a start, can't see them. Don't even know if they're there." I poked at my belly, wondering how many drinks Cassie had already had.

"Would you donate eggs to me?"

I spat my drink out in shock, watched as the liquid landed

on the expensive material of her couch. For once, she didn't care. I wiped my face and hands as she continued.

"You don't need to sleep with Guy or anything weird. They take your eggs, mix them up with his sperm, then put them in me! Easy!" She looked manic; she was crazy nervous about this.

"Cassie! Sweetheart, I know you're upset but that's not a good plan. How awkward would it be to know the baby was half mine? And I look nothing like you, we're about as opposite as can be. Don't you at least want a sibling who resembles your girls?"

"I don't want an anonymous egg donor who could be any old weirdo or psycho, selling eggs for money. I want good DNA and you have amazing DNA. Miss practically perfect in every way who has two absolute hotties fighting over her." Her forehead was bunched up in tension.

"I'm so far from perfect, you have no idea. Look, you're still registering the news. Have you talked about it with Guy?"

"The idea of using your eggs? No. He's up for trying egg donation, I feel weird about it being a stranger."

I rubbed at my face again, why did every day get more confusing. "When me and Zack have kids, they'd be half siblings, that's weird."

Her face lit up. "You said 'when' me and Zack have kids! You're choosing Zack, aren't you?!"

"Cassie, I'm worn out, can I go collapse in the granny flat now please? So much to think about. It's not a definite no, it's just… a big decision."

It was a no, it was a definite no, I needed the right way to tell her.

TWENTY ONE

*D*espite my mind being in overdrive, I fell asleep straight away, tucked inside the granny flat. A week of non-stop stress and sex would do that to you.

It was late morning when I awoke. I glanced at my phone, but it seemed everyone thought I needed to be left alone.

Maybe Cassie was trying to sweeten me up - she'd furnished the granny flat with my favourite bubble bath, enough wine to soak my problems up and enough chocolate to rot my teeth. She'd also left beautiful notebooks and pens, Cassie was a big believer that a list could solve anything.

Perhaps if I focused on one of them at a time, some epiphany would come to me? I made a coffee and grabbed a chocolate bar for breakfast, covering the important food groups as I slouched down on the bed.

I creased the sharp edge of a new, blank page and began to write down memories about Zack that made me smile.

<u>*Zack*</u>
Super patient when we first met

The amazing first kiss at the train station
Falling in love slowly and deeply
The amazing build up to the first time we had sex, in a castle!
I love his family, his sisters feel like my sisters
We live in a beautiful home that we chose together
We have great jobs together
Our eyes are identical, like mirrors to each other
Makes me feel loved and wanted and cherished

This felt like progress, or at least it wasn't doing any harm. Now onto Luke's list.

Luke
Literally saved me from the hardest time of my life
The deepest friendship I could hope for
When I did fall for him, it was fast and hard
As was the sex...
He already feels like family
I could do anything, be anyone and he'd support me
Those blue eyes...
Makes me feel strong, indestructible, desirable - like the centre of his universe

I looked at the pages side by side, therapeutic perhaps but no nearer a decision.

I felt too restless to just sit here. Wandering to the house I found that Cassie was out. I was alone with my thoughts... I rolled my eyes, fantastic.

And now my mind was empty.

Utterly empty.

I changed into my yoga stuff and leant my phone up against a tree trunk, heading to the 'YouTube' channel of one of my favourite instructors. Let's make the most of this empty mind.

Except, every time I moved to a new position and felt a muscle ache or stretch, I thought of Luke and the insanely good things he'd been doing to me.

In the end, the video kept playing but I lay on the grass. Letting the warm sun sink into my skin. Wishing I could just escape this.

What was worse? To have stayed as I was, alone but trouble free. Or to have had two amazing new lives opened up to me, one of which had to go. Maybe wine would help...

Yet an afternoon lying in the sunshine with a chilled glass of Pinot Grigio, did nothing. I jumped into the shower, frustrated at myself. Angry at the world in general.

A random idea occurred to me, to recreate some Zack magic. By early evening, I dressed in tight jeans and a sheer top, put the Gucci's back on and grabbed a cab to the restaurant we had shared our first date in.

A modern annexe had been built at the side, housing a stylish bar. I perched on a stool (tall girl win, no need to climb) and looked across at the main restaurant. I recognised the table we had been at together that night right away.

The new section was striking and modern, lots of glass and chrome lighting, plus those massively oversized wine glasses that I loved. It was the middle of the week and the place was just the right level of busy. Buzzing enough to stop me feeling self-conscious, but not packed.

I ordered a large Pinot Grigio from a tall barman with long brown hair in a ponytail. He looked to be in his early twenties which made me feel old as he smiled at me and swiped the credit card. Yes, I was still using the joint credit card.

"Just the one drink? Waiting for someone?" he asked.

"Only me tonight." I shrugged and took a sip of the cold wine, savouring the sharpness of it in my mouth.

"Oh, I'm sorry," he began. "I didn't mean to cause any offence."

I waved my hand, smiling as I placed the glass back down. "No, you haven't. My choice, I needed to think."

"Well, I do take my duties as a bartender seriously, so if you need anything let me know," he smiled and held his hand out. "I'm Jonathan." His hazel brown eyes focused on me, and I could see how confident he was in himself. I'd never been like that; it must be nice to not doubt everything.

"Lily," I shook his hand. "Please make sure I don't start doing shots, I have a bad history with shots."

"No shots allowed," he grinned. "I make a mean cocktail though so let me know if you want me to talk you through the list. Also, bartenders are great listeners, if you want to talk." He smiled as he moved to serve a middle-aged couple who had arrived.

I swiped through my phone as I enjoyed the sharpness of the wine. I read through old messages from Zack. Silly flirty comments and steamy suggestions. Mundane day to day tasks - what's for dinner? Are we going to the gym? Every message mattered to me. I looked through the hundreds and hundreds of photographs I had of us. We always looked so right together, we complemented each other. The sheer wealth of our life together hit me like a slap across the face. There were photographs of us with Cassie, my parents, all of his family, his university friends, our joint work friends, neighbours. Then on top of that a multitude of us together on nights out, cooking together, lazing in the garden, intimate ones that I swiped off as fast as I could with a blush. I landed on my favourite, the two of us in the castle together, with the sunshine behind us. It still took my breath away every time I saw it.

A voice pulled me out of my trance, startling me. "On the house." It said as another large wine was placed on the bar. "Don't tell anyone."

I looked up and saw Jonathan. "Thank you, that's so kind, and definitely needed."

I still had the phone in my hand, the photograph open. "Is that your boyfriend?" he asked.

"I wish that was a simple yes or no. Yes, I guess. We live together. We're just, 'on a break'." I did the air quotes. His laugh was warm as he looked at me.

"Think we've all been there. He doesn't look like he wants to be on a break. Was it your idea?"

"No, it was his. An argument got crazy." I took a long drink. Realising too late that I'd already had a lot, and it always gave me loose lips.

"Look at this picture and tell me what you think then." I swiped to a picture of Luke and I, cuddled up at his place a few nights ago.

"I think, you both look happy. They're genuine smiles, and your eyes look happy too which is the giveaway." He

passed the phone back. "Is this… how you spent your 'break'."
He did the air quotes too and I laughed.

"Yep. We go back a long way. I wondered what someone
outside of the situation would think."

"What's the situation?" Before I could reply the phone on
the bar rang. He mouthed, "sorry," as he walked away to
answer it.

Alone again, I went through the photographs of me and
Luke. There were a lot, covering a wider range of time, but
with large gaps which made me feel sad. I knew what those
gaps were. So many were in my flat to begin with, from
when I didn't go out and he and Cassie kept me company
there. Lots from work and nights out with the team,
gorgeous scenes from Snowdonia, The Lakes, Pendle, all
the places we'd hiked together. So many of us dancing
around, and coffee shop selfies. Then a huge gap, the
twelve-month gap in my phone was the busiest in his, I
realised.

This wasn't generating any revelations, but the wine was
good, and it was nice to chat to someone who didn't know
me. The bar was busier, I saw Jonathan glance at me between
customers. "What's your favourite spirit?" he asked.

I puffed out a breath. "Like them all to be honest! Probably… vodka?"

He nodded. "Nice choice. I'll use the good stuff. I finish
my shift in fifteen minutes, why don't you take a seat over
there, and I'll bring you one of my finest vodka creations." He
gestured to a table near the back, which seemed to be for
staff breaks. "Then you can tell me the rest, see if I can help?"
His eyes were kind as he spoke to me.

"Sure." I nodded as I gracefully hopped off the stool

(again, thankful for long legs!) and headed to the table with the last of my wine.

"I used my judgement to try to guess what you'd like." Jonathan smiled as he sat down opposite me a short while later, placing a beautiful looking drink in front of me. "This is a lemon drop martini. Hope you like lemon?"

"I love lemon!" I grinned. "Do they teach you this at cocktail school?"

He laughed. "I don't know if cocktail school is a real thing. I'm studying graphic design. Just good at reading people. Anyway, taste it."

I took a sip, licking the remnants of the sugar rim from my lip. "Oh my god, that's amazing."

"I get told this a lot." He took a drink from his own glass, a pint of honey coloured ale. His barman apron had been removed and he wore a faded t-shirt, his hair now loose and sitting on his shoulders. He tucked it behind his ears as he spoke to me. "You want to talk about these boys of yours?"

"It's hard to explain. I've been with Zack for almost eighteen months. We live together, we work at the same company. Love him to pieces, thought we were heading for the happy ever after, you know?"

He nodded. "So where did the other guy come from."

"Luke is… was… has been my best friend since my early twenties. We went through a lot together, as friends. Then he told me he was in love with me. Obviously, that went down well with Zack, who said I couldn't see him anymore."

Jonathan gave a subconscious nod, obviously in agreement. "Cue, me and him having a blazing row and him announcing that he wanted a break. About a week ago. Then I saw this…"

I showed him the picture of Zack and the blonde, it really needed to be deleted. "So, I thought, fuck it."

"And you fucked Luke?" he asked, with a raised eyebrow.

I nodded. "Lots of times. I have crazy, strong feelings for him. I need to choose between them, and I don't know where to begin. I'm staying at my best friends while I try to figure it out. She wants me to donate eggs for her to have a baby. I'm lost in my life right now!" I laughed at the absurdity of it all.

"Well, I wasn't expecting all that. I need a cigarette, come talk to me outside." He motioned towards an exit door near the kitchen, I followed.

"I think it's obvious who you should pick, but I guess that's easy for me to say." Jonathan stated as he leaned against the wall and lit a cigarette. "You want one?" He offered the pack, but I shook my head.

"How is it obvious?"

"You love Zack, and he sounds like a decent guy, all that stuff you told me. But Luke's the great unknown, the one that got away. Most people don't get a second chance like that. If you pick Zack, I reckon you'll spend your whole life wishing you were with Luke."

"I wouldn't, I love Zack." All the wine mixed with the cocktail was making my head spin now and his words were starting to irk me. I also realised I hadn't eaten for ages.

"I think Zack would be you settling. Everyone regrets settling in the end." He almost looked smug as he watched me over the cigarette smoke.

I took a deep breath and looked around, not sure how to respond to a total stranger commenting on my life like that. I noticed the restaurant was almost empty now, it must be later than I'd realised.

"I think it might be time to go inside." I pointed up at the dark clouds.

"It's not going to rain, don't worry. I learned that at cocktail school too. So, either way you aren't going to be on a break for much longer, are you?" Jonathan asked, his face poker straight.

"No, I'm glad, it feels weird. I was cheated on before, and this whole situation makes me feel unsettled to be honest." I said.

"Who'd cheat on you? You're stunning." He put the cigarette out underneath his foot.

"Not everything is about looks," I replied.

"Well, those two guys in your pictures aren't exactly average are they? I never see girls like you drink with an ugly dude."

"I'm not with them for their looks, that's not what this is." My head was getting foggier, fresh air always hit me badly when I was drunk.

"I have an observation about your situation. You seem to be bogged down in the emotion of this, I think you need to clear your mind."

"I don't do drugs, well, not proper drugs-" I started to explain but he cut me off.

"I didn't mean do drugs. I meant do me. No strings, no phone numbers, a night to take your mind off them both."

Before I could even think, he kissed me. The cigarette taste made me feel ill, his tongue so far down my throat, I was going to gag. As I felt his hand grope at my chest, I realised I needed to stop this now.

I kicked him in the shin, thankful again for the Gucci's

which seemed to connect nice and hard. "What the fuck was that for?" he cried out, clutching his leg.

"When did I ever give you the impression that I wanted you to kiss me?" I shouted.

"You have been giving me the eyes all night," he said, standing upright again.

"I have not! I thought you liked talking."

"Yeah...because talking to girls is my favourite hobby." he said sarcastically.

He started leaning in towards me again and I held my hand up to his face. "I can't believe you. Definitely not happening." I rushed towards the large doors of the main bar, ordering an Uber as I did. My mouth felt disgusting.

"Unbelievable." I muttered to myself as I climbed into the car, staying composed all the way back to Cassie's, before locking myself in the granny flat, feeling more tears springing from my eyes as I realised, I'd been an idiot once again. Why was my judgement of people so off? He wasn't interested in helping me, he just thought I was an opportunity for no strings sex. I didn't want meaningless excuses to sleep around. I wanted love, but which was the right love?

After brushing my teeth and swilling the mouthwash multiple times, I felt hygienic again. Cassie had left me a fluffy dressing gown, all parcelled up at the end of the bed like in a posh hotel. *Probably only because she wants to harvest your eggs!* My head never stopped.

I rubbed my temples and opened the notepad again. I wasn't going to be able to sleep, thinking about the past hadn't got me anywhere, I needed to think about the future, and what would happen with each of them.

Zack

We could be great together again
Wants a promotion and then we can buy a house together
I think he'd propose within 18 months
Huge wedding, massive family, crazy celebrations
Honeymoon somewhere luxurious and exclusive
He'd want babies straight away – even more reason to keep my
eggs to myself!
Life would be full of friends and family and love
Our home would be the centre of it all

Luke

Wouldn't need to forgive anything, jump straight into our 'real'
relationship
His house already feels like my home
I think he'd propose, but would be low key
Get married on a beach, just us, perhaps not even a legal ceremony
but symbolic
Honeymoon would involve travelling
Would he want babies? Would we adopt babies?
Life would be adventure, exploring the unknown

How could you choose between those two equally amazing, but utterly different lives? Still, it was progress, vague progress…

A thought occurred to me, that maybe a long, late-night phone call would help. Be like the old days? I didn't even know if either man would be free. I had started all my lists with Zack first, so got cosy in the bed, filled my glass up with water and hoped he'd answer.

He didn't let me down. "Wasn't expecting to hear from you, everything ok? It's late."

"Yep, all fine," I replied. "Just wanted to hear your voice. Are you busy?"

"Watching football at home, but you know you beat football every time." I could sense him smiling as he spoke.

"It feels like a long time since we just talked, do you know what I mean?" I asked.

"I do, but we're both on the phone now. So, I'll turn the football off, hey?"

"You are so well trained," I teased. "Who got you under the thumb?"

"Well," he was starting to flirt. I loved his flirty voice. "She's this absolute temptress, has me under a spell where even football can't break through."

"She sounds awful." I gasped, enjoying the playful mood. "How do you cope?"

"When she gets too much, I have this little trick, this thing I can do to her." His words made me breathe faster. "She can't deny me anything once I get started."

"How do you know she's really into it? Don't you worry she's faking?"

"You can't fake what she does." I could tell he was smirking.

"I'm going to hang up on you now Zachary." He took a breath as if to object. "Facetime me in five minutes, OK?"

"Wouldn't miss it." he replied, as he ended the call.

Well, that intensified quickly. Maybe that's the effect of

being apart? I remembered how we had calls like that every night when we first started dating. I dragged a brush through my hair and wiped my face, keeping the fluffy dressing gown on as I sat back in the bed. My phone began to buzz with a video call.

I smiled at Zack as I accepted the call. "Hello again."

"It's good to hear you sounding relaxed." Zack was on the couch in our living room. The lighting was dim and cosy, and his hair looked scruffy. He had stubble and looked beautiful to me. It made me homesick.

"Swap relaxed, for pissed." I admitted.

"Wish I was there, you're great when you drink." he grinned.

"I kicked a guy in the shin for trying to kiss me, so be careful!" I raised an eyebrow at him and smiled.

"What the fuck? Was it Luke?" He sat upright, paying more attention now.

"No, I'm not with Luke. I went for a drink, thought it might help me think. I went back to our first date date place. It was a random barman. Hope he has a bruise tomorrow." I really did.

"I worry about you. You walk around all gorgeous, not realising how good you look or the effect it has, you're too sweet and innocent sometimes," he sighed. "As long as you're safe. I'll come over if you need me?"

"I'm fine, promise. He was harmless, sort of. I wish you were here, but at the same time, I think this is giving me what I need I do miss you Zack. I'm glad we've stopped shouting too."

"I miss you too, that fight was stupid. Can we never do

that again? You feel close now though." I saw him take a drink from a beer bottle.

"I needed to hear your voice, to see you. I was remembering when we first met and how we fell in love and…" I paused, not knowing what it was I wanted. "It was amazing, wasn't it?"

"Not liking the use of the past tense there…" His eyes narrowed with concern.

"No, no I don't mean that. I just mean the feeling of falling in love with you," I smiled. "Used to love those phone calls every night too."

"Me too, still not as good as when we moved in together though."

"I remember when we went to see the house, and both loved it straight away." I relaxed even further, as I recalled walking up the driveway together on that sunny afternoon, holding hands and feeling giddy.

"I remember the first night when we moved in, and the second, and the third." He had a naughty smile on his face.

"Stop!" I knew I was blushing as I sniggered with him.

"Nice dressing gown by the way Lily."

"It was a gift. I think Cassie wants to trade it for eggs." I said.

"You're not making sense. Doesn't matter as long as you come home." His eyes were intense, and we just looked at each other for a moment.

"I'm trying Zack, I am. This is making me realise how much I miss being normal together." I admitted.

"I told you normal wasn't all bad," he said as he sipped from the beer bottle. "So how much wine have you had?"

"I don't know. Four? And a lemon martini?" I screwed my nose up as I thought about it.

"That's about the right amount that you'll love it if I start getting ideas about you taking the fluffy dressing gown off…"

I bit my lip before I replied. "Zachary that's an obscene suggestion. What type of girl do you think I am?"

"That's so unfair that I can't give you a full title like that." He rolled his eyes at me, but I knew he loved it. "As for what type of girl you are… I told you many times that you're my perfect girl. I seem to recall many, many nights when we weren't together but things… could still sometimes happen?"

I could hear that his was breath was coming faster and realised mine was too. His eyes looked so dark and intense, I wished he was with me right now. I was hit by waves of nostalgia. "I remember those nights, I remember I used to desperately wish it was your hand on me, rather than my own. I cursed myself for asking you to take it slow."

"Where would you like my hand now then Lily?" he asked, as he shifted around on the sofa, all thoughts of football now relegated.

"Unfastening this," I replied as I undid the dressing gown belt and slid out of it. He could only see from my collarbone up, but I knew the effect it'd have. "Whilst I was unfastening your jeans, hearing that satisfying thud as your belt hits the floor."

I smiled widely as I saw him stand up and then heard the same thud I'd just mentioned. "Obviously on the same wavelength here."

"I loved the way we went a little further every time we met, it was likes weeks of foreplay, it used to play on my mind all day. What your voice sounded like in my ear, what your next step would be." I told him.

"Me too, I struggled to concentrate on anything but you, still do." I could see the phone jolt as he got comfortable. "I've never wanted someone as much as I wanted you, but it wouldn't have been the same if we'd jumped right in. Those few weeks were indescribable, I adored them."

I closed my eyes for a moment, sighing as I remembered. Forgetting for a moment that Zack was watching me. His voice snapped me out of it. "You look amazing. I can imagine right now what your skin smells like, how warm you are. I know that anytime now you'd make the sexiest little noises in my ear as my hands wandered all over you."

"Zack," he was driving me crazy already. "You know my favourite way to make those noises, right?"

"I do," he sounded breathless. "You'd push me down, maybe right here on this couch, and climb onto my knee…"

"Take your face in my hands and kiss you, proper, sexy kisses." I continued the story for him.

"Then I'd run my hands up your legs, tease you with my fingers before…" He sounded so on edge as he spoke, I could almost imagine my own fingers were his in that instant.

"I love looking into your eyes at that moment Zack, as you pull me down onto you."

His voice was so low as he spoke. "That's when I forget the whole world. When only me and you exist. Feeling you gasping in my ear, the smell of your hair, your skin pressed against mine. That feeling of heat on the inside of you…" He stopped speaking and I knew that those memories had pushed him over the edge. I was feeling the same and caught up, the phone fell between the pillows as I did so.

I tried to control my breathing, smiling at Zack as I grabbed the phone back. "Thought I'd lost you there." Zack looked so relaxed, and insanely sexy as he leaned back on the couch. Our couch, in our house.

"Sorry," I bit my lip, embarrassed. "Got a bit carried away."

"As if you ever have to apologise for that. We shouldn't have stopped those calls."

"Be weird if we were in rooms next to each other though." I grinned.

"Nah, because I could come grab you when it got too much." Zack replied with a happy shrug.

I lay down with my head on the plump pillow, contemplating him for a moment. "I love you so much Zack. I'm sorry if I haven't shown it enough."

"Shh. I love you, always will, there's nothing in the world that could stop me." I blew a kiss to him as he continued to speak. "Listen, you need to look after yourself. You looked exhausted at work, and I worry about you. So, while you have that huge bed to yourself, and you're still feeling all orgasmic and dreamy, get some sleep, ok?"

I nodded. "I will. You too, Zack."

"Night Lily, love you."

"I love you too." I smiled as he ended the call and I snuggled down into the sumptuous covers, feeling at peace.

TWENTY TWO

I stretched and yawned, reaching for my phone immediately. Almost lunchtime again, this was becoming a habit. I smiled as I noticed a message from Zack.

Zack: Morning xx Wanted to say I hope you slept well, and last night meant so much to me. Not just for the obvious... to hear from you unexpectedly and to have you sounding like the Lily I first met, (and to not be shouting at each other!) Have a good day today, I love you xxx

I felt warm inside as I sat up, against the multiple pillows that I'd moulded into a cocoon around me as I slept.

Lily: Hope you don't think I've been ignoring you, just woke up, must've needed more sleep than I realised. I feel the same about last night. I'll be in touch soon, I promise. I love you too xxx

My stomach rumbled like thunder, warning me it was ravenous, and maybe slightly hungover. I quickly threw on black jeans and a stripy, cropped t-shirt. I felt on a high from the lovely moments with Zack but sensed it'd all come crashing down soon enough. It was as if my brain had a roulette wheel in it, which span constantly, the noise of it drained me as I waited to see if it would land on Luke, or Zack, Luke, or Zack. It never did land though, it kept spinning and spinning and spinning. Keeping me in an endless guessing game.

I strolled into the garden, ready to head into Cassie's house and make breakfast. She was already outside, hanging gorgeous, tiny dresses on the washing line.

"Thought you were never getting up!" she grinned. "Did you go out last night? What happened to staying away from them both?"

"I went out on my own, had a couple of drinks, kicked a guy, the norm." I shrugged.

"Lily, you'd never have gone out on your own, that's definitely not the norm."

"Everyone changes," I replied.

"They certainly do," she sighed and I noticed her glance down at her flat stomach. "Hang on, you kicked someone?"

"In Gucci shoes even!" I grinned. "Is it OK to grab breakfast?" I motioned towards her house.

"Sure, I've already had lunch, but go for it. I'm picking the kids up in half an hour, want to do baking with them?"

"Definitely!" I smiled. "It's been ages, I'll be out of practice."

Two hours later, my belly and heart full, I surveyed the destruction in Cassie's top end kitchen. Flour all over the worktops, eggshells on the floor, melted chocolate dripping over the hob… and two gorgeous cherub faces grinning up at me. "You two are the best cake makers in the world!" I smiled.

"Come with me and get cleaned up," shouted Cassie. "While Lily cleans the kitchen."

The smells from the oven were amazing as I cleaned up. I'd been too busy to bake lately, I missed it. Every Monday without fail I used to take treats into Draper & Hughes. The new place was so big though and it felt weird, I hadn't often bothered. Plus, in all likelihood Zack would finish it all on Sunday night anyway.

Another random memory flicked into my mind, baking 'special' brownies for Luke's birthday and us hysterically laughing on his living room floor about nothing for hours. Thinking about that night, it was a little hazy. I had woken up with my lips stuck to Luke's neck, all dry from being like that while I slept. I apologised for the dribble on him, and we never mentioned it, but had I tried to kiss him? I hadn't ever wondered until now.

The four of us sat in the garden, eating cakes still warm and gooey. Ruby and Emilia chased each other with sticky fingers and although Cassie smiled and laughed along, I could see she still had sadness in her.

"Do you want a boy?" I asked, flicking chocolatey crumbs off my top and onto the grass.

"I wouldn't mind you know, either way. I never thought I was done. It could be a girl or a boy and I'd be over the moon. Just to have a chance would be nice."

"Why don't you and Guy go away for a break? Book something, I'll look after the girls with... someone." I pulled a silly face. "The two of you can relax and decide what you want to do, have some space. I've heard it works wonders."

"That'd be so good, are you sure? I know you have enough stuff going on?" She looked hopefully at me.

"Positive. Just leave the wine fridge full."

"Are you any closer to knowing what you're doing?" she asked.

"No. Spoke to Zack for ages last night, I feel like I want to go home to him. But the price for that is not seeing Luke again. The thought of that tears me up inside."

"You can't have it all though, nobody can. If you chose Luke and brought your life back here, would you forget Zack?"

I shook my head. "No. The two of us have something incredible." I knew that as problems go, this was insignificant, there were people dealing with illness and debt and grief. It didn't make me feel any more positive in my outlook though. There was no magic happy outcome. "Someone said to me that Zack was the safe choice. I think they might have a point. I edge towards choosing Luke all the time, but I'm scared. I know Zack and I work, I want to be safe. But then... who makes me feel safer than Luke?"

"I don't envy you," she tucked my hair behind my ears. "Well, your ovaries maybe, not this."

"Once I'm settled with one of them... We'll look into it Cassie," I said as I hugged her tight. I hated her hurt, but I still wasn't sure this would be a solution.

As Cassie scooped the girls up for their afternoon naps, I ran to the granny flat, remembering a bag hidden there from ages ago. Forty-five minutes later I pulled an extra batch of brownies out of the oven. I parcelled them up in beeswax wraps and took them with me to the granny flat. These were not for little fingers!

I needed to speak to Luke, give him the same time I'd given Zack the previous night. My nerves were frayed as I waited for him to answer, all faith in my own thought process gone by this point.

"Lily? is everything OK?" Luke sounded out of breath and I instantly wondered what he was doing.

"Hi, I'm fine, I wanted to talk. Don't worry if you're busy." I apologised.

"No, I'm just out running, the bloody phone wouldn't pick up and I didn't want to miss you," he puffed. "Let me get my breath back."

"It's fine, don't worry. Run here if you like? I wondered if you wanted to come over?"

"I definitely do. I need a shower though, Give me forty minutes?"

"No problem. Love you."

"I love you too."

I lay on the bed until I heard soft knocks at the door. I teasingly held the brownie to my mouth as I opened it.

"Remember these?" I grinned as I nibbled at the crunchy edges.

"Well, that's going to cancel out the run," his laugh lit up his face. "You make these today?"

"Certainly did. One batch were child friendly. This batch – not so much."

"I would've run straight here if I'd known," he pulled me

into a delicious kiss. "Wasn't expecting you to call, every-thing OK? This feels like we're breaking the rules."

"I think that you and I burned the rulebook a little while ago." I said, seeing his face light up with a sweet smile. "Being alone here is good in some ways, and I'm getting lots of thinking done. I remembered the last time we had these, wondered if we had them and talked, this might make more sense?"

"Come here." Luke pulled me down onto the couch, so I was cuddled on his lap. I loved this feeling. I took a bite of a brownie, giggling as the crumbs fell down my top and Luke scooped them up with his lips. Was it me or did these kisses get better and better? We were like hormonal teenagers, all over each other on the couch at a party.

My head felt nice now, warm and cosy. I closed my eyes and leaned against Luke with a smug grin, so happy. "What did you want to talk about then?" Luke asked.

"Us really, past, present, future. What you feel, what you want?" I shrugged.

"Oh right, nothing major then?" he said with a laugh. "All I want is you to be happy. If that makes me happy too, then I'll be shouting from the rooftops with glee. But as long as you're happy and safe... that's the best I can hope for I think."

His eyes looked regretful. I reached out and stroked his face. "You should put yourself first, you never do, I worry about you."

"I'm never going to put pressure on you. The house hasn't felt right without you though. You say that I don't put myself first, but I'm thinking majorly selfish thoughts. Can't help but wish you and Zack were not speaking still. The maybe you'd just stay with me forever."

"Can you do something for me?"

"Anything." Luke replied with confidence.

"If all the problems were gone, and you knew it was me and you, Luke and Lily forever, what would you see in our future?" I asked him.

He blew out a long breath. "I may have thought about this in miniscule detail, and I don't want you to laugh at me." God, he was adorable when he was nervous.

"I'd never, I promise. I'm just trying to get my head around two potential futures and which is right." I replied.

"I think you'd move in with me straight away, because we wouldn't want to waste any more time being apart," his eyes sparkled at me. "I don't think you'd come back to work at the office, you'd take the opportunity to try something new. Something flexible, so you could come with me to travel. We could go around Europe together and visit all the romantic hotspots, but go off the beaten track and live like locals as well."

He placed a kiss on my lips before he continued. "I think we'd be in a gorgeous remote village, with stalls selling hand-made jewellery. I'd send you off to find coffee, I know you'd be grouchy without it. Then while you were gone, I'd buy a ring." I bit my lip and hugged him; this was exciting.

"Shh, stay with me until the end." Luke smiled as he spoke. "Then we'd go for a moonlit stroll, I'd ask you to marry me and be mine always. Back home we'd realise we didn't want a massive wedding with all the frills. Instead, we'd go somewhere beautiful, maybe mountainous, or maybe a deserted beach. Just the two of us and say our vows, swap our rings. I'd sob like an idiot, knowing I was the luckiest guy on the planet."

I kissed him, full of love, before letting him continue. "We'd spend maybe two years enjoying life together, filled with an abundance of love and hope, travelling whenever we could. I can't lie, there'd be a lot of sex, like an X-rated, ridiculous amount of sex and you'd need to prepare yourself." He grinned, and I laughed with him.

"That would, of course end up with my favourite image of you and me, at home together. Me stroking your gorgeous, massive pregnant belly. You'd think you looked like a blob, I know you would, but you'd look like heaven. We'd have perfect twin babies. A blonde-haired, blue-eyed girl like daddy. And a brown-eyed, brown-haired boy, like mummy."

I was silent, pressed tight against him. I knew if I spoke, I was going to cry.

"Lily? Have I freaked you out?" Luke asked with concern, his eyes troubled.

I shook my head as fresh tears started to fall. "No. I didn't know you wanted all that. That was so beautiful."

"Hey, don't cry, please. I didn't mean to make you sad." He held my face between his hands and peppered kisses across my lips, cheek and forehead.

"You haven't, you haven't at all. I can picture all of that in my head so clear, it's amazing." I smiled at him and wiped my eyes. "Why does life have to be complicated, why can't we have that?"

We were both silent for a moment before Luke spoke. "Because I was too late."

I stood up and poured two glasses of wine as I attempted to gather my feelings, which were flying through my head at speeds I couldn't comprehend. We both looked to the window as a flash of lightning lit up the sky, rain began to pour down, hammering against the windows as a rumble of thunder sounded far away. A perfect summer storm.

"Are you eating?" Luke asked. "You aren't just drinking are you?"

"Keep forgetting to eat to be honest. Assuming the brownies don't count?"

"They don't count," Luke confirmed. "I've made this weird, haven't I?"

"You haven't at all. That life sounds amazing, you said all of that so beautifully. I never thought we were going to get this complicated. I love you. You do know that, don't you?" I asked.

"I know, I feel it. I love you so much Lily," he sighed as though his heart was breaking right in front of me. "I wish I had a time machine. It's not even worth me hating Zack, it's not his fault. You were young, free and single and I was unaware my chance was expiring."

"It's not expired Luke," I sat back down, handing him a glass.

Luke's face shifted slightly as he looked at me. "I wanted to ask you for a while now, but I wasn't sure about bringing it up. Zack clearly knows about that night now, I wondered when you told him and why? When I left, you hadn't told him, and I thought that was how you wanted it?"

"I didn't like telling him, but he needed to know. We were getting serious.

I felt like it was something I'd want to know, in his shoes. Remember your last day at work? What a state I was in?" Luke nodded at me. "Well, by the time Zack arrived a couple of hours after work, I was a wreck. When you left the office, I fell apart, Petra had to shepherd me upstairs. I cried until I threw up. Felt like a vital organ had been torn out of me. I forgot Zack was even coming over until I heard the door go. When he saw the state of me, he knew this wasn't a normal falling out between friends. I needed him to know why the bond between us is so deep."

"What did he say?" Luke's eyes looked misty as he questioned me.

"Same as we all thought I think, thank god you were there. That silly, adorable what's for tea message system saved me. You saved me. Obviously, I can never, ever repay what you did for me, but I don't want you to think that it's only that one night that brought us so close."

I took hold of his hand, running my fingers over the soft bumps of his knuckles. "You were the only person who didn't try to fix me. You didn't tell me to get over it, or time would heal it or any of that crap. You travelled through every stage of it with me, do you know how rare that is in a person?" I rested my head in my hands, as if trying to hold back the memories that would sometimes float to my mind and haunt me.

"I'd do it a million times over. Look at me, Lily."

I looked up, huge, pendulous tears dripping from my eyes. "I love you so much."

Luke stroked his fingers down my cheek. "This is beyond love. I've said it before, you're everything. You're my whole world. There's nothing I wouldn't do for you."

As Luke pressed his lips against mine, a feeling passed between us. We'd kissed hundreds of times now, we'd explored every bit of skin and flesh, but what was happening now was different.

His kiss was drinking me in. I could feel him smiling as

his lips caressed mine. His fingers travelled with a painstaking slowness over me, as if he were memorising every patch of skin. I couldn't tear my eyes off his, they held the key to me. This was absolute paradise. I could've died here and now and not regretted a second.

Luke pulled away from me. "I forgot to bring condoms, I'm sorry. I can run home?"

I couldn't wait, I needed him now. "You got tested after you got home didn't you?" My mouth continued to move on his. He nodded as he kissed me. "I'm on the pill, you know I haven't slept around. It's fine."

"Really?" His lips paused as he asked me.

"Really, please just take me to bed now Luke."

We were silent as we undressed each other, heading to the bed in constant connection. If our mouths weren't touching, then our hands needed to be. I had to touch him. We'd had every type of sex imaginable over the past week, giving into all our fantasies about each other.

This though... The phrase made me cringe but making love... this was it personified. With every movement, every kiss, he filled my heart up with love until it overflowed. With that overflow I felt the agony of my heart breaking, before he filled me up with love over and over again. We had absolute reverence for each other. This was a torturous but addictive cycle that I seemed unable to break. I wasn't even ashamed of the tears rolling down my cheeks as he held me close to him. I never wanted him to let go.

TWENTY THREE

$\mathscr{I}$ stretched out to the side of me as my eyes sprang open. My hands found the other half of the bed empty. Luke had left, that wasn't like him. Did he have court again? I was confused.

I wrapped a sheet around myself and stepped outside onto the immaculate grass, it seemed even greener after the rainstorm. No sign of anybody. I wandered around the garden, my feet soaking wet as I cried once again. I couldn't bear to be without either Zack or Luke. I couldn't bear to hurt either of them. My head was in agony with the strain of it, I just didn't know what to do.

As I got back to my room, a message pinged onto my phone from Luke.

Luke: I'm sorry I had to go. I kissed you before I left, you looked beautiful. I had something to send you and it was too big for a text. I emailed you. Don't worry about anything, OK? xx

Lily: Sounds ominous. Everything OK? xx
Luke: It will all be fine, promise xx

I had a horrible sickness in my gut as I sat down on the bed and opened my email. I hadn't checked it for a few days and initially all I could see was spam before I saw his name, Luke Adamson, and pressed on the message to open it.

Dear Lily,
I tried so hard to stop myself falling in love with you, but I couldn't. You were so hurt and vulnerable. If I'd told you then I'd have either alienated you, or I would've become a rebound. Then we became such good friends, I've never had so much fun with someone. We'd go on a night out and I'd feel like we were a couple, dancing and laughing, heading home together, but it was just friendship for you. At one of those points... that's when I should have progressed it. A night when we were in a club, pressed together and hot, I should've braved a kiss. Remember the night all the trains were off, and we stood in the pouring rain trying to get a taxi, laughing our socks off? You hugged me and looked into my eyes, so alive and beautiful - that would have been an ideal point to tell you. I remember the weekend before I went to Uganda, the chat we had about being brave. Why wasn't I brave that moment?! I thought it'd be stupid to start something with you when I wouldn't be around for a while. I was furious at Cassie for encouraging you to meet Zack, but it wasn't her fault. She was right. You're young and

beautiful and clever, why waste that time? She was trying to help you blossom. I thought you and Zack were so new, that if I told you how I felt... I don't know... would you abandon him and come running to me?

Yet there was something there in you, something that made you message me that night, was it the way that kiss felt on my last day? Until that point, I'd concentrated on forgetting you. Instead, I now began to concentrate on keeping you in my life. It's felt magical us being together, talking and laughing, making love, hearing those words from you. I held back so I wouldn't hurt you. Maybe that was my mistake, but I can't apologise for putting you first. I loved knowing you would be there when I woke up, and that we would go home and cook dinner together. I want this to be your home Lily, our home, together.

I want to hate Zack, but he hasn't done anything wrong really. He fell in love with the most incredible girl in the world, how can I blame him for that? I know we have love and happiness, but this situation is hurting you.

Please believe me that it's shattering me to write this. I need you to understand and do what I say, please. We could take on the whole world together, grow old together and be as much in love the day we die as we are now. Making this choice between Zack and I, it's making you ill. You're losing the shine from your eyes, you look weary. I know your heart is going to feel broken whichever way you choose, and I know that in spite of your own hurt, you're more concerned with not hurting either me or him.

I want to ease that burden. Forget how I feel, if you're happy, that's all I need. You to be happy, safe, loved, healthy. And you will be, with Zack. He loves and adores

you and he'll look after you, I'm one hundred per cent sure.
You don't need to make the awful decision, I'm taking that
away from you. I love you so much, and it's because of that
I know I have to let you go. Please go and be happy and live
an amazing life with him.

We can't be a part of each other's lives anymore. This has to
be goodbye. The most heart-wrenching goodbye I could ever
imagine, but for all the right reasons. If the universe wants
it, maybe one day we'll be reunited. In our next lives Lily,
it's you and me forever - don't ever forget that. I'll be
searching for you, wherever and whenever that may be. For
now though, live this life, be happy. I will always love you.
Always.

Luke xxx

I gasped for breath, the panic choking me. My face was drenched with tears my mind wanted to shut down. I couldn't swallow, I couldn't speak, I couldn't move. Numbness overwhelmed me, but at the same time joined by absolute agony. Curled up in the bed like a baby, my tears soon saturated the pillow below me.

I read the email five, ten, fifteen times but I couldn't digest it. How do you act on words like that?

I managed to calm my breathing down and tried to think what to do. I needed to talk to Luke.

Lily: I want to call you, but I can't speak, I literally can't speak. I don't know what to do anymore. I love you so much, this is too hard. I can't be without you x

Luke: I've wracked my brains about this Lily. This is the only thing I can do for you. I know it's hard, the hardest thing in the world. But it will get easier for you. Just go and be happy, go and live your best life, let me do this for you x

Lily: I can't imagine my life without you Luke x

Luke: Then imagine our next life together, this isn't our time. If it was then it wouldn't be this painful. You still have clothes at mine, I will leave them with Cassie over the weekend x

Lily: Luke please, please don't do this x

Luke: It's the only option. I've been round and round it in my head a thousand times. It's because I love you so much that I'm doing it. You're strong, you're amazing, you can handle this. You can go back home and put your heart and soul into your life with Zack. I know you can, you don't need me, you've got this xx

Lily: But I love you. I love you so much it's killing me Luke x

Luke: And I love you, I always have, I always will. I honestly believe what I wrote, this isn't our time, our place. But when it is, we'll find each other. Stay strong. Don't ever forget how loved you are. Goodbye for now Lily xxx

After that, he didn't reply, I messaged him over and over, begging and imploring him. I called him more times than I could count, but just got voicemail. Eventually I threw my own phone across the room in a temper, noticing myself in the long mirror on the opposite side of the room. I looked like a shell of my true self. Pale, blotchy, tear stained and crushed, small and worthless. if someone tried to paint heart break, I would be it. How could I go home, cope with this, explain it to Zack, none of it seemed possible.

I kept imagining Luke in absolute pieces and that set me off again. He'd done this for me though, that was so typical. Why couldn't he be selfish for once? Just be selfish and not let me go. Should I accept what he was doing? Should I march round there and tell him no? What then though, go and break Zacks heart? There was no right answer here.

Luke had put himself through hell to make that decision, to write those words, to explain it to me. Maybe the kindest option was to accept it, rather than make him go through it all again? *You should've left him alone.* This was all my fault. I felt like my heart was being stretched out on a rack when I thought of never seeing him again, but when I switched the roles and thought of never seeing Zack again, I felt the same.

I heard gentle knocking on my door as Cassie popped her head around.

"I spoke to Luke."

I looked up her, barely able to focus on her through the tears as she locked me in a tight hug.

"I think it's for the best sweetheart, I really do," she kissed my forehead, rocking me backward and forwards slowly in her embrace, like she would when her little girls had scraped knees.

"Is Zack expecting to hear from you today?"

I nodded, still unable to speak.

"There's no rush at all. If you want to go home today, or not for two months, I don't mind either way. If you want driving though, just tell me. I'm going to make you a cup of tea. Why don't you jump in the shower?"

She headed back to the house, but I couldn't take a shower. His lips had touched this skin, his fingers had caressed it... I didn't ever want to wash that away.

Cassie and I sat together a few minutes later with extra strong cups of tea, the grass still wet against my bare toes. There was nothing to say. We were both going through utter heartbreak over entirely different situations. I wished someone would take my heartbreak away, I could at least help with hers.

"When I'm home Cassie, I'm going to talk to Zack about the egg donation idea."

She squeezed my hand tight. "Thank you, but you two need to get back on track. No rush."

"I know you want tall kids, it's all a ruse isn't it You want my tall genes?" I managed a sad smile.

She laughed. "Shall I drive you home beautiful girl?"

I nodded. "Not fair on Zack to drag this out. Can we take a quick detour?"

An hour later I was outside a coffee shop, although I wasn't a pretty sight I had managed to stop gulping and sobbing like a banshee. Luke had gone through so much to make that decision, I needed to honour it, I needed to wrap my head around that.

His phone was *still* switched off, I wondered if we'd ever speak again. I couldn't bear the thought of not seeing his beautiful smile again, not hearing him laugh at my silly comments. Never feel his arms pull me up the last few steps of a hike, ignoring my insistence that I couldn't make it. How could it be I'd never wake up in his arms again?

Sitting on an uncomfortable metal chair which dug into my legs, I inhaled the scent of my double shot latte and opened the three memory cards I'd just bought from the shop next door. I put one card into my phone, and downloaded every message I had from Luke, along with every photograph and video, and that email, that reality ending email. Then I made two more copies and zipped them inside my bag.

Cassie watched me with worried eyes as she blew on her cup of tea. "Do you need a hand?" I shook my head and continued with the task at hand.

The tremors in my hands made my progress slow, as I clicked delete on everything in the phone. I couldn't have it there, at hand so I could look whenever I wanted. I had to avert my eyes, I couldn't read the lovely messages, I couldn't see our happy faces together. Every press of the delete button felt as though I was wiping us out of existence. I was tempted to read that email once more, but I didn't have the strength to. I had to face this, as hard as that was. I also had another person I needed to message.

Lily: Cassie is driving me back, should be home in a couple of hours
Zack: That's good news, wasn't sure when or if I would see you...
Lily: I'm coming home Zack. I'll talk to you when I am back
Zack: Lily, I love you so much. Get back safe. Can't wait to see you xx

I could never tell him it hadn't been my choice. Luke had made the decision for me. It was out of my hands and I felt crushed. A memory came back to me, of watching a movie with Luke, a couple of years back when life was simpler. We were lying on cushions on his living room floor, buttery smelling popcorn strewn around from an earlier game, trying to catch it in our mouths. The winter weather was bitter, and I could see the streetlights on through the window, illuminating the dark evening. It was warm as toast in his house as we lazed around in shorts and t-shirts, our legs aching from the day's exertions. The group of friends in the movie were trying to escape from an old temple. One of them needed to hold the lever to wedge open the exit so the others could escape. One selflessly stepped forward, knowing they'd be trapped and alone. Even at that time I'd laughed and said that would be Luke. The others were so busy trying to convince him not to, they almost missed their chance, meaning his sacrifice would've been pointless. Luke got so frustrated at them.

Now, it was Luke making the sacrifice. I wanted to be locked in the temple forever with him, but I knew that would defeat everything he was trying to do for me.

I tried to look at his Instagram, but I could see that he had removed me. This was it. This didn't feel real, this couldn't be happening. I turned my phone off as I finished the last dregs of coffee. Once back in the car, I set the air conditioner to its lowest temperature, and blasted it on full, wanting to feel it sting my face and focus me.

It felt like the longest drive home I had ever known, yet at the same time, as Cassie pulled over, I couldn't remember it. I could see Zack inside through the window, he looked happy. I felt numb.

I think I was in a kind of shock. I watched myself from the outside, not present in my own mind. I said goodbye to Cassie, who was looking at me as if I was about to collapse.

I saw myself go into the house, be scooped up in a gigantic hug by Zack and covered in kisses. He wrapped a blanket around me and rubbed my cheeks with a gentle touch, worried by how cold I was. Then I sat on the couch and he brought me coffee whilst placing soft kisses over me, asking if I wanted to talk.

"Zack," I sighed. "This has been the hardest experience. It'll be fine, I know it will. I need time to get to grips with what's in my head. I'm sure you have stuff to work through too?"

"I thought I was never going to see you again. I feel like I never want to let you out of my sight."

"What happened in Iceland-"

"It was nothing," he cut me off. "Can we leave it behind us? I just want to forget all of this."

I didn't have words to respond with or thoughts to comfort him with. I rested my head on his chest, feeling his arms wrap around me, knowing he wanted to make it all better. I knew we weren't really addressing any issues, but I didn't have the strength.

This wasn't the same as the chest I rested against last night...

Later still, I watched myself soak in a long bath and go to bed early with a dreadful headache. I noticed how I checked my phone every five minutes but the message I longed for was never there. I saw myself go to work, hold hands with

Zack, eat sandwiches together at lunchtime. I watched life happen around me, not sure I deserved it.

I was very conscious that even after a week, Zack and I did no more than kiss. I couldn't bring myself to replace Luke as being the last person who touched me that way. That last time we were together…

I turned up at Cassie's the next weekend, as arranged, still numb and vacant. Guy had taken the girls to the park, Cassie and I sat in the living room. Her eyes were wary, I think she was expecting snot and tears, but I'd retreated into numbness. I think my mind was protecting itself, being an empty shell was easier than living with the pain.

"All your clothes are in the two boxes by the door," she said softly. "Some from Luke's and some that you left here."

"Thank you," I replied, gulping the hot coffee she had given me. It was too hot to drink but the distraction of the burning sensation on my lips was helping me. "Can you please do something for me?"

"Of course." Cassie replied as she squeezed my knee softly.

I pulled two of the memory cards out of my handbag, the third one was hidden at home, at the back of my wardrobe. I didn't know if I'd ever look at the contents again, but I wanted to know the option was available to me. "Can you please look after one of these, forever for me, in case I ever need or want it?" Cassie nodded at me. "The other is for Luke, if he wants it, it doesn't matter if he doesn't, please don't tell me either way. Every photo, message, 'us' I have from my phone. I can't keep them there, I can't pretend it didn't happen either so…"

"I can do that," she said. "Are you OK? You don't seem it?"

I felt desensitised, tears ran down my cheeks, my body suffering through the physical motions of this grief, but my mind wasn't in sync with it. I wasn't sobbing, or consciously feeling those tears, I was detached from them. "I don't know," I replied. "I'm not bothered about me to be honest. Is Luke OK?"

"He will be, I'll make sure."

"I'm going to go now." I said as I stood, suddenly wanting to be anywhere but here. Luke's house was a few minutes' walk away, I couldn't be this close.

"Stay for a while, we can talk, we can eat full tubs of ice cream, whatever you need." Cassie offered.

I shook my head and wiped the fresh tears away. "I need to go. I'm taking the clothes to the charity shop on my way back, I can't take them home."

"Not the shoes?!"

I looked at Cassie in confusion. "All of it, too many memories."

"But they're Gucci!" Cassie looked at me, as if this fact would alter my opinion.

"Do you want them? You can have them, just don't wear them when you're with me."

"Yes, you cannot send Gucci to the charity shop!" Cassie smiled, and a little, lonesome light came on inside me.

I smiled back and she pulled me into a tight hug as I whispered to her. "You need to know; I had a lot of sex wearing those shoes."

She pushed me away from her, laughing whilst she pretended to gag. "We still come back to the same point, Gucci! Why don't you keep them, put them away safe? You won't always feel like you do now, I saw a smile then, that's progress."

As I drove back home, autopilot kicked in once again. I watched myself, halfway home, stop at a charity shop and leave all the beautiful, expensive clothes that Luke and I had bought together. All except the shoes which I knew could also find a home at the back of my wardrobe.

I saw a reflection of myself in the window, tear streaked make up, pale, vacant eyed and definitely too thin. The staff in the shop may have thought I was insane, but I didn't care. I stood there for ten minutes, watching myself. I needed to do what I had done before, compartmentalise this. I needed to focus on Zack. He didn't deserve one more ounce of hurt from me. He'd been so patient with me, but I couldn't carry on like this.

An hour later, I walked into our home. Inside I felt the same, but I knew I needed to try to fix our relationship. I'd cleaned my face and stopped to buy fresh bread and coffee, which I handed to Zack with a smile as he kissed my cheek.

"I was thinking," I began. "Maybe we could go on a date date tonight?"

Zack's face lit up into a smile. "I'd love that. I'm so worried about you, about us."

I thought back to Cassie's words about her own heart-break. It was a grieving process she was right. "Zack, there'll be good days and bad days, but as long as we both want this, we'll be OK."

Loving two people was brutal, I hadn't asked for it, but I hadn't been able to stop it.

I knew I needed to focus on what was in front of me. I still had more than most people are ever lucky enough to, right here with me, holding my hand. A man who adored me. A man I loved. A man who would build our future alongside me.

That night, I slipped the memory card into my beautiful shoe box and pressed it to the back of the wardrobe. I made a promise to the universe, "Next life Luke. It's me and you. We'll find each other. I promise."

Zack's face broke into a contented smile as I came back downstairs wearing the red dress that he loved so much, the red dress that reminded us both of the wedding and everything that had passed between us during that weekend.

I wrapped my arms around him and hugged him tightly, burying my face into the crook of his neck and taking deep breaths, as much as I might be missing another... Zack was everything to me as well.

"I love you so much." I whispered as his hands stroked my arms.

"I love you more Lily. Come on, date date time." He grinned and took my hand as we headed out of our front door together. We had so much future ahead of us, just waiting to be written.

———

AFTERWORD

I hope you enjoyed reading The Missed Kiss as much as I loved bringing it to life. When my early readers read the story, I was amazed to find a fifty-fifty split between people who preferred Zack and people who preferred Luke. I'm as bad as Lily, my preference changes by the day!

I would love it if you let me know your favourite via socials or email (details on About the Author). Who knows... it may even affect their future!

Team Zack, Team Luke, or even Team Lily? Was she better alone?

There are many more stories to come - I promise that Lily, Zack and Luke's journey isn't over. Watch out for updates on the sequel. (Sneaky peek in the next couple of pages!)

Lastly, as an independent, debut author, it would mean the world to me if you could leave a review on *Amazon* and

Goodreads. I want to continue writing, I have so many potential books in my head, just waiting to spill out onto pages for you all.

ABOUT THE AUTHOR

Nicola lives in North West England with her family. She has three daughters, and therefore will never be rich or sane but does have a house full of hormones and hair bobbles!

Turning forty during lockdown spurred her to pursue her dream of writing. Once she began, she realised she couldn't stop.

Like her characters, she loves a glass of wine with her best friends, but sadly cannot walk in gorgeous designer heels!

www.nloweauthor.com nlowe.writing@gmail.com

facebook.com/NicolaLoweAuthor

twitter.com/@nicswriting

instagram.com/nicolaloweauthor

BOOK TWO SNEAK PEEK

*W*hy had it seemed a good idea to come to the zoo on the hottest day of the year, slap bang in the middle of the school holidays? My nerves were frayed from making sure Ruby and Emilia didn't get lost or dangle over the Black Bear enclosure. There were so many people milling around, oblivious to being completely in the way, it was making me super tense. Being responsible for two children for a full weekend was far more stressful than anyone had warned me. Cassie, my best friend since high school, was far from a helicopter parent but she seemed to take all of this in her stride.

I smiled with relief as I saw Zack heading back towards us with ridiculously big ice creams. The girls ran to get their treats, and I pointed them towards a shady patch under a large tree. Thankfully I'd remembered sunscreen, it was like the sun knew how stressed I was going to be and wanted to just add to it with August temperatures exceeding twenty-six degrees.

Zack took a seat on a wooden bench, carved with beautiful animal figures, just a metre away from where the girls sat comparing whose ice cream was the biggest, and which sprinkles were superior. He patted the seat next to him and I sat down slowly. The wood feeling as though it would scorch the bare part of my legs beneath my denim cut off shorts.

He held his ice cream out to me with a grin. "Want some?"

I surveyed it, and him, cautiously. "What flavour is it?"

"Cookies and cream on top, salted caramel underneath. You can even have my flake if you like?"

The flake was melting as I looked at it, the heat of the sun taking no prisoners today. It made me feel slightly nauseous. "It's OK, you have it. Unless they have a wine stand around here somewhere I'm fine." My eyes darted back to the girls, making sure they hadn't moved.

Zack took my hand in his. "They're fine, they're having a great time. Everyone is having a great time. You just need to relax." He shrugged as he slurped at the ice cream, and for the first time I found it irritating rather than endearing.

"I just want to keep them safe, its more stressful when they're someone else's children. More pressure." I tried to explain.

"Interesting." Zack ran a cold finger down my arm. "So, if one day we come back here with our children, you might relax?"

Ruby and Emilia now had their arms linked together, like a couple with champagne at a wedding, tasting the others' ice cream. They had the same blonde, bouncing curls and I could see sticky ice cream caught in the ends. I couldn't help but grin at them, but I think Zack thought I was grinning at him. I may have been doing a good job at pretending all was fine, but inside I was feeling far from it.

It had only been three weeks since it happened, three weeks since the email from Luke. In fact, tomorrow at about eleven forty in the morning, that would be exactly three weeks since he stepped away from my life. I felt my eyes betray me with tears even as I thought about it. *Thank god for Ray Bans hey Lily?*

It was two weeks since I'd gone to Cassie's to collect my things, then hidden the Gucci shoe box at the back of my wardrobe. I'd sworn to myself that day that I wouldn't hurt Zack anymore. I'd been slowly teaching myself to put everything that had happened into a back room in my brain, a place I didn't have to go often. That way it didn't have to be a sharp, immobilising pain, more of a dull ache and sting that plagued me when I was least expecting. I could barely think Luke's name, it almost didn't feel real already.

"Lily?" Zack was watching me.

"Sorry! I went in a bit of a daydream. Was just wondering if we would have girls or boys." It sickened me how easily I lied, I didn't used to lie to anyone. But I was doing it for him, I tried to reassure myself. If I kept carrying on like everything was fine, it would be.

Zack pulled me close to him and kissed the top of my head. "Did I tell you how much I love the zoo?" He grinned at me like an excited schoolboy.

"I think everyone here knows how much you love the zoo Zachary…" I let his name play out on my lips longer than necessary, sliding my sunglasses up into my hair and watching his dark eyes meet mine. "You have been running around faster than the kids."

He whispered into my ear, as I continued to watch the

girls. "You know how it makes me feel when I get the full title."

"I don't know what you mean." I leant forwards on the bench, running my hands up the salty heat on the back of my neck and up into my slightly damp, dark ponytail.

"What time do they go to bed again?" Asked Zack as he motioned towards the girls with a smile.

I stood up, squeezing his knee as I did so. "Come on, they want to see the sealion show."

After being absolutely fleeced at the gift shop we headed home and cooked pasta for everyone. Bedtime was thankfully brief as the girls were exhausted from the long day and the hot weather. Zack and I sank into the huge U-shaped sofa that dominated Cassie's expensive but homey living room. Two tall fans whirred and span, blasting cold air at us. The August evening was just getting stickier and clammier by the minute.

"I love them, but they're exhausting." Said Zack, his eyes closing for a minute.

"Absolutely!" I agreed, as I took a long sip of the cold, sharp wine. Cassie had told us to take whatever we wanted from the wine fridge, my life needed a wine fridge. I made a note to myself that if Zack and I ever moved, wine fridge was a must.

"They're asleep now though. It's just me, you and a mini mansion. What could possibly go wrong?" Zack turned his head to me, watching me carefully. Cassie knew we called her place the mini mansion, think she loved it really. The house was huge, decorated so stylishly and located on one of the poshest streets of my hometown.

Zack looking at me like that set off feelings and sensations that I wasn't ready for. My body always reacted to him, but my mind was a little more guarded at the moment. I quickly thought back, this was approaching four weeks without having sex now which was completely unheard of for us, four nights was pretty much unheard of to be fair, until now. He hadn't said anything, but we both knew it was hanging heavily between us.

Zack and I had been 'on a break', then I was with Luke. I just hadn't been able to face it since I got home. It was as though my body remembered that Luke was the last person who kissed it, touched it, loved it. It scared me to let someone else overwrite that.

Zack had tried to broach the subject a couple of nights back and I'd just clammed up. He was incredible and it was so like him to be patient and understanding, to put me first and wait until I was ready, but perhaps that just meant the problem was being ignored. Luke wouldn't have done that, Luke would have just grabbed me and…

"Lily?"

As I met Zack's eyes I could see the worry in them, almost a fear. "Sorry, sorry I was just feeling crap from the heat. What is it with this country? Either boiling or freezing?!"

Zack smiled and shuffled closer along the plush material. "I know. Guessing it's too hot for the hot tub?"

"Definitely. I love the hot tub in winter, when you have to jump out and leg it across the grass into the house before you freeze." I smiled widely, remembering Cassie and I doing this on many occasions, not just me and Cassie… "Maybe we could just stick our heads back in the wine fridge for half an hour?"

He took a deep breath and reached out for my hand,

wrapping his fingers around mine. "I was thinking maybe, we could just go to bed? Been a while since we had an early night." My eyes darted between his. I was still ultimately drawn to him, I loved him from the bottom of my soul. I was just also going through deeper grief than I could have imagined. I loved Luke just as much as I loved Zack, and he was gone. My love was gone. My best friend was gone. "We need to get back to me and you Lily."

I pressed a soft kiss to his lips, my eyes closed, the taste of the sharp wine mingling between our mouths. "I know."

He stood up and took my hand, pulling me up from the deep, squishy couch. "Come with me."

I grabbed our long-stemmed wine glasses, Zack smiled as he led me across the sumptuous grey carpet, up the wide staircase and into the spare bedroom. The spare bedroom at Cassie and Guy's felt as big as the whole downstairs of our house, with its own en-suite, super king size bed and built-in wardrobes with matching shoe racks.

Zack softly closed the door behind us, conscious not to wake the children. The lights were out but the August sun hadn't fully set yet, the room was filled with a deep orange light seeping through the wooden shutters. He ran his hand across the exposed skin of my stomach and around to my back, before lifting my cropped white t-shirt over my head. His mouth dipped to my neck and kissed at every crevice as his fingers deftly unfastened my bra and pulled it loose, letting it drop to the floor.

"This is a look I like on you." His eyes flashed brightly as he took a step back. His eyes roaming up my bare legs to the cut off denim shots on my thighs, and the naked skin above. "May I?" He asked, as he reached behind me and ran his fingers amongst my long ponytail. I nodded and he pulled the band down the length my hair, his eyes never leaving mine. I shivered slightly as my loose hair hit my skin. He continued to watch me, and I bit my lip nervously. My body was still going absolutely crazy for him, but my mind just couldn't relax.

Zack handed me the wine that I'd put down on the bedside table. As I took a deep sip, he slowly undid the button on my shorts, his fingers teasing at the warm skin of my stomach. "You look insanely inviting, you know that?" I shrugged and smiled shyly, feeling more exposed than sexy. There was a moment of silence that lasted just a little too long. "Am I undressing myself today then?" He asked innocently, but I detected a note of irritation behind it. He knew I wasn't one hundred per cent with him right now. I knew the same, but I needed to make him think everything was OK. *Snap out of it Lily!*

I look forward to sharing the rest of book two with you soon! Keep watching the website and socials for updates.

Nicola x

Printed in Great Britain
by Amazon